THE LONG NIGHT

JESSICA SCOTT

A haunting novel about the sacrifices good men must make in war.

"An unsettling but captivating look at the dark and painful effects wrought by war on the minds and bodies of soldiers caught up in the moral and ethical dilemmas they face while trying stay alive" ~ Night Owl Reviews

"This one will haunt you." ~ Bestselling author J.D. Rhoades

Whatever it takes, just come home to me. Promise me, Sam.

In eight months, Staff Sergeant Sam Brown will become a father. But first, he has to survive his fourth tour in Iraq. On his last night home, he tries to pretend that everything is fine, that the war is fine, that his life is fine.

But as he returns to the war zone, things are anything but fine and the promise he made to his fiancé takes on a desperate edge. As things spiral down, Sam starts to wonder about that promise.

How high is the price he will pay when the long night comes to an end?

Note — these books are fiction. Any resemblance to real people or events is purely coincidence

Learn More At…
http://www.jessicascott.net
Follow Jessica on Twitter
Like Jessica on Facebook
Sign up for Jessica's Newsletter

ALSO BY JESSICA SCOTT

The FALLING Series

Before I Fall

Break My Fall

After I Fall

Catch My Fall

Until We Fall

The HOMEFRONT Series

Come Home to Me

Homefront

After the War

Find My Way Home

The COMING HOME Series

I'll Be Home for Christmas: A Coming Home Novella

Because of You

Anything For You: A Coming Home Short Story

Until There Was You

Back to You

All For You

It's Always Been You

NONFICTION

To Iraq & Back: On War and Writing

The Long Way Home: One Mom's Journey Home From War

BOOKSHOTS

Dawn's Early Light

CHAPTER ONE

Faith was soft against him. He groaned low in his throat and inched closer, pulling her body flush against his. He stroked his hand over her fur, wanting to get clos—

Fur.

He opened his eyes as Maggie's tongue scraped over the side of his face. He was snuggled up to the yellow lab in a deeply inappropriate manner.

"Ugh!" He scrambled back, shoving her out of the bed. She landed with a thud. "Damn it, Maggie!" Her tail thumped on the floor and she twisted her golden head to rest it on the bed and look at him with adoring eyes.

Never mind that he'd just sexually assaulted his *dog*.

"If you ever tell *anyone*," he muttered. Her tail slapped the floor harder. Clearly, he was already forgiven.

Sam sat up slowly as the light from the hallway attempted to pierce his retinas. He cradled his head in his hands and waited for the pressure to ease off his stomach. He still wasn't entirely sure he was going to make it through the morning without puking his guts up.

A quiet knock made him lift his head. Faith stood in the doorway, already dressed and fully functional. She had tied her hair back, away from her face. She looked far too alert and perky for first thing in the morning. "Your mother called," she said.

Sam closed his eyes again. "What did she want?"

It wasn't that Faith and his mother didn't get along. It wasn't that they had a difficult relationship. It wasn't even that Catherine Brown was the Sainted Mother of all long-suffering parents.

No, it was much simpler. It was that – according to his mother -- he'd shacked up with the Whore of Babylon and Catherine Brown didn't bother to hide her condemnation of Sam's future wife.

That was only part of it, though. The rest of it…the rest of it was purely Sam's fault.

He groaned and cradled his head in his palm some more. One of his last days in the States, and he was going to spend it refereeing between the woman who'd given life to him and the woman who had chosen to spend her life with him.

And he was nursing one hell of a hangover. He was not in the mood for this shit. "Why is she calling so early?"

Faith shifted and smiled from the doorway. "It's almost noon."

"Oh." He scrubbed his hands over his head. "Guess I don't really have a response to that, then."

"Not really. Now if you're done molesting the dog, you might want to take a shower."

Sam scowled as heat crawled up his neck. He looked up at her. "You saw that?"

"I woke up and you were spooning with Maggie instead of me." Her lips pressed into a smirk that was just shy of a full-blown laugh. "I'll try to contain my jealousy," she said dryly.

Sam made a sound and reached down to stroke Maggie's head. She arched her neck to put her head against his palm. Her tongue lolled out of her mouth. "You said you weren't going to tell anyone, mutt."

Thump. Thump. Thump.

Sam straightened and stepped over the dog. He stopped a foot in front of Faith. "I'd ask for a good morning kiss, but I'm afraid you left a cat in here last night."

She lifted her hand to cover his mouth. "Yes, a toothbrush would be wonderful first." Her eyes danced and he stole a quick kiss anyway.

"Thank you for playing nice with my mother. I'll be down in a few." He paused. "Can you bring me up some Motrin?"

Faith smiled and held out her hand. Four little white pills rested in her palm. Sam swallowed them dry and immediately regretted it. "You're a saint. You know that, right?"

She patted his shoulder. "Hurry up or I'm not responsible for my actions."

Sam ducked into the bathroom and turned on the shower. The pipes creaked in the wall, groaning in protest as they forced hot water from the cellar through the aging pipes and into the shower. He stepped into the hot stream, savoring his last hot shower for who knew how long.

Showers were few and far between on the shitty base he occupied. Oh, they were there and available, but the fungus on the floors was so thick it took a braver man than him to walk into it. It wasn't like anyone was around to complain about his balls smelling like something died in his pants if he went a few days without bathing.

The Iraqi heat could do that to a guy.

Well, Lewis complained, but Lewis bitched about everything.

Even listening to Lewis bitch was better than braving whatever unkillable diseases were growing on the inside of the shower stalls in Iraq. The last time his feet had started itching, he'd lost a toenail and had attempted to kill whatever it was growing between his toes with lighted gasoline. His brigade surgeon had been somewhat less than impressed. But the burned skin had grown back fungus free. A little pain had been worth it.

Sam soaked his head and tried to stop thinking about Iraq. He had one goddamned day left at home. He didn't want to spend it thinking about the fucking war.

He was reaching for the faucet when a crash exploded in the bedroom. Maggie's bark was muted by the steam, but it sent his pulse racing. He grabbed a towel and damn near broke his neck slipping on the floor before he caught himself on the porcelain sink. He skidded into the bedroom.

And froze as Maggie lowered her head and snarled at him. She stood on the bed, the lamp and the alarm clock twisted on the floor. Her hackles were a rigid line down her back, her teeth exposed and wicked.

She was snarling. Not at the threatening lamp.

At him.

His throat closed off. He lifted his hand, palm out.

"Maggie?" He'd been the one who'd brought· her home to Faith when she'd been a puppy.

She lowered her head and took a single menacing step closer. One paw hung in the air as she hesitated, ready to strike.

Sam's breath was stuck, his lungs refusing to work as all the blood in his body pushed to his limbs.

He reached for his weapon.

It wasn't there. It was a half a world away, in a weapon's rack in his company arms room.

He was unarmed.

"Fuck me," he muttered. The emergency room hadn't been on his to do list for his last day home, that was for damn sure.

She took another step toward him, a low and threatening growl rumbling deep in her body. Her hackles were spikes of anger along her spine.

Footsteps pounded on the stairs.

Faith stopped in the doorway. Maggie's intense stare didn't waver from his. "Sam?"

"Stay away, Faith." He ignored her, focusing entirely on the dog's twisted muzzle and deep black eyes that had looked at him with love only a moment before. "Maggie. Maggie, listen to me.

It's just me, Mags." He held up his hands, hoping the towel stayed in place. He wasn't so scared that the idea of his dog biting his dick off wasn't a pressing concern.

Her throat rumbled, deep and savage.

He was ninety percent sure he was about to have his throat ripped out by his own dog.

"Maggie!" Faith's voice snapped from the doorway.

Maggie paused. Her tail dropped, her hackles lowered and she fell into a crouch, before rolling over onto her back, exposing her belly. Her tail fluttered in apology.

Just like that Maggie was back.

Sam looked up at Faith, fear rolling back in waves like a receding tide. "What the hell was that?"

Faith's skin was parchment white. "I don't know. She's done that a couple times to people."

"Do you think she's sick?"

"I took her to Doc McLauren's. She couldn't find anything wrong with her."

Maggie's tail thumped on the quilt that Faith had bought from the church sale a few summers ago. *Thump. Thump.* Sam gripped the towel and crouched down, ashamed to see his hand tremble as he reached for her. She rolled further onto her back and showed her belly, no trace of the snapping, snarling menace who'd just threatened him.

"Okay, Mags," he whispered, patting her belly. Her fur there was soft and thin. Her paws twitched and her tail wiggled as he rubbed her. She groaned and wriggled happily. "Okay." He lifted his gaze to Faith. "Well, that was exciting."

"Heh. Not so much." She picked up the lamp and set it back on the table. "That was really strange." She bent back down, lifting a small pendant from beneath the bed. "Your mother gave me this for you. Glad I found it." Faith looked up at him. "I don't think she'd believe me if I told her the dog knocked it off the table."

"What is it?" Sam was willing to bet dollars to donuts it was something religious that she'd picked up on the Home Shopping

Network or whatever it was that fleeced old ladies out of their retirement money. He hesitated then retreated. His mother's religion wasn't his.

It couldn't be. Not any more.

There was no God to forgive the things he'd done.

"Just tell her you gave it to me and throw it away." He turned his back on her extended hand. He couldn't take it from her.

If there was a God, he'd be more likely to get struck by lightning than have his soul saved.

"Something must have spooked her." It was easier to talk about the dog and her potential schizophrenia. "She's fine now."

"You think she had a nightmare?"

Sam shrugged. "Not sure. Not outside the realm of possible," he said. "I suppose my parents would now be convinced she's possessed."

Faith smiled and tucked an errant blond hair behind one ear. "No, only your mother. Hurry up and get dressed before I molest you." She crossed the small space between them. "You're not allowed to stand there all wet and sexy and not expect me to get turned on."

"You've been awfully needy of my cock lately," he said with a smile, hooking his index finger in the waist of her jeans and tugging her closer.

"I'm blaming the pregnancy hormones." She slid her arms around his neck and pressed her body close to his.

"You're so much sexier than the dog." He covered her laugh with a kiss, wishing like hell that he wasn't going back to Iraq so soon.

It was Faith who broke the kiss. "Seeing how you get to leave for Iraq tomorrow and I'm left dealing with your mother, please come downstairs and make arrangements for tomorrow. For me?"

"Of course. But we'll finish this later, or I am not responsible for my actions."

Faith left him alone with the dog. Maggie had jumped off his bed and now laid on her dog bed in the corner, her head down, her eyes calm and brown.

Sam pulled on a pair of pants, occasionally glancing over at her. She was asleep. But he couldn't shake the feeling that she was somehow watching him.

CHAPTER TWO

"When do you go back?" Tommy held a Sam Adams in one hand, a Marlboro unfiltered in the other. Sam couldn't believe Tommy still smoked those. Sam had given them up when he'd discovered how hard they were to find in the post exchange. They were even harder to find in the desert. But Tommy had spent his life in the tiny Maine town where they'd grown up and Sam…well. Sam had run off and joined the Army at the precious age of seventeen. Tommy worked at the mill and bitched about the jobs drying up.

And Sam? Sam held his breath during thunderstorms and waited for the boom.

When the rain came on suddenly, like buckets of nails being dumped over a thin tin roof, Sam paused. And waited. The lights in the shitty hole-in-the-wall bar flickered and threatened to quit.

Sam tensed and waited for the explosion that followed the burst. It always came. He held his breath. When the boom came, distant and feeble, he took no comfort from its weakness.

Real explosions came with a concussion wave. And sometimes with shrapnel.

He tried to relax and have a drink like everyone else in the Elks' Lodge. The wood paneling glistened with years of spilled grease and cigarette smoke. The giant moose still hung in its traditional home next to the big screen TV, which was currently blaring a Patriots game. The Patriots were losing.

Sam couldn't summon the energy to care. It felt like he was the only thing that had changed in the Elks' Lodge in ten years. He glanced at Tommy, whose mouth moved without words. Tommy was fatter than when they were kids, his face rounder, his nose red from too many Maine winters and too much coffee brandy.

Sam was leaner and stronger than when he'd lived here, his face marked with a permanent tan line around his eyes. He figured it would fade at some point. After the wars stopped.

If they ever did.

Sam gave himself a mental shake, pushing the war away. For a few more hours at least. Tommy's voice and the buzzing noise of the bar rushed back, like the pounding of rapids over the falls.

"Tomorrow night," Sam said, to Tommy's repeated question. The entire time Sam had been humping the streets in Baghdad, he'd thought about home. Now that he was here, all he could think about was being back over there.

Home…wasn't, anymore. Except when he was around Faith. When he was with her, everything felt better. Not right—no, Sam didn't think he'd ever feel right again. But he definitely felt less wrong around her.

He didn't say those words out loud. Tommy would mention it to his mother, and then his mother would worry and try to take Sam to church. His father would tell him to toughen up.

And Faith? Faith would flitter and try to fix things that weren't broken. Things that weren't her responsibility to fix.

Things that she would be better off not knowing. Just like his mother.

He supposed he should keep that similarity between the two women in his life to himself. Neither would appreciate the comparison.

So he kept his thoughts to himself and pasted on a smile. It felt fake, but Tommy didn't seem to notice.

Sam took another pull off his Coors.

"That must be a bitch of a flight," Tommy said. He motioned toward the bartender, Curtis Lethe. They'd gone to high school with him, but neither had spoken to him the entire four years. Curtis was still the same dark, gothic, angry guy Sam remembered, except now that seemed to make him popular with the ladies. He'd graduated from a single piercing made by a needle sanitized with a lighter to a gauge in both ears and colorful South American gods tattooed over each forearm.

"Yeah, it sucks."

Tommy lined up four shots of tequila on the bar. A fifth had an ominous-looking worm hanging out at the bottom.

Sam grinned. "Some things never change," he muttered.

The first time they'd ever tried tequila, Tommy had explained that—according to his uncle who was an expert on all things involving alcohol—it was mescal with the worm and not tequila. Sam hadn't cared then and didn't care now, but Tommy had insisted it mattered.

He grabbed his first shot and tipped it back. The mescal burned all the way down and got stuck halfway between his mouth and his stomach. He hurked and almost puked it up but managed, through the desire not to be fucked with for his last few hours in the States, to keep it down.

Tommy laughed at him as he tipped his second shot and swallowed it like a smooth cube of Jell-O.

"Fuck," Sam muttered. That last shot with the fucking worm was going to put him under. Faith was going to be pissed.

But the worm went down smooth and easy. Easier than Sam had figured it would. Now if it would just stay down. He wasn't in the mood to listen to Tommy fuck with him if he puked.

'Course, in 24 hours, puking would be the least of his worries. Getting blown up in the middle of the Surge was a much more relevant fear. With luck, the mother of all hangovers would make sleeping on the plane a no-brainer. The ride to Bangor was going to be lovely in a few more hours.

"So." Tommy cleared his throat. "Tell Faith thanks for letting you out to hang with your old high school buddy."

Sam ran his hand over his too-long brown hair. He needed a haircut before he went back. He'd probably take care of that in Kuwait. Guaranteed that plan was going to get him ripped apart by the first sergeant major he ran into on his way to the barbershop. Maybe he'd get Faith to buzz him up before he left. There was that same familiar warmth every time he thought of Faith.

"Yeah. She's cool like that." He glanced at his watch. "But she's picking me up in a little bit."

"Well shit, there goes my plan to get you well and truly shit-faced." Tommy held up his beer. "Hey, listen up!" His accent was thicker now that the liquor was slowly pulling him under. "My buddy Sam here is heading back to Iraq tomorrow. Fighting for all you fucking pussies' freedom. So buy his sorry ass a beer and thank him for his goddamned service."

Tommy's words sounded like *fahkin pousies*. Sam had never realized how much thicker Tommy's accent seemed now that Sam didn't live here anymore. He wondered if that was how he sounded to the guys back in Iraq.

The people in the bar collapsed around him while the storm unleashed hell on the suspect roof. Everything sounded far away.

His hands moved in slow motion as he lifted the beer to his lips. The bottle was cold and smooth against his bottom lip. He no longer felt the beer as it slid down his throat. He looked down, fully expecting to see his legs somewhere other than attached to his body.

He hiccupped and burped into his hand as the wave of slapping hands and saluting his service continued far too long. Sam looked into his beer, hiding his resentment. These people slapped him on the back, said "Thank you for your service", and went back to turning off the news because it was too upsetting to watch. Nobody gave a shit about the war. Not unless they had someone over there.

Everyone wanted to cheer the soldier on.

No one wanted to actually *be* the soldier.

His cell phone vibrated in his back pocket. He slapped Tommy on the shoulder and motioned toward the door. "Time to go."

"You're an old married man and you're not even married yet," Tommy said. "I'm never getting tied down."

Not much had changed with Tommy in the ten years since they'd stumbled, partly high and mostly hungover, across the stage at their high school graduation at Penquitomis Community High School. Come to think of it, not much ever changed at home. Except when they tore down the old Mason's building to make room for the Rite Aid in the middle of town. That had been a big change.

But the same people were still pumping gas at the Irving. Maybe they weren't the same people, but it felt like it.

He slung his arm around Tommy's neck as they stumbled toward the door. The rain fell in huge splats as they stepped into the piercing darkness, illuminated only by occasional too-bright headlights and distant flashes of lightning in the hazy black sky.

"You know what, Tommy." Sam's words slurred together. "I missed you. When I was over there, I used to think about skipping school and going fishing out at Hartland Pond."

They staggered into the rain and splashed toward Faith's waiting Subaru. Sam stepped too hard into a puddle. Water sloshed over the toes of his shoes and sank into the fabric, cold and wet. His shoes squished as he walked. He yanked the door of her car open. Relief unclenched in his guts when he saw her face, smiling. She wasn't pissed. At least not yet.

God, what would he do without Faith? He leaned over and kissed her cheek. She slapped at him playfully, her blond hair clinging to her face from the wet he brought into the dim interior with him. But she wasn't pissed.

Tommy leaned into the car and slung his arm around the seat. He leaned across Sam. "Take care of him. He's one of the good ones."

Faith offered a long-suffering smile. "I will, Tommy."

Tommy leaned dangerously into the car and stuck his finger up in Sam's face. "No, I mean it, Faith. Forever. You need to take care of him." Tommy gripped Sam's neck, the finger dangerously close to Sam's nose. "Don't get blown up or shot or anything."

"I won't, Tommy." A lie. Or at least a futile promise. "I'll see you around, Tommy."

Tommy slammed the door shut and staggered back to the bar. Sam wished he didn't see his friend's head dip or his shoulders slump. The door opened and Tommy disappeared into the smoke and haze of the Elks' Lodge. Back to his normal Friday night out.

"You okay?" Faith asked as she pulled out onto the main road, back toward their place.

"Yeah." He looked at her and offered a weak smile. "Just really, really intoxicated."

She laughed quietly and shook her head. That was his Faith for you. Just quiet patience. No railing lectures. No freaking out over some things.

He didn't feel sad driving away from Tommy and the bar. He felt…something…but he couldn't really put his finger on it so he let it slide. The only sound in Faith's old Subaru was the *swish-click* of the wipers and the blast of the defroster on the windshield.

He leaned the seat back with a click and closed his eyes, trusting Faith to take him home. Their home. He hoped it would feel like that again some day. Maybe after the war. Maybe then.

He floated on a tequila cloud. Around the bend and across the river and down the muddy dirt road. *Click, swoosh. Click, swoosh.* The silence was comforting. Not the silence of anticipation of the next explosion or the ball-clenching fear of being out of ammo.

Just silence. Simple silence.

And then it ended.

CHAPTER THREE

"I'll help you inside." Faith's voice was a whisper on the silence. Not a note of condemnation in her words. Nothing but what she said. Straight shooter. That's what his Faith was.

He thought he said something about being fine, but the sound came out garbled even to his ears. She said nothing, stepping into the dark rain and sloshing around the car. Her boots squished in the mud. He should have put down more gravel in the driveway while he was home. Mud season was going to be a bitch come springtime.

He'd be home again in seven months. He'd fix it then. He didn't want Faith dragging the mud into their home. Even if their home was a worn-down old farmhouse that cost more to heat than he made in a month, it was still her home that she tried to make his whenever he could get enough time to come up to Maine from Georgia. It would be her home until he came back and took her away to a military base in some far-off state like Georgia or Texas or Washington.

He wondered how Faith would like living in the South. He should probably ask her, if she planned on being his wife. The Northeast had a shortage of military bases, which meant that when she'd said yes all those months ago, she'd essentially signed up to live in the South. He should probably ask her again.

Too bad he couldn't convince her to marry him before he went back. But she had some screwed up ideas about how people would look at her for marrying him right before he deployed.

They'd called her a slut in high school because her clothes had been too tight and her mascara too black.

Guess those wounds still hurt, because she was still worried about what people thought.

Which didn't make a damn bit of sense. How could being a single parent be less bad than being his wife?

But that didn't matter. She was set. She'd marry him when he came home and not a minute sooner because she wasn't going to be the girl that married the soldier before he went off to war. Right now, the driveway was muddy and Faith was standing in a puddle, waiting for him to heave his drunk ass out of the car.

Maybe he'd ask Tommy to fix the driveway while he was gone.

His hands and legs weren't working right. He looked up at her. Her hair ran down her face. Her breath froze in the air in front of her. A cold front was chasing the storm across the state. He needed to get her out of the rain before she got sick.

Couldn't have her sick. Not with their baby growing inside her.

The lights flooded the porch, casting their shadows on the old steps. And still he didn't move.

It was a miracle that he was able to stand without staggering into her. She slipped her arm around his waist and helped him as he walked—if you could call it that—toward the house.

Maggie waited at the top of the stairs, her tail thumping slowly on the old wood floor.

Sam hesitated. Waited for her to bare her teeth. Or bolt down the stairs at him.

Then the moment passed and Maggie was all yellow lab and happy tongue and wagging tail again. She was two, just past the age of complete asshole for labs, and right now, she was really fucking happy to see him. She jumped on his shoulders as he bent over to yank off his shoes. The damn mutt knew she wasn't supposed to jump. The weight of the dog combined with the booze knocked him off balance and he went down, in a puddle of wet man and happy dog.

He pushed her off. At least, he tried to.

"Maggie!" There was Faith, yanking the dog back. Forcing her to sit when she wanted to jump. Maggie's entire body trembled with the effort of listening to Faith. She tried to be a good dog, she really did.

He hoped she calmed down before the baby came.

Sam sat up and kicked off his shoes. "Aw Mags, why'd you do that?" His voice sent her into a frenzy again. She wriggled her seventy pounds into his lap and licked his face.

Faith held out her hand. "Come on, soldier boy. Let's get you to bed."

Sam looked up at her. Her face was shrouded in a halo from the hallway light, but he knew what he'd see if he could see her clearly. Perfection. Everything about her was better than he deserved. Her body was curvier than it had been in high school. Less perfect than it was now.

She said she was the luckiest girl in the world the day he flew back home to see her after months of email. He wanted to kiss the random-ass spammer who'd hacked his email account and had caused her to email him to tell him that no, she did not want to see his dick, thank you very much.

Somehow, he'd managed to convince her that no, he really hadn't sent that email. His dick wasn't all that impressive to be emailing it around the world. It was a humble dick. Functional and all that, in the way that dicks were.

And somehow, she'd emailed him back.

She'd picked him, despite his being gone to war and his failure to promise he would come home and sometimes not being able to *call* home. Despite missing her birthday three years in a row and only making a video call for one Christmas.

She was coming to Fort Benning with him when he came home this time. She'd finally agreed to be his wife once she could be sure that marrying him wasn't a death sentence for him. She'd gotten it into her head that if she said yes before his deployment, he would die over there.

Saying no was her way of controlling the universe.

But he couldn't promise her he'd come home. He couldn't make that promise – whether he survived this deployment wasn't up to him. If he did somehow make it home, he'd get a twofer out of the deal: a wife and a baby.

He lurched to his knees and wrapped his arms around her waist. Her belly was a firm mound beneath his cheek. He kissed the lump. "Hey, Peanut. You being good for Mommy?" he asked.

Faith laughed, one hand resting on his wet head. "I think Peanut has enough sense to be asleep at this hour." A shudder ran through her.

He hoped to hell that wasn't her hiding crying. He hated seeing her cry.

Sam stood. "Go get warm. I need some water and I'll be up."

She tipped her chin, not convinced.

He shooed her toward the stairs. "Go. Shower."

She called Maggie to follow her, padding up the stairs, which were covered with secondhand stair treads she'd picked up from the Methodist Church yard sale. Sam listened to the thump of her feet across the floor above his head. The old house was full of sound. Creaks and groans. The pipes squealed when she turned on the shower. The sounds of home were so much better than the sounds of war.

Sam made his way to the kitchen. The counter was lined with food for his flight the day after tomorrow. The red and brown Slim Jims and Almond Snickers Bars mocked him, marking time as the last nights of his R&R came to an end. He'd be back in Iraq soon. The sand and the dust and the grit would be back. Being home would be nothing more than a memory. Hell, maybe he was dreaming of being home right now and was already back in the desert. That would be a fitting fucking nightmare.

The Slim Jims stared up at him while Sam waited for the water in the sink to clear up. He held his cup beneath the stream. "Diet of champions," he muttered.

The chocolate would be gone before he hit the desert sand. Chocolate didn't stand a chance against 117 degrees in the shade.

He frowned as a faint glint of silver caught his eye. Lifting the front lip of one of his pockets on the assault pack, he found a small metal pendant. It might have been stainless steel or sterling silver. It was a small crest on a heavy silver chain, with the words "St. Michael" on a scroll across the top and "Protect Us" across the bottom, beneath the feet of the warrior standing on the neck of a dragon.

It had to be from Mom. She'd do something like that. He closed his fist around the small pendant. Unwilling to throw it aside. Unable to put it around his neck. Somehow, it felt hollow and false to be asking all the angels and the saints to watch over him when he wasn't entirely sure they existed in the first place.

There was no angel guarding over him. Not now, anyway.

The water was cold on his throat as he swallowed, trying to ward off that mother of all hangovers. He leaned on the counter, gripping the pendant tight, trying to sort through the riot of emotions twisting in his guts like bad food.

"Fuck."

He sucked in a deep breath until the pain in his lungs faded, replaced by the dead sensation of alcohol purring through his veins. He wanted to crawl into bed and wrap his body around Faith. He wanted to smell her shampoo, that ridiculously expensive shampoo she used that took the hard water minerals out of her hair.

She'd be warm and wet from the shower right now, snuggled beneath her grandmother's quilt. Someday he'd buy her a bedroom set from Sears or JC Penney but right now, they had hand-me-downs and heirlooms, and that was okay.

The pipes protested as Faith turned off the shower. Sam summoned the common sense to turn off the lights in the kitchen and stumble upstairs. Faith was in the closet. He caught a glimpse of her pulling on a pair of faded blue sweat pants and a cream-colored tank top. He loved watching her move, the way her belly just slightly bulged beneath the pants.

He made it to the bathroom. The walls were wet with steam. The toilet paper was wilted on the roll, the mirror coated with fog. He had the half-cocked fantasy that Faith would step into the bathroom, wrapped in nothing but a towel and a smile.

He'd probably pass out before he got his dick out of his pants. But the thought was nice.

He finished his business, then stripped off the rest of his clothes. He swore when he stubbed his toe on the bedpost. Bright pain exploded up his calf to his brain. When the pain in his toe subsided from *motherfucker that hurt* to merely *sonofabitch* throbbing, he climbed into bed.

Faith was already there. She was just as he'd imagined: warm. Moist. Her skin radiated heat and smelled like Ivory soap. Clean. Crisp.

Warm.

He nestled against her back, pulling her against him. Breathing in the smell of that expensive shampoo in the faint hope that maybe, the warm scent on her neck could banish the burn of sulfur seared into his memory.

CHAPTER FOUR

He padded downstairs some hours later, badly hungover and in need of butter and toast and greasy eggs. Because isn't that what everyone wanted when they'd had a little too much to drink the night before.

He heard his mother's voice carrying up the stairs. He stopped at the edge of the steps, wanting very much to have a last day home that wasn't a Jerry Springer episode.

He didn't hold out much hope that it would actually go that way.

No matter how much he tried, he often found himself arguing with his mother. All because she didn't understand all the things he didn't want to say. Things he didn't want to talk about.

She wanted to believe their war was just.

It wasn't.

Dad didn't ask as many questions. At least, not as many hard ones. Sometimes he wondered how his dad stayed married to his mom. But then he remembered his parents' religion: divorce was a mortal sin.

Sam was their biggest disappointment. At one point, he'd been convinced his mother wanted him to be a priest. Instead, he'd turned toward war and the man the Army had made him. No disappointment in the world was as great as disappointing your parents and abandoning their faith was about as bad as it came.

Funny, he'd never remembered them being so devout when he was growing up, but Mom signed all her emails now with "be blessed" and regularly sent him prayers through Facebook. Sometimes he had this vision of a modern-day Jesus, reaching the masses through memes.

He'd never really thought of himself as devout but any shreds of faith in God had been left behind in the desert.

And nothing about the war had convinced him of any master plan. It was nothing but chaos and death and stupid, violent acts dressed up as heroism.

If God did exist, He had a hell of a lot of explaining to do.

His mother was chopping onions. Faith's expression was tight and tense, her back to Catherine. If she hadn't been pregnant, Sam was sure his fiancée would be nursing a beer instead of wearing the long-suffering expression on her face.

The two women in his life were squared off around the small kitchen island. Faith's mouth was pressed into a flat, hard line. Oh lovely.

In the Gospel According to Catherine, Faith hadn't been raised right. The fact that Faith had lived with her father after her mother had run away to join the Texas National Guard had made her an object of pity in high school. Now that the girl from the wrong side of the tracks was going to be his wife, Saint Catherine had turned her back on the fallen woman he'd asked to be his bride. Guess all those stories about Jesus and the prostitutes didn't actually apply in real life. Catherine swore the apple didn't fall far from the tree: Faith would run off and leave Sam the first time something better came along.

Walking into his kitchen felt only slightly less nerve-wracking than turning down a loaded alley.

He wondered if he would ever gather the courage to tell his mother to back the fuck out of his life. But even if his faith in the God who wrote it hadn't been destroyed, the fourth commandment had been drilled into his bones from birth. He wasn't likely to break it any time soon.

He walked across the linoleum floor, feeling the cold penetrating his bare feet. It was October in Maine—not as cold as it was going to get, not by a long shot, but his blood had thinned since he'd been gone. Iraq was the other end of the thermometer, the one set to "inferno". That was the temperature range his blood was used to.

He'd never felt heat like that. But now, the cold was simply too much.

"Please tell me there's coffee," he said as he leaned in and kissed his mother on her still-smooth cheek. "Sorry I overslept."

His mom smiled thinly, her face a mask of tolerance worn by martyred mothers everywhere.

"Fresh coffee. Down East Coffee Breakfast Blend," Faith said, handing him a cup without looking in his direction. She was focused on stirring the scrambled eggs on the skillet in front of her.

"All packed?" His father broke the awkward silence. Sam could have kissed him.

Sam poured his coffee and held the pot out in offering to his father, who leaned on the wall arch near the fridge. His father extended his cup, a worn Irving mug ringed with stains.

"Not really. I'll do it in a little while. I think my uniform is still in the dryer."

"It's in the wash now, actually," Faith said over her shoulder.

Sam glanced at his mother, who was being unusually quiet. She stood to one side of the small island in the middle of the kitchen, skinning carrots. It was probably a safe assumption that he would find carrot sticks in his assault pack later. If she replaced the Snickers with carrot sticks, however—

"Morning." She didn't respond to the greeting.

Clearly he'd missed some fireworks already.

Awesome. "Did I miss something?" He didn't want to know.

At the same time, he needed to get peace between Faith and his mother before he left.

Faith might need her when he was gone.

She blinked, her eyes shimmering. "You've been home for two weeks and you're going back to war today. I've barely seen you. What could possibly be wrong?"

Sam's dad circled the small island, standing next to his wife. He placed his hand on her shoulder. His dad's hand was spotted now, the veins standing out in a way he'd never noticed before. "Don't start with him."

Sam sniffed, rubbing one bicep with his free hand and tried to keep his tone civil. "Him prefers not to fight on his last day in the States," Sam said mildly, reaching into the fridge for the half-and-half.

Another thing he was going to miss: real dairy products in his coffee. Not that Coffee-mate didn't have its own magical goodness, but there was just something delicious about real half-and-half. Or better yet, cream.

He dumped enough in his coffee to turn it the color of mocha ice cream, then scooped sugar into his cup. "I'll be fine, Mom. It's just another war."

His mom's brown eyes shimmered when she glanced up at him. Her hair never changed. She'd worn it the same for as long as Sam could remember. She kept it short, a perm around her face. It framed her face like a brown halo. "You're not sleeping well."

Sam made a noise over the edge of his coffee cup. "PTSD does that," he said. At his mother's horror, he backpedaled. Quickly. "It was a joke. Jeez, don't start planning my funeral, for fuck's sake."

He wondered what it said about him that part of him was yearning for the simplicity of the war. If he got into a pissing contest with another dude, they'd take it outside. Couldn't really do that with his mother.

"Watch your mouth around your mother," his dad said softly. Behind those mild words was the memory of a not-so-mild belt in the woodshed.

His dad had never even lost his temper back then. To this day, Sam wondered how his father had slid the leather from the loops so calmly and swung it across his son's backside.

Sam was never going to hit Peanut. Never.

The sound of claws on the stairs announced that Maggie had finally realized that breakfast was almost ready and decided to join the party. But she didn't come into the kitchen immediately. Sam saw her peeking around the corner from the bottom of the steps.

What the hell was wrong with that dog?

He sniffed and decided to change the subject from his foul language to something less likely to cause an argument. "So how's retirement treating you?" he asked his dad.

Maggie slunk around the corner and eyeballed the bacon with soulful brown eyes. This was the dog he loved. Not the snarling demon who'd threatened to rip his throat out yesterday.

When Sam didn't acknowledge her mooching, she let out a single pitiful whine.

He slipped her a piece of bacon. It might be the last piece of bacon he could ever slip her. How was *that* for a depressing thought? But he kept silent about the fear that sidled up his spine and wrapped around his shoulders like something from *Aliens*.

"Retirement is good," his father said. "I get to volunteer with the Knights of Columbus more than when I worked at the mill."

His mother started chopping potatoes. Her hands were as quick and efficient as any line cook's. "Do you go to mass over there?" she asked, looking up at him while her fingers flew over the newly naked carrots. If Sam attempted that, he'd lose a finger, or at least the tip of one.

"If I can fit it in." Not entirely a lie. Only mostly. "We don't have a Catholic chaplain on my base, and he only gets to our base every couple of weeks."

His mom scooped up the potatoes and dumped them into a pot filling with water in the sink. "How can they not have a Catholic chaplain at your base?"

"Because there aren't that many Catholics in my unit. Not

compared to some of the other denominations," Sam said. He fought the urge to get a beer out of the fridge. Considering he'd just dragged his corpse out of bed at noon, he didn't think his mother would approve. And he really didn't want to fight.

"How many are there?" Catherine asked.

"I don't know, Mom." Frustration leaked into his words. He felt like he was thirteen again, caught with that *Hustler* he'd stuffed between the mattress and the box spring. "I'm in the infantry, not the chaplain corps."

"I was just asking."

Cue guilt trip, he thought. Faith leaned past him, taking the opportunity to rest her palm on his heart as she did. Her touch was warm and comforting. Calming.

The anger eased back. Just a little.

His dad, though, finally put out the fire by handing him a beer and heading out onto the back porch. Sam followed.

The cold was damp and thick. It slapped at him as he leaned back against the wall and kicked one foot up on the Adirondack chair.

"The news makes it look pretty bad over there," his father said, twisting the top off his beer.

"It's not Disneyland, that's for sure."

"How bad is the fighting in your sector?"

It killed him when his father tried to speak his language. Sometimes he suspected his father regretted missing out on Vietnam, as if it would give them something of a shared experience to talk about. Instead they pretended Sam was still the same kid who'd run off to join the Army after high school. That four tours in Iraq hadn't left a mark.

But Sam said nothing, appreciating his dad's effort at keeping the peace more than he could ever say. If he acknowledged it, though, he'd have to answer questions.

And he didn't want to answer questions.

"Bad enough that Mom probably shouldn't watch the news."

Dad sniffed. "She prays for you every day. Has half the parish praying to St. Michael for you. You've got lots of folks watching out for your immortal soul."

Sam smiled and took a sip of his beer. St. Michael couldn't help him. But Sam said nothing because his father wasn't kidding, not about the group of old ladies praying for his soul or his father's worry about it.

"You should go easy on your mother, Sam. She does the best she can."

Sam took a long pull of his beer. "I'd be fine if she wasn't constantly trying to convert me. Ever since I told her I didn't want to go to church any more, she's been relentless."

"It's not easy to see your son turn his back on your faith." His father sighed. "We raised you to be a good man."

Sam was tempted to ask if the belt had been part of that. Why the hell was that bothering him now, all of a sudden?

"And I can still do that without going to church every weekend and listening to some hypocrite talk about some useless scripture." The bitterness was back, sharp and black and potent.

"Your mother just wants what's best for you."

"Sure," Sam muttered. Then the frustration was coming in a flood of words that he might have stopped if he'd thought for a second about the consequences. "Nothing is ever good enough for Mom. She wants me to find a nice girl; I do. She hates her. She's going to be a grandmother, but she's pissed that our kid won't be born to married parents. She can't ever just be happy for me."

A clink that sounded like metal on glass. Sam turned to see his mom standing in the middle of the slider, her lips pressed into a flat line, her eyes filled with hurt.

"Mom—"

"No." She held up one hand, turning her face away from him. "You're too good for my faith. Continue to mock me. It's fine." Her voice broke and she disappeared into the house, her movements rigid and stiff.

Guilt and shame wrestled in his belly. Guilt won. "Ah fuck," he muttered. "Mom!"

She didn't turn around. Sam stalked into the house and slammed the remains of his beer into the trash before he rushed out of the house after her. "Mom, damn it, stop." He grabbed her arm and stepped in front of her.

"I'm leaving, Sam. I should have gotten the hint when you didn't come around while you were home."

"Mom, will you just stop for one minute?"

"Stop what, Sam? Wanting the best for you?"

"Stop judging me for every failing. Stop making me feel like I'm thirteen every time you're in the house." He dropped his hands. "Stop making me feel guilty because I couldn't use the toys you sent over."

"They were perfectly good toys."

Sam sighed hard. "You really can't see what's wrong with giving a little Muslim kid a teddy bear that says Jesus loves you?"

"Jesus loves all the children."

His temper snapped. "Goddamn it, no he doesn't! He doesn't fucking care about the Muslim kids or the Christian kids or any of them."

She sucked in a scandalized breath. "You watch your mouth, young man. You can mock my faith all day long, but don't you dare speak ill against the Lord."

He wanted to keep fighting. He wanted to tell her that her God was dead, that He didn't exist.

No God would ask him to do what he'd done in the name of Duty, Honor, Country.

But he bit his tongue until it bled. Because the fight wasn't worth it. All it would do was take his mother from him.

And despite it all, she was still his mom. And he missed her. The woman she used to be, before he left for the war.

Or maybe it was him who'd changed and she was still the same.

"Can you please come back inside, Mom?" He dragged his hand through his hair. "Please?"

It was a long moment before Catherine the Martyr walked stoically toward her pyre.

———

"Well that was about as pleasant as an enema made of napalm and rat poison." Sam took a pull off his beer, grateful that his hangover had finally started to fade. Even if it was six hours too late to make the family afternoon bearable.

"What, being told your unborn child will burn in hell if we don't get him baptized isn't your idea of polite dinner conversation?" Faith glanced over at him, fatigue showing in her eyes.

"I thought the Pope changed the whole babies-in-purgatory thing." He flopped onto the bed, knocking over a pile of uniform t-shirts and a couple of pairs of socks.

Faith glanced over at him. "Do you believe her?"

Sam took another pull from his beer. "That Peanut will go to hell or limbo or anything else if he doesn't get baptized?" He rubbed his thumb on the edge of the label. "You'd have to believe in an afterlife for that. So no, I don't think I do."

Faith turned away, tucking his t-shirt into the duffle bag near the door. He wasn't so dense to think that she was merely folding laundry.

He pushed off the bed and crossed the worn hardwood floor. Wrapping his arms around her, his hands cupped the slight bump of her belly where Peanut was nestled safe and snug. "I kind of hoped she'd change with the news of the baby."

Faith leaned back against him, trying to swipe at her cheeks without him noticing.

He noticed. "Ah, honey, don't cry," he whispered. He nuzzled her neck. Her palms slid to rest on his forearms. Her hands were soft against his rough skin. He liked the contrast.

He missed the contrast when he was gone. A lot of the guys bitched about their wives and girlfriends back home. Sam didn't.

He knew he was damn lucky a woman like Faith had settled for him.

He wasn't about to screw it up. He believed in karma, even if karma sometimes took her sweet time in righting the wrongs in the universe. He frowned against her neck as memories from the not-too-distant war slithered out from the depths where he'd tried to lock them away while he was home.

Except that his lock sucked, and they'd tormented him when he lowered his guard.

"Faith, it'll be okay. I'll be home in a few months and then you can move to Georgia with me. You won't have to deal with my family."

She sniffed. "If you think dealing with your mother is why I'm upset, you're an idiot."

He turned her in his arms, resting them on her shoulders. "I'll be okay."

"I'm afraid, Sam. Every night the news says it's getting worse and worse over there. You said yourself it was worse than your first tour. What if something happens to you and I have to raise Peanut by myself?"

"Then marry me. Let me at least go back knowing that you'll have all the benefits of being my wife if something happens to me."

She held up one hand. "I won't marry you as insurance in case you die. It feels too much like signing up for your death."

He buried his face in her neck, needing to burn the sweet, clean smell of her skin into his memory. "I never took you for overly superstitious."

"I'm not. I just…" Her voice cracked and broke his heart a little more. "Promise me you'll come home?"

He leaned back and brushed his thumb over one cheek, swiping at the damp tears that tumbled from her eyes. "I can't promise that."

She lowered her eyes and plucked at his shirt. "I—"

He kissed her, cutting off the sob he heard building in her voice. Her mouth opened beneath his, her tongue dancing across his lips. She was intense, wild, more fierce than he could remember as he stripped her clothes off and lowered her to the bed. Her little gasps and cries penetrated his own sadness at leaving her and for a moment buried the fear that he might do exactly what she worried about.

He didn't tell her that as his hips moved and he gripped her hands over her head, pinning her. He didn't tell her about the dark and twisted things that fought for supremacy in his head as he fucked his fiancée for the last time. He didn't tell her about the horrible things he'd done or worse, the terrible things he hadn't done. Good or bad, the results were the same: death.

Her orgasm trembled and exploded over him, drawing him deeper into the little death. And when he came, it was tainted with the fear he'd tried to ignore.

That she was right.

CHAPTER FIVE

Faith slipped from the bed as the storm broke over the old farm-house. It surprised him that she was still awake. She was more tired since she'd gotten pregnant, but as lightning flashed, illuminating the ancient clock on the wall, he listened as Faith padded downstairs, as silently as she could with the stairs creaking beneath her feet.

He sat up, searching the shadows for any movement before he followed her.

The intermittent flashes of lightning added to his fear and loathing of the dark. Funny, he'd never been afraid of the dark before the war. Now? Now the shadows held real bogeymen who went boom in the night.

A white mass in the shadows sat on Maggie's bed near the door. His heart pounded against his chest. The white shadow lifted its head, its eyes soulless black pits, it's body ragged and skeletal.

He stopped, unable to move. Waiting, waiting for the thunder to finish rumbling. Praying for the next round of lightning, that followed a moment later.

Illuminating Maggie. Just Maggie. He blinked and looked again, sure he had just seen a skinny, ragged beast where his dog had been a moment before. No, it was only Maggie, thumping her tail on the floor.

Sad that the war had even stolen his love for her. Would he lose Faith, too?

He followed the echo of Faith's footsteps and found her curled up on the couch, cradling a coffee mug. He assumed it was decaf tea. She'd given up all bad things the minute she'd suspected she was pregnant.

She was going to be a good mom.

He said nothing as he slid onto the couch with her and tugged her against him. She didn't protest, but nestled up against him. He rested his cheek against the top of her hair, breathing in the clean, sunny scent of her shampoo. It was something expensive she got down at the Rite Aid. He still cringed remembering the first time she'd sent him in for it. Twenty-three dollars a bottle for the shampoo and twenty-five for the conditioner. They weren't so flush they could easily afford it, but Faith was vain about her hair. She'd had frizzy hair in high school. Apparently this had scarred her for life.

It was a simple thing he could do for her.

Now, sitting and breathing in the smell of her, he tucked her scent away into his memory, hoping he could remember it when he was surrounded by dirt and dust, burning tires and rotting garbage.

"Didn't mean to wake you up," she said softly.

"It's better that I'm up. It'll help me sleep on the plane."

She shifted, her palm covering his heart. The heat of her hand penetrated his thin t-shirt. "I'm scared, Sam."

"I know." He kissed the top of her head, her hair like silk beneath his lips. He'd managed to stay hydrated since he was home on leave. No dead skin on his lips caught on her hair.

"You don't have to go back," she whispered. "We can move to Canada. Seek asylum. Protest the war."

"Well, aside from being a felon for the rest of my life, you'd have healthcare for Peanut."

She slapped his chest. "I'm not joking." Her voice broke over a sob. "I don't want you to go back."

"Baby, I don't have a choice," he whispered.

"Yes, you do."

"No, I don't." An edge came into his voice, a tight twist of anxiety. He hated fighting. Especially with her. "I have to go back. I have men counting on me. I can't leave them to fight the war alone. Lewis and Hale would kill each other inside of a week without me."

She pulled away from him and stood up. She moved like a caged wolf, angry and protective. He thought of Maggie, her head down, her teeth pulled back in a snarl. "I don't care about Lewis and Hale. I don't care about any of them. I only care about you. I want you home, Sam."

He stood and tried to pull her to him. Nothing in the war had taught him how to deal with a hysterical female. At least, not how to deal with a hysterical female *appropriately*. Thunder rumbled over the house, shaking the frame. It reminded him of being too close to an IED. He waited for the concussion of the blast a moment later.

It came, shaking the old wooden house around them.

"Faith, I'll do everything I can to come home."

"That's not good enough!" She ran her hands over her hair. "I want you to promise me. Promise me that you'll come home."

"I can't control that, Faith. You're asking me to make a promise I can't keep."

"No, it's a promise you *won't* keep." Her voice was higher than normal, her eyes wild. Tears streamed down her cheeks, causing dark blue splotches on her tank top as she choked back a sob. "Whatever it takes. I want you home, no matter what."

"Faith—"

"I don't care what your mother says. I don't care what you have to do."

He finally managed to capture her, pulling her against him. She was stiff and unyielding.

"You don't mean that." His skin was cold.

"Yes I do. I don't care what you have to do. I don't care if it's a little kid holding a puppy, if that little bastard has a gun, you blast the fucker." Her words were fierce. Sam wondered whether she'd say such a thing if she'd ever stared down the sights on her weapon and seen exactly that.

He didn't think she'd be so determined for him to act then. But he didn't tell her that.

He didn't think she'd understand.

Her sob broke against his chest. He tightened his arms around her. He held her while she cried, her hushed grief and fear chipping away at the lock he held on his own emotions. The weight of his sins—those things he'd done and failed to do—threatened to break him.

He moved them both to the overstuffed chair they'd bought at a garage sale a few years ago. She'd fixed it up with a slipcover that had cost more than the chair.

Concern licked the base of his spine when she was still sobbing minutes later. He whispered soothing nothingness against her hair.

"Promise me?" she begged.

Sam closed his eyes. Knowing it was a lie before he even spoke the words, he nonetheless whispered into the darkness. "I promise."

The storm stopped abruptly. No rain. No distant thunder. The house was shrouded in darkness and silence except for the sound of Faith's sniffle against his chest.

He shifted, cupping her wet cheeks in his palms. "I promise, Faith. I'll come home to you."

Her bottom lip trembled a moment before she kissed him. He felt the relief in her body, her mouth. But there was no relief for him.

Instead, a deep fear rumbled in the distance as the storm moved away. But it left behind the nagging fear that Sam was going to die.

The universe was fucking with him.

Fog blanketed the house, an ominous thick soup of heavy air.

It felt as if he was stepping into the seventh level of uncertain Hell as he stepped off the porch to start Faith's orange Subaru.

He'd be on a plane before the sun came up. The last thing he would remember about his visit back home would be the headlights reflecting back into the vehicle from the thick wall of fog.

He walked back into the house, where Faith was filling his assault pack with snacks. He didn't have the heart to take the Clif bars out of the pack and leave the Slim Jims and Snickers unmolested by the alleged health food. He'd just give them away on the plane.

He supposed it was a sign that she cared, right? Health food meant she didn't want him to die of a heart attack at twenty-nine like his Uncle Chet.

He stood in the archway of the kitchen for a moment and watched her flitter around the small space. He tried to memorize the shape of her body beneath the thick grey sweater, the tiny bulge of her belly. He wanted to take the shape and smell of her back with him. Maybe it would give him something to think about during the long patrols other than the worry of getting blown up around the next corner.

He shifted and hitched up his pants. He'd lost weight while he'd been home on leave, which was the opposite of what normally happened. He was tempted to punch another hole in his Army-issued belt before he got on the plane. It would drive him nuts, constantly hiking his pants up while wearing his body armor.

Faith turned and smiled. The smile did nothing to mask the sadness in her eyes that she'd tried to hide beneath makeup. "Sorry I fell apart on you," she said, offering him a cup of coffee.

He kissed her lightly on the cheek. "That's what I'm here for," he said. "I'm good in stressful situations."

"You must be used to a heck of a lot worse than me crying in your arms."

He smiled and dumped a bucket of cream in his coffee. "I won't have cream in my coffee again until I get home."

"They don't have it over there?" Faith asked.

It was an excruciatingly normal conversation. They were both trying so damn hard not to think about what was coming.

"The main chow hall on the big base a few hours away has Coffee-mate sometimes. The closest thing to cream is half-and-half and to get that, we have to convoy five hours and cross a bridge that's known for ambushes." He grinned up at her. "Somehow, it doesn't really feel like it's worth the trip, ya know?"

"I can send it to you. If I put it on dry ice, it'll make it."

"It's okay. I get used to drinking it black." And he'd like it that way because if he complained, the rest of his men would complain. And all that complaining would lead to something stupid, like trying to convoy for cream and sugar or dip and smokes. "Besides, the one and only time we actually risked getting blown up for smokes and cream, the PX on Balad had been out of cigarettes and the Coffee-mate was expired." He shrugged. "So it's not something we're going to repeat. Not when Hale still sits funny from the shrapnel in his ass."

"You make it sound so…ordinary. Like getting blown up going to the store is just a normal thing." Her voice was quiet. Her words, hesitant.

He didn't know why he was telling her this. Maybe he wanted her to know all the stupid shit that happened over there. Maybe he wanted her to understand a little more when he needed a break and couldn't pretend that everything was normal when it wasn't.

And it probably never would be again.

Satisfied with his coffee and knowing it was going to be the last time he tasted heaven for quite a few months, he pulled his combat t-shirt over his head and stuffed it into the belt on his pants. He surveyed his stuff. His assault pack on the table. His duffle bag by the front door.

His gaze landed on Faith. Who wasn't sobbing. Wasn't making a scene. Steady, reliable Faith. He reached for her then, tugging her close and simply needing to hold her for a moment.

Her arms slid around his waist, her palms flat against his back.

Faith breathed out a trembling sigh. "Guess this means you're ready?"

"Yeah. Want me to drive?"

She shook her head. "I'm fine. I'm used to driving in this stuff. You're not."

Sam slung his assault pack over his shoulder and stuffed his wallet into his front pocket. He picked up his coffee and sighed. "Well, I suppose." He hesitated, hating that he was questioning whether he should say good-bye to his dog. And hating even more what that thought meant for his mental health. He scrubbed his hand over his face. Jesus, he was losing his fucking mind. "Maggie!"

The yellow lab came trotting down the stairs, her butt wiggling as she descended. Sam hesitated, then crouched down. "Be a good girl, 'kay?"

Thump thump. Her tail thumped on the floor; her big brown eyes looked at him with adoration. He rubbed her head and she lifted her paw, setting it on his thigh to keep him from stopping. He scratched beneath her chin where she loved being scratched, then stood up.

He followed Faith out into the fog and to the waiting Subaru. The tires crunched on the gravel driveway as she pulled out onto the main road that led from the middle of nowhere toward town and civilization. Or as much civilization as could be said to exist in the middle of Maine, hours from Bangor.

The road was dark and winding. They passed the occasional logging truck, barreling up the road toward the logging trails deep in the great north woods. The fog was thicker when the road dipped right before Charleston Hill. The bog at the bottom of the hill was spooky in the daylight, but in the dark, the fog seemed to swallow the headlights.

Faith flicked the lights to low beams and slowed down as she approached the hill.

"Why are you slowing down?" he asked.

"It would really suck to slam into a deer. Even if it would mean you got to stick around because you missed your flight." She glanced at him, her face lit by the dashboard. "On second thought—"

Sam reached over and stroked the back of her neck. Her skin was warm and dry. Not like the viscous fog. He was tempted to close his eyes but the fog danced between the evergreen trees, casting shadows where there shouldn't have been any.

They were at the airport far too soon. Faith pulled into the brightly lit parking lot and turned off the car. Silence fell over the vehicle when she reached for the keys.

He stopped her, his hand covering hers. The words he needed were locked in his throat.

Harder words he'd never spoken.

"I don't want you to come in."

———

Silence, cold and thick like the fog. Sam knew he was being a selfish prick. That didn't make his next words any easier to speak. Worse still for Faith to hear.

"I need to make the break clean, Faith. Dragging it out only makes it harder for me to leave."

Still she said nothing. He felt smothered, tense, waiting for her reaction.

She wouldn't be wrong if she slapped him. She was stronger than she looked. Her palm would be wet and hard against his face. She'd leave a mark if she hit him. He'd deserve it. He wasn't about to encourage that course of action, not by a long shot, but that didn't mean she wasn't thinking about it.

He'd seen Faith moved to violence only once in his life: they'd been in high school and the captain of the soccer team had told the entire senior class that Faith—then a freshman—gave horrible blowjobs.

She'd slapped him. In the middle of the cafeteria, when the soccer captain's hands had been otherwise occupied by a tray of sloppy joes and Mountain Dew, Faith had hauled off and decked him. Travis Paulson had never lived down the split lip. And no one else had spread rumors about her, at least not for the rest of her freshman year.

She'd gotten in trouble, of course. She wasn't from one of the good families in town. Her father hadn't even bothered to show up and defend her. She'd served in-school suspension—with Travis, no less—and then gotten on with her life.

But when she didn't move, didn't speak, Sam wondered what she was thinking. Her expression was blank. The only movement was the tapping of her thumb against the steering wheel.

Finally, she broke the silence. "That's an asshole thing to ask of me," she whispered. "I'm not going to see you for seven months. I'm probably going to have this baby without you. And you can't wait to walk away?"

Sam shifted to look at her. Faith did not bother to hide her anger or her hurt.

"It's not like that," he said softly.

"Then tell me what the rationale is for taking away the last thirty minutes we have together."

Sam sighed hard, releasing a tiny bit of tension bound in his chest. He saw it then, a brief flicker of emotion in the quiver of her bottom lip.

"Aw, honey, don't cry." He reached for her, pulling her as close as he could over the center console in the small car.

She resisted, pulling away when he would have offered comfort. "Don't," she sniffed. "Don't offer comfort when you won't be here in an hour. I can cry by myself, thanks."

"You don't understand how fucking hard it is to walk away."

She looked at him then, her eyes shrouded in darkness.

"I love you. So fucking much. It rips my soul out knowing

you're going to have our baby without me. I'm terrified of leaving you alone." He paused, rubbing his hand over his clean-shaven jaw. "But I've got to put away everything I feel for you and focus on the mission. I've got to turn it off, put it away. I'm not going to play cards with the locals." He tried to reach for her hand. She didn't pull away, and he covered it where she still gripped the steering wheel. "I can't be thinking about you when I'm over there."

Because you're everything that is good about this world. And over there life is empty and dark without you.

But he didn't say that. She didn't need to know that she was his hope and fear all bound into one. That was too much to ask of one person. Too much to ask of anyone. So he kept silent, hoping his explanation was enough.

"Sam—" She leaned into him, resting her cheek against his shoulder awkwardly. She wiped her face with the back of her hand. "I'm going to miss you."

He kissed the top of her head, inhaling the smell of her shampoo once more.

He didn't want to taint her with the filth.

"Me too."

He squeezed her hand and stepped out of the old Subaru. For a second, he thought she wasn't going to follow him, but then she stepped into the darkness.

He dropped his duffle bag on the damp concrete and pulled his assault pack out of the back. He slammed the hatch. The fog seemed to swallow the sound.

He didn't want to drag this out. Didn't want her to see the emotion that threatened to choke him. It wasn't easy for him to walk away from his future wife and child, no matter how much she seemed to think he was anxious to get back to the war.

The war was simpler. Easier somehow. And the addiction it fed was something sinister. Something Sam wanted to pretend did not exist.

Something he wanted to leave behind when he finally came home.

He opened his arms and she didn't hesitate. She stepped into his embrace, resting her head against his heart. Her breath was warm on his neck.

He kissed her eyes. The tip of her nose. Her mouth. Then he dropped to his knees and kissed her belly. "I'll see you in a few months, okay, Peanut? Be good to your mommy. No weird cravings or anything like that."

Faith's hand rested on his shoulder. Her fingers flexed when he rested his cheek against her belly.

"I love you," he whispered.

She said nothing as he slung his duffle bag over one shoulder then hefted his assault pack in one hand. Without a final look, he turned toward the terminal.

"Sam?"

He stopped. Looked back over his shoulder.

"Whatever it takes." Her soft words broke with fresh tears.

"Whatever it takes," he whispered into the fog.

And then he walked away.

CHAPTER SIX

The flight from Bangor to Atlanta wasn't bad, considering they sat on the runway in Bangor two hours, then on the approach to Atlanta, circled for another half hour before they were allowed to land. By the time Sam made it into the terminal, he'd eaten three of his twelve Snickers bars and contemplated breaking into the Slim Jims.

Except that if he ate the jerky, he wouldn't shit right for a week. He wasn't quite ready for that fun side effect of deployment to start up again.

His hands were shaking as he counted out the change for an egg-and-cheese bagel and large coffee. The bagel disappeared in record time, but his hands still shook as he waited for the food to hit his bloodstream.

He'd been hungrier before. The last mission before he'd gone home on R&R, he'd been at a remote combat outpost that had been cut off from supply routes. Actually, those fucking civilians in charge of their logistics had refused to convoy to their location because they got attacked every time they crossed over that goddamned bridge that kept getting blown up.

The day before the patrol had arrived to shut down the base

and escort them back to the main base, Sam had eaten two ketchup packets and half an MRE cracker. It had been the best fucking cracker he'd ever eaten. Other than remembering the ketchup, that entire mission was a blur. At least he kept telling himself that.

Wishing he could forget the parts that weren't a blur.

He still saw that one little girl with aching clarity. He wondered if she'd haunt him for the rest of his life or if he'd ever forget about her.

He dragged his hand over his face, then reached for his cell phone. No calls. Hopefully, Faith had gone back to bed. He shouldn't have kept her up that late. It was probably bad for the baby.

He shouldered his assault pack and made his way to the Admirals Club. One of the perks of fighting his nation's war: the corporations who sponsored it got good PR from giving soldiers free shit —in this case a chair that reclined while he waited for his flight back to Hell.

He signed in at the front desk and wrote down his flight information when asked. The young woman at the desk looked like she was barely out of high school. When had he started looking at twenty somethings and feeling like an old man? Or worse.

He wasn't the only soldier in the dimly lit Admirals Club. A skinny kid with bad skin was deeply involved in whatever he was reading. His lips moved while he read. The entire airport could have blown up, and Sam doubted the kid would have been jolted from the words on the page of the leather-bound book. It was probably a Bible. Lots of kids heading to war the first time found Jesus. Or God. Or whatever power they felt would get them through the relentless terror of combat.

Sam dropped his assault pack near a chair close to the back of the room. Recess lighting created a soft mood, one that beckoned him to pull a blanket over his legs and enjoy the last few hours of comfort. He settled back in the chair, plugged his headphones into his ears and picked up a copy of *Psychology Today* from the side table.

He flipped through the pages absently, until an article on schizophrenia caught his attention. They'd had a soldier thrown out of the Army for that right before they deployed. Goodman. The kid had been a known drug user, but he'd told his squad leader that the voice told him to kill Britney Spears and eat her heart.

Sam had been sure he knew what normal was, until he'd met Goodman. Goodman had sworn the devil was real and whispering in his ear.

Sam's commander had thought the kid was bullshitting to get out of deployment. The doctors had diagnosed him as a paranoid schizophrenic and that had been Goodman's speed pass out of the military. Sam wasn't sure whether the kid had been telling the truth or not, but he'd freaked Sam the fuck out every time he was around him. Something about him had just not been right.

He was damn glad that fucking lunatic wasn't on this rotation; that was for damn sure. What Goodman was doing now, Sam had no idea. He hoped whatever it was, it involved Goodman taking his meds.

What was it like to live with that kind of crazy? To look at the world and see things not like everyone else. Who was the crazy one?

The next thing he knew, a thin woman with too much makeup was jiggling his boot. "Sir?"

He opened his eyes, tugging one ear bud out of his ear.

"Sir, you need to catch your flight."

Sam squinted, then glanced at his watch.

He bolted upright. "Shit." Slinging his assault pack over his shoulder, he dropped the magazine and headed for the door. "Thanks," he called over his shoulder.

He made it to the gate with five minutes to spare. Which meant he hadn't stopped for a piss. He slid into his seat, stuffed his pack under the seat in front of him and prayed that he would not be smooshed between two big fat majors who smelled like burritos and grease and day-old body odor. If he was really lucky, the flight wouldn't be full and he'd have an entire row to crash out in.

He had one Ambien pill he was planning on having a deep and serious affair with as soon as the plane took off. He needed to take a piss first, though.

His wish was denied when the skinny kid from the Admirals Club swung into the seat next to him.

"Hi, Sergeant."

Sam blinked. He hadn't been called Sarn't in almost two weeks. Two blissful weeks of pretending he was a civilian. He'd almost forgotten that to the people he'd left in combat while he went home to fuck his girlfriend and get shit-faced drunk—not necessarily in that order—his first name was Sergeant.

Sam grunted. He hoped the kid wasn't going to chew his ear off the entire flight.

"Are you heading back from R&R?"

"Roger that." He paused, not wanting to be a complete asshole. "You?"

The kid shook his head, giving Sam an eyeful of the inside of his pores. "I'm new. I'm supposedly linking up with my unit. They're in a place called Tangi. Tongi."

"Taji," Sam said. "It's a big logistics base north of Baghdad. What unit are you going to?"

"Black Knights? It's a fuel company. I think."

"Are you a fueler?"

The kid shook his head again. "No, Sergeant, I'm a radio specialist."

Sam frowned, but it wasn't for him to decide the machinations of the Army personnel management system. Or to figure out why this kid was on his own with obviously no idea where he was heading. "Oh."

The kid's skin flushed with relief. At what, Sam didn't know. A smile teased at the edge of the kids' lips as he flipped open his book. Faint gold letters were etched into the worn leather: King James.

Sam ran his tongue across his teeth, bracing for what he guessed was coming next.

The kid didn't disappoint, staying true to stereotypes that Sam had both grown up with and grown to hate. The kid turned a thin, tan page softly and started reading out loud. And not quietly, either. "*Because if you confess with your lips that Jesus is Lord and believe in your heart that God raised him from the dead, you will be saved.*"

"Don't do that, man." Sam tried to keep the irritation from his voice. That verse was too familiar. Sam didn't read the Bible—he was Catholic after all, even if he was highly lapsed—but he knew that particular verse because Chaplain had been arguing with one of the captains in the TOC about it one night. According to Chaplain Cloud, the Book of Romans was all hellfire and brimstone. Too much Paul, not enough Jesus.

But Chaplain Cloud wasn't here to stop the kid from proselytizing and Sam damn sure didn't feel like spending his entire flight listening to this kid read out loud.

"Why not?" The kid seemed genuinely shocked.

"Because other people have to share this space with you, and not everyone shares your beliefs."

The kid tipped his head, his skinny neck bending at an angle that made Sam think of a goose. "You find my faith offensive." It wasn't a question.

Sam answered without thinking. "Yes. I do."

"Why?"

Sam took a deep breath and counted to ten. It was either that or throw the kid out of his seat. "Because your God doesn't exist," he snapped.

The kid's eyes went wide, then narrowed to a dangerous glint. "You've been to combat. How can you say that?" He folded the Bible reverently against his chest. "There are no atheists in foxholes."

"Get another sound bite." Sam stretched his legs out in front of him, tucking his feet around his assault pack. His Snickers bars were probably mashed into paste at this point.

The kid looked down at his Bible, his voice less certain than the words he professed. "Why are you so bitter?"

"I'm not bitter." Of course not. "I'm a realist. People say there are no atheists in foxholes like there's some kind of religious transformation that happens the first time you get shot at. The only transformation you're going to go through the first time a round hits the wall next to your head is whether or not you shit yourself."

The kid opened his mouth to protest, but Sam cut him off. "You don't get to sit there and preach the gospel out loud and drive everyone batshit crazy. Shut your mouth, get some sleep and start thinking about what you're going to do the first time shit pops off. Because when the first round goes live is not the time to arrange your world views on pulling the trigger."

The kid sniffed. His index finger rubbed across the spine of the leather. Up and down. Up and down. "I know what my world views are on killing, Sergeant."

Sam looked at him. A fanatic's glint lit the kid's eyes. "Do tell."

The kid puffed up with pride. "'For we wrestle not against flesh and blood, but against principalities, against powers, against the rulers of the darkness of this world, against spiritual wickedness in high places.'"

"Great, so you can read."

"I'll do my duty when necessary, Sergeant."

It was unnerving, hearing him say the full world 'sergeant' as opposed to the abbreviated 'sarn't' like everyone else who had been in the military for more than a day did.

"Will you? It's one thing to sit in the pews on Sunday and listen to what some preacher tells you. But when you're staring down the barrel of that weapon? Or worse, when you don't have time to think about taking that shot?" Sam looked at the kid with his bad skin and over-sure eyes, so certain about the way of the world. "Your religion won't save you over there. Nothing your

Sunday School teacher taught you means anything in a firefight. There are no good choices. They're all the same: they all turn out bad."

"Jesus will guide my hand."

Sam leaned forward into the kid's face. The kid flinched, and Sam felt a twisted flicker of satisfaction. "You don't get it. Jesus abandoned you the minute you got on this plane. He's not guiding your hand, he's not watching your back. You're on your own, kid, and you better figure out what you can live with and what you can't. Right now. This flight. Before you get to the desert and before you ever think about going off the base."

The kid licked his lips and leaned away from Sam. His thumb slid over the leather. "There is a higher purpose," he whispered.

Sam shook his head. "There is no higher purpose. Even the good choices you make in war come back to bite you in the ass."

"'Be strong and bold; have no fear or dread of them, because it is the Lord your God who goes before you. He will be with you; he will not fail you or forsake you. Do not fear or be dismayed.' Deuteronomy 31:6,8." The kid looked over at him, certainty in his eyes. "We are but servants in service of the Lord."

"I'm in service to Uncle Sam. Now take your religion and keep it to yourself. I get enough of that shit from my mother."

"Your mother —"

Sam held up his hand, silencing him. "What part of 'I don't want to talk about it' do you not understand?" He balled his fist in his lap, fighting the urge to grab the kid by the collar and twist until the words died in his throat. "Now, if you would like to talk about the Patriots—or maybe the Broncos?"

The kid looked down at his Bible.

Sam sighed. "Great. I'm sitting next to Jesus' sidekick." Sam leaned forward and dug the Ambien out of the front pouch of his assault pack. "I'm going to sleep. Wake me up when we get to Kuwait."

It was a long trip, making it back to Iraq. Pity there wasn't a direct flight from Baghdad to Bangor. That would have made life easier.

"You don't want to deplane if we stop somewhere?"

"Not if it means I've got to get a sermon," Sam said, folding his arms across his chest and closing his eyes. Goddamn but all this talk about Jesus pissed him off.

Fucking idealists heading off to war, thinking they were serving some part in a giant cosmic plan.

More like a cosmic clusterfuck.

He still had to piss, but they hadn't even closed the front doors of the plane. He'd go once they'd taken off. If he was still conscious.

"You really don't believe that God has a plan for you?"

The drug gently gripped his consciousness and pulled him under the heavy darkness.

"There is no master plan," Sam mumbled. It was only one step away from *there is no God.*

———

"The chow hall is out of regular Cokes again." Hale's voice penetrated the haze caused by too much wind and not enough rain.

The dust was everywhere. Ground into his pores. The crack of his ass. Beneath his toenails. His lips were chapped. He bit a piece of loose skin and tasted blood as it tore free.

"Diet Coke sucks balls," Lewis mumbled.

"You suck balls." Hale's fist shot up in the air. The entire formation halted.

Sam dropped to a knee, waiting for Hale to assess the intersection. A long moment hung in the haze. Then, he motioned for their squad to continue.

He expected Lewis to start bitching about having to walk to their objective. Lewis hated walking. He was fond of reminding everyone that he was in the Cav, which meant he'd planned on taking a tank or a Bradley wherever he needed to go.

Walking had not been part of his life plan.

Lewis was a husky kid with black hair and meaty fists and a temper that often needed defusing. Sam knew the power in Lewis' fists all too well. They'd gone a few rounds in the combatives ring, and Lewis had damn near knocked Sam's teeth out more than once.

He didn't dare let Lewis and Hale go at it. At least not without Hale having a mouth guard in. Hale thought he was tougher than he was, and Lewis had him by at least thirty pounds of pure mean.

"Ladies, will you shut the fuck up about Diet Coke?" Sam hissed. "I'm more concerned with getting to our objective on time."

Lewis shot him the bird. "Someone's panties are in a bunch. Don't be pissy just because the chow hall is out of Butter Pecan Baskin Robbins."

Sam flipped Lewis the bird back as Hale's fire team moved down into the alley, leaving Sam on point with Lewis' fire team. Sam inched to the edge of the building. The haze had swallowed all but the faintest shadow of Private Pillow's fat-ass head.

Shapes twisted in the haze. The wind whistled over the top of the building, stirring the haze.

The team's whispers carried on the wind behind him. The radio was silent. His heart pounded in his ears.

A dog barked in the distance, a hungry, desperate sound. A boot crunched against the dirt.

Hale's team was lost in the darkness, swallowed by the desert.

He called over the radio to Hale. The response came back broken. Unreadable.

"Chaos Red. Chaos Red."

Silence greeted his call. He keyed the mic again. Static.

He motioned for the remainder of the squad to get to their feet and sent two dudes to cover their rear while Sam and Lewis headed down the alley.

Side by side, they stepped into the haze.

A sound like a claw scraping against concrete grated through the air.

Something made of shadows and hate burst out of the haze.

———

The plane's tires skidded onto the asphalt. Sam jolted awake, his heart slamming against his ribs. His lungs refused to expand to allow a full breath.

His skin was stretched too tight over his bones. He closed his eyes. Focused.

And breathed. A deep, full breath of recycled air, but it was a breath so he was happy.

The seat next to him was empty, the cabin dark. His Bible-thumping seat companion was nowhere to be seen. Which was good, because it meant his nightmare had gone unseen. Always a plus not to have the soldiers around you wondering if you were crazy.

He was perversely glad that little fucker wasn't there to see it. Undoubtedly Jesus' sidekick would have told him his immortal soul was at risk.

The pilot braked and the plane slowed dramatically. Sam's body strained against the seatbelt. He reached for his cell phone to call Faith before he remembered that it wouldn't work other than as an alarm clock for the rest of the year.

He wanted badly to turn it on and see a missed call from her. Or better yet, a voice mail. Anything to remind him that there was still good in the world.

The plane slowed to a stop and everyone stood and started pulling down their bags. Sam watched, not anxious at all to get off and back to the shit and the grime and the dirt of the desert.

A young female soldier shrugged on an assault pack with a stuffed pink unicorn in the straps. Another kid, who looked like he was about twelve, had a video game guitar hanging out of his pack. Must be nice to have that kind of time, to play video games.

It was probably the reason the network sucked so bad that he couldn't get a decent video call through to Faith.

He could only imagine the sheer amount of shit that Lewis would give Hale if he caught him playing with a pink unicorn or a music video game. Or worse, if Hale caught Lewis playing with the unicorn. Sam smiled faintly, the tolerant smile of a tired uncle. Lewis and Hale fought like siblings but in the end, they had each other's backs. That was never a doubt in Sam's mind.

They started debarking the plane and Sam stood, stretching until his spine popped and his knees protested from sitting for too long. That sleeping pill had been no damn joke. Which was good, because it was probably the last good night's sleep Sam would have in a while. Like seven months.

He fiddled with the time on his watch while he waited, setting the time zone to Iraq time. He'd slept the entire flight. Which was awesome, except for the nightmare. That had sucked. And it wasn't even entirely a nightmare. One of the benefits of combat-induced insomnia was no nightmares. Had to sleep for that to happen and they were always too fucking busy to get more than a couple of hours here or there.

He finally took a deep breath and slung his pack over his shoulder and prepared to shuffle off the plane and onto the bus for a short ride to stinky porta-potties and then another ride to Camp Buehring for processing. It would be a day, day and a half until he ended up back at his base near Taji, depending on how the roads were.

He hoped Hale hadn't gotten the squad in any trouble. Hale was next in charge when Sam wasn't around because he couldn't count on Lewis to keep his temper in check with the platoon sergeant. Find out if he'd managed to fuck the girl working the call center with the pink hair.

A cold edge curled around his guts and squeezed tight. He tapped his thumb against his thigh as he waited in the line to get off the plane. Anticipation rolled through his fingertips. He fucking hated it here, hated the war, hated the goddamned people.

But yeah, that was excitement running through his veins now. The pure fucking adrenaline of the fight. He was looking forward to seeing what kind of shit Hale had gotten into.

The war was the one thing he was good at, and no matter what he told Faith or his parents or anyone else, the futility of it didn't matter when you were shoulder to shoulder clearing a building. The only thing that mattered was the man next to you.

And there was no higher calling than that.

CHAPTER SEVEN

The familiar sign of the Green Bean Coffee shop was the first thing he saw when he landed at Taji, and it was a welcome sight indeed. Sam briefly considered genuflecting in front of the green and white lettered sign, but figured the skinny kid with the Bible might take offense. Wherever he was. And why the fuck was he still thinking about that little shit stain?

He still had a good fifty minutes before he could expect to get his duffle bag from the mountain of duffle bags at the back of the plane, and then who knew how long before someone from his unit would show to pick him up.

If he was lucky, it would be someone in a base runner instead of a shitty three-mile ride in a gator, where you felt every fucking pothole and speed bump. Yes, Iraq had speed bumps — big ones meant to slow down Abrams tanks and Bradley fighting vehicles so they wouldn't run over their own soldiers. The potholes didn't really do much other than tear up the suspensions of the non-tactical vehicles used by anyone who could get their hands on one. Anything was better than walking in the ungodly heat.

Luckily it was October, which meant it was slightly cooler than the inside of the sun at night and only mildly oppressive during the day. The sandstorms were worse in the winter, which was why it had taken Sam two days to get from the base down south back to home station.

He ordered a large black coffee and grimaced as the bitter liquid scorched his tongue and made his taste buds want to curl up and die. He was reasonably certain he'd grown three more chest hairs from the strength of it. It was pure caffeine.

That was good, because Sam needed it. His head was still fuzzy from the sleeping pills. He'd taken another one last night to get over the jet lag. The fuzziness was why he didn't take them very often. He shifted his assault pack and walked outside into the haze. It swallowed the lights from the community events center, where Salsa Night was apparently happening.

Salsa Night. In the middle of the war. Good times. He sipped his coffee and contemplated crossing the courtyard to see about picking up a dog-eared paperback. Maybe he could find a new thriller. Maybe a mystery.

Who was he kidding? He didn't have time to take a shit properly, let alone read a full book.

He might have felt at ease at getting back into theater, but the truth was he could already feel the stress building in his shoulders. Nothing was simple here and yet, the routine of it all was something familiar. He knew exactly what would happen when he showed back up to work. His company commander liked to circumvent his platoon sergeant, which left Sam in the awkward position of having his commander's trust and stabbing his platoon sergeant in the back every single day. Not a good place to be, considering how many people were armed. Like, oh, everyone.

He dropped his assault pack onto a nearby picnic table and leaned on the nearby stone pillar, watching the headlights flicker through the darkness. Spectral shapes floated on the haze.

It was worse than his nightmare because this was real. He hated the fog. Night vision goggles illuminated the dark, but man had not yet invented a way to see through fog and haze and sand.

The brownouts were worse than the dark. Sam sipped his coffee as the shapes twisted and writhed on the mist. His fingers itched for the familiar curve of his weapon.

A conversation drifted closer as two troopers walked by. One of them had some frou-frou drink that smelled like cinnamon. It made him think of Faith and her flavored coffees.

"Blew a hole in the roof of the chow hall," the first one said.

"No shit?"

"Yeah. No backpacks in the chow hall anymore."

"Next thing you know, they'll be saying you can't wear bloody uniforms in the chow hall."

"You're an ass; you already can't do that."

"Saw the sergeant major doing it last week."

"Whatever. Sarn't Major is crazy. Chow hall guards don't want to get shot arguing with him."

Sam frowned as the conversation moved off and out of earshot. Which chow hall had gotten blown up? He tapped his thumb against his thigh, anxious for the air load team to get the pallets of bags off the plane. He wanted to get his duffle bag and get back to check on his boys.

After what felt like forever, the load master called them forward to get their baggage. Sam found his duffle bag easily from the big orange tag on the strap. He dropped it against the column and sat on it, leaning back against the cool concrete. He'd just sat down when a light blue pickup rolled into the courtyard in front of the airfield waiting area.

Sam stood, a slow grin spreading across his face as he recognized his ride. "Chaplain Cloud?"

"I am your faithful servant," Chaplain said, his eyes shining behind his silver, wire-rimmed glasses. "How was leave?" He lifted Sam's duffle bag before Sam could protest. It landed with a thud in the bed of the truck and Sam climbed into the back seat.

"Leave was good. How were things here?"

Chaplain climbed in next to his driver, then twisted in the

seat. "Not so fast. You just got back. I want to hear about home before I start depressing you with news of war and rumors of war."

"Was that a reference to the apocalypse?" Sam leaned back against the stiff back seat, more relaxed than he'd been on the entire journey back to the war.

"The Book of Revelation, to be exact," Chaplain Cloud said.

A couple of empty magazines bounced around on the floorboard. At least Sam hoped they were empty. "I'm good. Leave was good. Faith is pretty good. Baby is healthy."

"And how was your mom?"

Sam sighed. He'd opened up to Chaplain one night on a long walk around the perimeter of the base. He couldn't keep his frustration with her bottled up any longer. He didn't know how to get her to hear him when he told her he couldn't listen to her sermons any more.

He supposed it was odd to talk to the chaplain about his lack of faith in God. But Chaplain Cloud was one of the good guys. "Mom was Mom. We argued my last day there. Then patched it up before I left." He opened his eyes. Chaplain's grey-blue eyes were warm and compassionate, so unlike his mother's judgmental gaze. How could two people claim to worship the same God and be so different? "Other than that it was good, Chaplain. Now what's this I hear about a chow hall?"

Chaplain's driver pulled them away from the airfield and headed down the gravel road, which was in desperate need of being graded. It was as if potholes were a point of pride for this fucking country. Sam's tailbone protested each time the driver steered toward the next divot.

"Suicide bomber blew up the chow hall a week ago."

"How?"

"Local national security force. They're still looking into how he got through the headcount guard."

Sam swallowed. "That's not good." It meant there was a hole in their security somewhere. It was the somewhere that had Sam worrying. A known hole they could mitigate. Unknown? It left them vulnerable.

"No. No, it's not."

Sam scrubbed his hand over his mouth. "So what's been going on out in sector?"

"More not good things. We're pushing into the cities and building walls around them. Small outposts. Trying to clear two neighborhoods and hold them."

It was the Surge – they were trying out this new thing called clear, hold and build. Some officers got their panties in a twist that whenever someone brought it up – clear, hold and build was not a doctrinal task or some bullshit. Sam didn't really give a shit about doctrine beyond battle drills.

He supposed that was why he was a staff sergeant and not getting paid to be one of those big brained planner dudes.

Except it was the big brained planner dudes who kept stretching the force thinner and thinner. Clear, hold and build took boots on the ground – boots they didn't currently have.

"We don't have the manpower to do that." A sick feeling soured the coffee in his guts. "Not to hold them, anyway."

Chaplain Cloud nodded, pushing his thin glasses higher on his nose. "Yeah. That's the consensus."

"But we're going to shut up and color, aren't we?"

Chaplain's smile was grim. "Of course."

"That's easy for you to say. You've got Jesus as your sidekick."

Chaplain laughed and shook his head. "And we're back. That didn't take long. Glad to see your sarcasm didn't stay on vacation." He twisted back around and focused on the dark road ahead of them. "You're going to need it."

———

"You coming to the fight?" Chaplain's question caught him off guard.

Sam pushed his sleeve up and looked at his watch as the

truck pulled to a stop in front of the life support area where Sam and his platoon lived. They'd taken over a bunch of staff officers' quarters when they'd conducted a relief in place. The officers' quarters were much nicer than the enlisted bays across the base.

"That's today?" He'd forgotten about the combatives tournament one of the Marines had coordinated. It had official sponsors and ring girls. Sam suspected half the reason everyone was so excited was because of the ring girls.

Okay yeah, probably more than half.

"Yep. And if I remember correctly, Lewis and Hale are both in the ring."

"Why the hell are they both fighting?" Sam jerked his duffle bag out of the back of the pickup. "I can't have them knocking each other silly. It would leave Private Kadoush in charge of the whole squad."

Chaplain laughed. "It wouldn't be the first time the Wonder Twins got in trouble, now would it?"

Sam slung his duffle across his chest. "Nope. Leave those two idiots alone for two weeks and this is what they get into. Let me drop my gear and pick up my weapon from company ops."

"No weapons at the fight."

"Are you fucking serious?" He flushed with guilt at swearing in front of Jesus' right-hand man. "Sorry, Chaplain."

"I've heard worse. And yes, I'm serious. They tasked Delta Company with security. Everyone else? No bags, no nothing."

Sam's skin crawled. "Half the base is at this event."

"Probably more than that." Chaplain held out his hands, palm up. "Are you going?"

If the shit and the fan decided to have an orgy, tonight would be the night to do it. What could possibly go wrong in the middle of a hostile country with a war going on outside the wire? Did they honestly think they were safe *inside* the base?

"Oh sure." He didn't want to go anywhere near it. Nothing like mass chaos to draw the bad guys' attention. And having the majority of the base separated from their weapons was a bad, bad idea. What kind of fucking moron had made that call?

Probably someone already surrounded by his own personal security detachment. They weren't the ones who would be trampled in the chaos.

Sam climbed back into the back of the pickup and rode the distance to the fight in silence.

———

Chaplain was wrong. Half the base wasn't at the fight. The *whole* base was there. The crowd was thick, bunched up in pockets up a sprawling hill. The ring looked tiny from where the chaplain parked the truck. Sam pulled his cap on and waited for the driver.

"I think Tomas wants to stay with the truck."

Sam shrugged, scanning the hill for possible egress routes if he needed to make a quick escape. The porta-potties offered concealment but not cover. The stands where the colonels and senior enlisted guys were watching the fight would provide a small amount of cover. But the hill gave any shooter a massive advantage. It offered an unrestricted field of fire to take out the entire crowd. One crew-served weapon could do a shitload of damage.

Sam shoved aside his concerns as he descended the hill. The officers were paid a hell of a lot more than he was to figure out these things. If they figured no weapons was safe, then who was he, a lowly squad leader, to question it?

His rationale didn't really help soothe his anxiety. Not at all.

His misgivings faded as he approached the pit where the fighters—and two of his team leaders—waited.

Lewis saw him first. He grinned and held up a hand in a closed-fist salute. Hale turned around and jerked his chin in greeting. The sun was slowly sinking behind the concrete barriers. The floodlights illuminating the ring worked overtime to penetrate the encroaching darkness. The crowd dotting the hill overlooking the ring ceased to be made of soldiers and instead transformed into shapes and shadows.

"Welcome back," Lewis said, pulling his mouthpiece out. "Just in time to see me whip Pussy Boy's skinny ass."

"Fuck you, Lewis," Hale said with a grin. "You might be bigger than me, but I'm quick."

"Gotta be pretty quick to duck one of his fists," Sam said, tucking his thumbs through his belt loops. He felt naked without his weapon. "You two are fucking idiots. If either one of you ends up on sick call for this stunt, I'm going to court martial your ass."

"For what?"

"Damaging government property," Sam shot back. But he didn't mean it, and they all knew it.

"Whatever." Hale shrugged and swiped his forearm over his mouth. "How was leave?"

"Too short."

"Isn't it always?" Lewis said. "How's the old lady?"

"Faith is good." He didn't want to talk about her. Didn't want to pull her out of the box where he'd locked away the soft and tender feelings that did him no good over here. "What's been going on back here?"

"Same old shit. You tracking the new mission that starts day after tomorrow?" Lewis took a pull from his water bottle and swished it around his mouth before spitting it into the dirt at Sam's feet.

"Ah, shithead, I literally just got back from the airport. What mission?"

"Battalion is the main effort for a raid into the Karadah district. We're providing support."

Sam didn't get a chance to ask any more questions like what his platoon would be doing on this mission. He supposed he'd have time to figure that out after the fight. It sounded like they were sitting this one out, though.

The announcer called Lewis and Hale into the ring, leaving Sam alone with too many questions and an unsettled feeling in his guts that had nothing to do with his two team leaders beating the shit out of each other in front of the entire base.

The fight was over before it started. Hale hadn't been joking about being quicker than Lewis. Hale slipped around behind him and choked the bigger sergeant out before Lewis had even figured out where Hale had gone.

The shit-talking was never going to end. Sam spat into the dirt and scuffed sand over the glob as Hale celebrated and Lewis threatened to knock his teeth out.

The next few days were going to be oh, so much fun.

———

It was still dark when Sam finally gave up attempting to sleep. Dark, but not quiet. Nothing in Iraq was ever quiet. From the constant grind of the generators to the crunch of boots outside the walls of Sam's trailer, there was a constant whir of noise. The containerized housing unit's walls were thin as paper. He heard every crunch of boots on gravel, every porno some ass clown four trailers down decided to play too loud.

He'd gotten used to the silence at home, he realized with regret. The silence and the warmth of Faith curled next to him. He rolled onto his back and scratched his stomach, staring into the darkness. He'd been lying there for three hours. He supposed he'd dozed? Maybe? He'd pay for that later, he was sure of it, but that did nothing to convince his body to go back to sleep. He wished he wasn't out of Ambien.

There were a couple of ways to deal with the brutal jet lag. He could try to go back to sleep, which didn't appear to be a viable option. Or he could get up and head to the company ops to see what exciting stuff was happening on the night shift. The sergeant major had completely lost his shit when he'd discovered the night-time crew had been playing Risk in the ops. Sam couldn't say that he blamed him but then again, he'd pulled more than his fair share of night shift duty and sometimes it was boring as hell.

Still, he might get some good intel on the upcoming raid. Added bonus if he started to feel like he had a handle on things instead of feeling like he was still playing catch-up.

He rolled out of bed and got dressed, pulling on his pants and banging his boots on the ground before pulling them on to make sure nothing alive decided to take up residence in the dark. He cleared his M4 before slinging it across his chest. The weight was comfortable and familiar, like sliding on his glasses. Eye protection was their purpose, not style or comfort, but after months down-range, Sam just liked the feeling of them. After the foreignness of being home on leave, things finally felt like they were back in their place.

Sam stepped into the cool night air. The haze coated his skin in grit and he could practically feel the moisture being pulled from his exposed skin. He knocked his cap back on his head and looked around. The smells were familiar. Dirty, rough. Dusty. The dirt burned his nostrils.

He headed across the flat, dusty earth toward the call center. He figured he'd try to give Faith a call before he headed to the ops. It should be late afternoon at home. With luck he could catch her on her cell phone.

At least there was no line in the middle of the night. He slipped onto the smooth black stool and dialed the AT&T opera-tor, then jammed in his calling card information. A long silence stretched out in the ether before the phone started ringing. Two rings, then disappointment punched him in the belly when he was clicked to her voice mail.

"This is Faith. Leave me a message." Her voice sounded clean and fresh, out of place in the desert.

"Hey babe, it's me. Just trying to catch you before I head to work." He cleared his throat. "Miss you."

He hung up before he said anything else. Before the ache in his heart consumed him. He wanted to go home. He wanted to curl around her in their bed and feel her belly move beneath his palm.

It was sappy, but it was what he wanted. Lewis would bust his balls forever and a day if he knew Sam was thinking like that. 'Course, this would be from the guy who'd married a stripper, then bitched when he'd caught her blowing a guy behind a dumpster—literally—at a shitty dive bar back in Columbus.

He still called her, which baffled Sam to no end, but hey, there was no telling some guys. At least Sam had managed to keep Lewis from giving her Power of Attorney before he'd left. Some nights Sam wondered if Lewis had done it anyway and just hadn't told him. They'd find out soon enough whenever they redeployed, and Lewis checked his bank accounts. It wouldn't be the first time some girl had given a guy his first piece of ass and he'd given her his checking account. Poor dumb bastards came home from war and found their lives ruined.

Sam pulled his cap on and walked out of the call center, wishing he'd heard more than Faith's voice mail. He was lucky, he knew. Incredibly lucky to have found a girl like Faith. How she would adjust to life as a military wife? What would it be like, going home to her?

The moon was a sliver in the sky overhead, peering through the clouds every so often as Sam ducked through the maze of twelve-foot high concrete barriers on his way to the ops. They lined the roads, circled the buildings. Some were decorated with graffiti. Others bore wounds from encounters with military vehicles.

Concrete and dust, that was his home now. It surrounded everything of even moderate importance, and what wasn't protected by the massive barriers was barricaded by walls of sandbags.

Things lived in those sandbags. Creeping things. Along with massive fucking camel spiders. One had attacked him two weeks before he'd left for R&R. He'd thought about shooting the damn thing before it had skittered into a hole beneath a sandbag wall. The thing had been the size of his fist, and apparently pretty pissed that Sam had dared walk by its cave.

He'd never cared for spiders, but he fucking hated them now.

What made it worse was that Benning had some of the biggest fucking spiders he'd ever seen until he'd gotten to friggin' Iraq. He was convinced that he was going to go take a shit one day and a spider was going to latch on to his balls.

He dragged a hand over his face. He needed a cup of coffee if he was going to start contemplating vasectomy by spider. He hoped the ops sergeant major had gotten over the cinnamon-flavored coffee fetish he'd had going before Sam had gone home. He rounded the next barrier as the sliver of moon disappeared behind a bright cloud.

Something skittered in the shadows. Fear tingled up Sam's spine and he turned, half expecting to see something charging from the shadows. He fucking hated the feeling of being chased.

When he'd been a kid, he and his Uncle Horace had been out fishing in the bog late into the evening. Uncle Horace had thought it would be funny to hide from Sam in the woods. Sam had been nine.

He'd been leading the way back up to the clearing that night when he'd realized he was alone. His uncle had disappeared into the trees. A dozen doves had lit from their roosts, coos mixing with the rustle and flap of wings.

A twig had snapped behind him and nine-year-old Sam had spun, convinced it was the devil himself.

He never knew what had stepped out of the woods. All Sam remembered seeing was a shadow melting from behind a tree and he'd taken off, tearing through the trees until he'd run out of breath and adrenaline.

He'd slammed face first into a low branch. His eyes watered but he kept running away from the shadows that had nipped at the back of his neck and chased him into the clearing and across the field to his mother's kitchen.

Now he swallowed the fear that prickled at the base of his spine and made his guts clench. His fingers tightened on the butt of his weapon. He didn't call out but it was a close thing. Primitive terror rose up and whispered that he was a coward masquerading as a warrior.

Nothing moved in the silence except the rapid pounding of his heart against his chest. Sucking in a deep breath, he turned and headed back toward the company ops.

And was grateful that no one was around to see him pick up his pace just a little bit.

CHAPTER EIGHT

It was hot as balls and it was only 7:00 a.m. Sam hadn't managed to get any more sleep and he hadn't managed to eke any information from the staff officers riding the night shift at the battalion headquarters. He was fucking irritated, on his way back from the chow hall with shitty food weighing on his guts and a piss-poor attitude.

He walked into the company ops and immediately noticed the changes. The first sergeant's office was empty. Not missing-a-person empty, but missing all of a person's stuff. There was a blank desk and an empty chair. The humidor that First Sarn't Gnash had kept on his desk was gone, along with the Maxim calendar he'd pinned up by his monitor. Gnash had always sworn that Mila Kunis was his future ex-wife, a statement that had prompted some uncomfortable visuals.

But now his office was empty and Sam wanted to know why. He knocked on the commander's door.

Captain Lehr looked up from where he was swearing at his computer. "Fucking SIGO can't make the goddamned fucking computer talk to the fucking printer."

Sam leaned on the doorframe and hooked his thumbs into his belt loop and waited for his commander to stop beating up on the signal officer. His M4 bounced on his hip. "Someone having a good morning?"

"Fuck you, Brown."

Sam jerked his head back toward Gnash's office. "Where's Top?"

Lehr's nostrils flared. The vein in the center of his forehead throbbed. Sam wondered if it was possible to have a heart attack from a temper tantrum. Lehr was known for those — the tantrums, not the heart attacks. The vein was the warning sign that he was approaching blast-off.

"He got moved down to Camp Victory."

"For what?"

Lehr sniffed roughly. The muscle in his jaw pulsed as he slammed his fingers into the keyboard, trying to use brute force to make the computer do his bidding. "For pissing off the sergeant major."

"Huh?"

Lehr swore and threw the keyboard across the room. Sam leaned back to get out of the way of any other projectiles. "First Sarn't decided to tell the battalion commander his plan for the mission we've been working on was fucking stupid. So now he's guarding the burn pits with the other rejects who didn't have sense enough to keep their fucking mouths shut."

"The Surge is going well, then?"

Lehr stopped what he was doing and stared at Sam. Everything was quiet and tense. The commander looked at Sam like he wanted to nail him square in the jaw. Lehr was an angry bull, and Sam felt like he was wearing a bright red cape.

The silence hung on. A thousand emotions flickered across the commander's face. His chest rose and fell in hard, deep breaths.

His nostrils flared a final time before he spoke. "Swimmingly," Lehr said, his voice dangerous and low, his temper barely restrained. "You hear about the latest plan?"

"Yeah. Mostly just rumors, though."

Shifting the conversation away from the first sergeant, then, was a wise move.

"It's not going to be easy," Lehr said. The vein in his forehead stopped throbbing as he picked up the pieces of his keyboard and tossed them on the ratty chair in front of his desk. "We've got a briefing in about an hour. I need all the squad leaders there."

"Okay." Sam paused. "Who is acting first sergeant?"

"Tick."

Tick was Sergeant First Class Tykowski. He was built like a pit bull and had the disposition to match. He was also known for having a porn addiction. Rumor had it that Tick had gotten caught jerking off in the middle of their fifty-man bay on the initial invasion. Sam didn't really want to know either way, and he always had second thoughts after Tick slapped him on the back or wanted to shake hands. But what he did on his off-time was his business. Tick was an asshole, but he was a competent asshole. So the resident whack-off king was now Sam's first sergeant.

He shrugged. "Anything else I need to know before I go round up my guys?"

"We're doing a joint op with another unit."

Sam raised both eyebrows. "Huh?" That didn't sound like a raid.

"There's a unit attached to the other brigade. We're going to conduct a relief in place into their sector during the operation."

Sam frowned. "I'm confused, sir."

Lehr pointed at a map. "Our battalion has been ordered to move into this battle space," he said, pointing at an area covering several kilometers in a particularly shitty part of town. "The unit holding it has been there for fifteen months. We need to replace them so they can redeploy. So rather than do two separate operations, we're going to send our folks out to transition with them while providing support for the raid on this mosque."

Doing a joint operation with an outgoing unit was not unheard of. He'd seen it numerous times over the last few deployments. The problem was, joint ops always raised confusion about who was actually in charge. No matter how many times the guys in charge clarified it, someone didn't get it—usually some dumb shit lieutenant who ended up getting left in sector.

"So they get to go home and we get left holding the bag of shit in the form of an area that's too much for us to hold with the number of people we've got?"

He wasn't surprised. He just wished it felt like more of a plan. Maybe he'd feel better about it once he had an idea that was better than the current muddy-water visual.

Then again, he was never sure what the higher-ups were doing. He went where they told him to go, shot what they told him to shoot, and hoped he managed to bring all his boys home in one piece.

Lehr nodded. "Pretty much."

"Pretty much sucks, sir. Top was right. This plan is fucking stupid."

"Yep. And I need you to keep that to yourself because I don't need any more of my sergeants getting fired."

Sam pressed his lips together until a split at the edge opened back up. He needed to remember to get a new ChapStick the next time he was at the shoppette. "Roger that."

He headed back up the hill toward the squad bay where the platoons hung out between missions. The squad bay had a giant television for video games—the violent cathartic kind, not the music video kind—along with a raggedy old couch they'd stolen on their first patrol.

Captain Lehr had merely shaken his head and walked off when they'd come rolling back through the base defense checkpoint with a couch strapped to the roof of the Bradley. They'd sprayed it down with Febreze and pretended that because it smelled clean, it was clean. Sam was pretty sure he didn't want to know any of the things that might be growing in the fabric.

Sam walked into the squad bay in time to see Lewis take a swing at Hale. Hale ducked and danced out of his reach, laughing.

Sam waited for the shocked look on one of the new privates'

faces to spread through the crowd. Guilty looks flashed through the formation. The last two to notice were Lewis and Hale, and not until Lewis attempted to knock Hale's teeth out one last time.

"Honestly, will you two just make out and get it over with?" Sam said, hooking his thumbs into the loops on the front of his pants.

"Ha ha, fuck you, ha ha," Hale said flipping him the bird. "Finally done making the commander's coffee?"

Sam returned the gesture and everyone relaxed. "I need you guys to stop making googly eyes at each other and get your shit on. We've got a mission brief in"—he glanced at his watch—"twenty-six minutes."

A subtle shift passed through his squad. Huggins put down the video game controller and adjusted his pants. Jinx shifted his weapon higher on his shoulder. One by one his boys stopped fucking around. Sam preferred it when they were fucking around but it was oddly calming to go through the ritual of getting everyone kitted up in their body armor.

"Jinx, start getting everyone loaded up and doing our pre-combat checks. Twitch, get with the maintenance guys and make sure we're fully mission ready on all counts. Go get the commo guy out of his fucking trailer and off the video games and make sure our comms are wired tight. I don't want another episode where we lose radio contact with half the convoy."

His boys peeled off, each on their missions as Lewis and Hale picked up their weapons where they'd stacked them against the couch. Lewis popped his knuckles, a dangerous glint in his eyes.

"So what do we know?" Hale asked, slinging his weapon across his chest at the low ready, muzzle pointed at the ground.

"Joint mission with Quarter CAB."

"Not those fucking cowboys," Lewis said, tucking his t-shirt into his pants before the sergeant major caught him and went balls-deep on him for looking like a slob.

"Yes, those fucking cowboys," Sam said. "We don't get a vote on who we're running around out in sector with. And after what happened to First Sarn't, I'm thinking we need to just shut up and color."

Hale looked at him, his cheeks flushed from sparring with Lewis. Only his eyes belied the seriousness of his question. "And when do we argue that this is fucking stupid?"

Sam looked the younger sergeant in the eye. "When it's time to argue, we'll argue," Sam said quietly. "Now get your shit and let's head to the ops."

Sam didn't want to remember the time they hadn't argued. Not when Captain Lehr had ordered them to clear and hold the school in the middle of the sector. They hadn't argued when the order had come down to secure it because there was a weapons cache inside.

Sam had wished with everything he was that he'd disobeyed that fateful order. But he hadn't. And only Lewis and Hale knew what had happened because of that order. The fact that both men were still unflinchingly loyal to him said more than any words ever could. He would go to the wall to protect them after what they'd done for him.

He could never repay their silence.

The guilt, though. The guilt was his alone.

———

The company ops was no longer empty. It no longer smelled like fresh coffee and dust, either. Instead, it was packed full of dirty men and smelled like balls that hadn't seen the wet side of a baby wipe in a long, long time.

Sam didn't usually notice the smell, but crammed into the small space, everything was concentrated. The stench was a thick, greasy taste on the tip of his tongue. He could almost consider dipping to rid himself of the flavor.

He slipped a piece of gum in his mouth instead.

He squeezed his way to the conference room. It wasn't really a conference room—more like a plywood lean-to that had been nailed to the back of their ops. The table was another piece of rough plywood balanced on two homemade sawhorses. The single light dangled from a dirty orange extension cord and a thin green piece of 550 cord hammered into the wood with a rusty nail.

Sam made his way to Tick, who was sweating profusely. On any other man, Sam would have thought it was nerves. On Tick it was normal. Tick could sweat in thirty-below-zero weather. It was just how the man was built.

"Nice crowd," Sam murmured.

"Tell me about it." Tick spat into a soda bottle.

"So what are we doing?"

"We're support for this mission." Tick pointed at the sand table, a mock-up of their sector. "We've been running through the different routes all week, trying to make sure we don't tip them off that we're coming." He stuck his finger into his bottom lip and fished out the dip only to replace it instantly with another wad. "Merrick is going to be in charge of your sector," Tick said.

"Which one is Merrick?" Sam scanned the partially hidden nametapes on upper arms, but none stood out as the name he sought.

"I'm Merrick."

Sam turned and looked into the face of a man who had no business being anywhere but eating. He was skinny, his face lined and weathered from too many years in the vicious sun. The man was constant motion. His hand tapped against his thigh. His eyes darted around the room before landing back on Sam.

Merrick was taller than Sam, forcing Sam to tip his chin to look into the bigger platoon sergeant's face.

"Brown," Sam said, offering his hand.

Merrick glanced at Sam's outstretched hand and nodded before returning the grip. "Merrick. Nice to meet you."

It was an oddly pleasant greeting in a place where manners weren't often on display. Sam couldn't say what made it stand out in his mind, other than that.

Sam dropped his hand to his waist, tucking his thumbs into his belt loops. "So, what's our task and purpose?"

"Our task is to provide support to clear this block and provide security for communications support for the main element. We've got intel that there's a weapons cache behind this mosque." Merrick leaned over Sam to the table to watch as Tick briefed the mission on the sand table.

"Wow, actual information about the mission," Sam muttered. "I'm forever in your debt." From what he'd gathered from the conversations around him, Sam wished they were going out in elements that were better prepared to defend themselves.

"We're pulling security on the tactical command post," Merrick said. His voice was low and scratchy, as if he spent too much time smoking. Or breathing in the grit and sand in the desert. "Two squads."

"We're jumping the TAC?" Sam asked. They hadn't launched the TAC since they'd arrived in country. This was a much bigger operation if they were pushing out the TAC as opposed to just controlling the battle from the main headquarters. "To secure this entire area?"

He looked again at the area he was tasked to secure. With less than a platoon. It was almost two full blocks. "Two squads aren't nearly enough to properly secure the building with an inner and outer cordon, let alone keep from getting overrun if the enemy decides to get froggy. And you can fucking forget trying to hold all that battle space."

"We'll have enough men. The mission will be fine. We've got good support from the locals here." Merrick's voice didn't waver. Didn't flinch. Didn't hold the edge of panic Sam felt licking at the base of his spine.

He kept trying to get his brain around the nagging detail that was escaping him. Something wasn't right, something more than the lack of manpower.

It flittered away, just out of reach.

Damn, but he wished he'd gotten some sleep.

Merrick continued, ignoring the tension in the room. "We're going to take two squads and secure this area around this orphanage. We're security for the TAC, which will establish the communications relay point and monitor the battle. And then we will pack it all up and go home. Questions?"

"Yeah, a lot of them, actually," Sam said, bristling under Merrick's calm façade. He couldn't be that calm, could he? This mission sounded like a world class clusterfuck.

"You have a problem, Sergeant?"

Sam frowned at the way Merrick said the full word "sergeant". The same way that fucking weirdo on the plane had said it.

"Yeah, I do."

Across the table, Lewis looked up from the map. Silence fell across the room. Sam could have sworn he heard crickets chirp.

Merrick blinked and leaned back, folding his arms across his chest. "Let's hear it, then." He spoke in a way that sounded like he genuinely wanted to hear Sam's opinion as opposed to letting Sam skewer himself on a pike of his own making.

"This area is too big to properly secure with less than a platoon. Even if we go out loaded for bear, we'll leave holes in the perimeter. The terrain works against us because the house you're talking about using is at a low point at the edge of the neighborhood. We'd be better off securing this building and using it instead." He pointed at the satellite image of a building next to a mosque.

"This building you're so eager to use is an orphanage," Merrick said quietly. "It's off limits."

Sam flinched at the thought of little kids in the middle of a clearing operation. Still he drove forward, hating the point he was about to make. "Not if the insurgents are using it as a base of operations," he said. "Then all Geneva protections are off."

Merrick's lips cracked a cold smile. "Mighty bloodthirsty, are we?"

"Not particularly anxious to die in the middle of a poorly planned mission."

"As opposed to dying in a well-planned mission?" Merrick asked. His smug tone grated.

"I prefer the not-dying-at-all option." Sam straightened, bristling. "There is absolutely no point in pushing the TAC out to this location. We're holding a couple of city blocks just to hold a couple of city blocks."

Merrick stared at Sam, his eyes glittering black in the low light. Sam lifted his chin, refusing to be cowed by a man who looked like a walking skeleton.

"I realize this is less than ideal," Merrick said, "but I assure you we have enough men and the locals are helping us. We'll be fine with what we have."

Sam refused to be sucked into the calmness surrounding Merrick. "This plan sucks and I'm not going to just sit back and do nothing while you drag my boys into a shithole fight with no objective."

A moment later, Merrick was in his space. His breath was hot on Sam's face and smelled like cigarette smoke and coffee. "You think you get a vote here? You'll play your part, Sergeant," Merrick said, his voice a soft hiss.

"Or?"

Merrick's smile was merciless. "Or you'll let your men go out on this mission without you."

"Are you fucking threatening me?" Sam growled.

"Take it however you like." Merrick patted Sam's chest with both hands. "But you're still going to do the mission whether you like the plan or not. So how about you—how would you say it? Shut up and color?" He glanced over at Sam. "You don't have any problem obeying orders, now, do you?"

Sam tightened his fists by his sides and said nothing.

"Sarn't Brown, I trust you're playing nice?" Captain Lehr's voice penetrated the brewing shit storm in Sam's head. He'd stepped into the company ops with another captain on his heels.

Sam took a step back from Merrick's smile. Merrick brushed his sleeve off with one hand. "Your sergeant didn't mean any harm, Captain Lehr," Merrick said. His lips curled slightly at the corners. Sam's fists bunched by his sides. "He was just expressing his opinion."

"I wasn't worried about him," Captain Lehr said to Merrick. The shorter captain stepped into the conference room behind him, a small blond man who looked like he was about twelve. "I was worried about you."

Merrick's smile didn't waver. "I wouldn't. I've got a long history of getting people on board with plans far less ideal than this one." He tapped the edge of the table with his knuckles.

"If we're all done with the get-to-know-you phase, would we all like to get back to the mission?" Captain Lehr said.

———

An hour later, Tick elbowed Sam in the ribs when he caught Sam watching Merrick. "Cut the shit."

"The elbow delivered that message loud and clear," Sam snapped. "I didn't need a neon sign."

"Apparently you do. If I leave this room to work with Second Platoon, are you going to act like a fucking adult or do I have to babysit your stupid ass?"

He thought about arguing, he really did; there was something about Merrick that set Sam's teeth on edge. No one was that calm out here. It wasn't fucking natural.

"All right then." Tick waved his hands at the table. "You two play nice and work on the defense plan for the TAC."

Lewis and Hale moved closer to the sand table on one side while Merrick's fire team leaders leaned on the other side.

"Clearly this mission is off to a good start," Sam muttered.

Merrick ignored the comment. He pulled his knife out of a sheath on his hip and marked a circle around the building they were planning on using as the tactical command post. "We'll set defensive perimeters here, here and here. Main guns will go at the major entry points."

"Manning those guns takes half a fire team off mission," Sam said. "We'd be better off putting the big guns here and here, then using smaller crew-served weapons like the 249 here and here. Gives better coverage with smaller manpower requirements."

Merrick looked up sharply. "You're not understanding me. We're not taking the Bradleys. We're rolling in Humvees."

"You're fucking kidding me, right?"

"In case you didn't already gather, I don't have a sense of humor to speak of. No, I'm not fucking kidding you." Merrick traced a line in the sand with the tip of his knife. "This isn't a big enough operation to warrant the Brads."

"Why aren't we bringing the big guns?"

"Ask the planners at brigade. I don't know and I don't fucking care. We don't have them. Get over it."

"You honestly expect us to just roll into the neighborhood in thin-skinned vehicles and be fine?"

"Well, I could lie to you, you know. Tell you it's all unicorns shitting rainbows. Would that make it easier to sleep at night?" Merrick tipped his chin and narrowed his eyes. The calm was gone now, replaced with an intense focus. Sam thought of a cat watching a hamster as it scurried for a crumb. "But you don't sleep well now, do you?"

"Listen, Gandalf, knock off the mind-reading shit," Sam snapped. But the question unsettled him. "And I'm glad you think this is a goddamned joke. We're the ones who have to stay in this area when you head the fuck out of here and go home."

Merrick's smile was flat. "We've been here for fifteen months. If you think you know the situation on the ground better than me, by all means, have at it." He took a step back and gestured toward the sand table.

Sam straightened and folded his arms over his chest. "I'm not sure what game you're playing here but I'm pretty well not interested in it. I don't trust these fuckers as far as I can throw them."

"And that's why, when we leave, you'll see an increase in attacks. Because these fuckers, as you call our allies, can tell when you don't trust them. And trust is the foundation of everything we do. Every agreement."

"Dude, cut the shit," Hale whispered. "He's been out in this neighborhood more than us. Stop pissing him off."

Sam scowled at Hale. "You're on his side?"

Merrick smiled. "You should listen to your team leaders."

"I do," Sam snapped. "Do yours even speak?"

Both of Merrick's team leaders looked up at the same time. Their faces were cut in shadows from the single light bulb. They looked hungry. Like beasts on the edge of humanity.

"Woof," the dark-haired one said.

Sam bit back a smart-assed comment and shrugged off Hale's disloyalty. He rolled his shoulders, trying to release the tension squeezing the back of his neck. "So we're putting mounted security here and here. We've got fifty-cal mounts on some of the Humvees. We'll take those. It won't kill us to man those in two-man teams."

Merrick nodded and marked an *x* in the sand. "We'll string up the concertina wire around the entire building three strands high. The signal guys will be able to get the antenna up on the roof. We'll have security on the roof, too."

Sam surveyed the mock-up of the city. "This building is going to block our communications."

"The antenna will be able to get over it."

"Barely," Sam said. "It would make more sense to occupy this building and put the antenna on that roof."

"That building is off limits per our working agreement with the mayor. We go in there, we risk killing a shitload of women and children." Merrick looked up, directly at Sam with those calm, penetrating eyes. "And we wouldn't want that to happen, now would we?"

Sam held his expression immobile. He couldn't know. There was no fucking way he could know what had happened back in that school. "Sure. Whatever. This building is a major vulnerability in the security plan." Sam looked back at the sand table, avoiding

Merrick's eyes. The fucker knew. He *knew*. How the fuck did he know? Sam's heart slammed against his ribs.

Sam looked up. Merrick was watching him, those black eyes unblinking in the flickering light.

The hair on the back of his neck stiffened as cold wound around his spine.

CHAPTER NINE

"I have a bad feeling about this," Hale said as they walked back to the life support area.

"You have a bad feeling about every mission," Lewis said. He flicked the wad of dip out of his bottom lip and spat into the dirt.

"It's part of my natural sunny disposition, smart ass." Hale elbowed Lewis, but with no force behind the gesture. "You okay, boss?"

"Not really." Sam pushed his Eye Pro higher on the bridge of his nose. "I don't like this mission any more than either of you." He sucked in a deep breath, trying not to choke on the dust in the air. "But we need to keep that shit to ourselves. We don't need to get the guys wound up. They need to focus and so do we."

"No shit, Sherlock," Lewis said. "But why couldn't we just get the commander to overrule that guy about that big-ass building?"

"We don't want a repeat of the school mission," was all Sam said. Silence fell, an uncomfortable memory filling the gap in the conversation.

Hale kicked a rock down the path. It bounced off the Jersey barrier and landed in a small hole. "Yeah, well, kids on the battlefield are always bad news."

Lewis pulled his dip can out and slapped it between his thumb and forefinger. "There won't be any more kids on this mission. God can't be that cruel twice."

Sam swiped his hand across his mouth and said nothing. They rounded a barrier and came up short.

A dingy brown dog sat in the middle of the path. She lifted her head.

Sam couldn't look away from the wretched suffering etched in the lines of her ribs. He could count them clearly. Her teats were empty sacks beneath her belly, flaccid and empty. Her eyes, though, were sharp and filled with bitter misery.

She tensed when she saw them but made no move to get up. They had no way around her, either.

"Where did she come from?" Sam asked.

"She's a stray some of the guys have been feeding," Hale said.

"We're just violating GO1 with impunity now?" Sam asked. General Order Number One prohibited feeding any of the local wildlife, along with any form of fun and other good stuff.

Lewis shrugged. "She's a good mouser. Our rodent population has gone down dramatically since she moved in."

"How long has she been around here?" Sam wasn't comfortable with the idea of a feral dog in the life support area. Nothing against dogs or cats in general, but he wasn't a fan of adopting the local mutt. Having pets in the life support areas was asking for trouble, especially since the last rabies outbreak at a nearby base had gotten three soldiers evac'd out of theater to the hospital in Germany. Only one had come back, according to the private news network.

Sam's squad was already short two dudes. He couldn't afford to lose any more. Not to feed a goddamned dog. He barely had enough personnel to establish a proper perimeter.

"About two days before you came back, actually," Hale said.

The dog stood and stretched, her narrow body extending until it looked as if her spine would snap.

"There's a captain at battalion who is just dying to catch her, but she's too smart. She's avoided every trap, and every time

Vector Control comes around, she's nowhere to be seen." Lewis stuffed a wad of black dip in his bottom lip. "Some of the guys think she's a ghost."

Sam snorted as she trotted off, dust kicking up from her paws. She disappeared around one of the barriers. Sam wondered if she usually hung out in the middle of the paths or if this was something new. He deliberately avoided the idea that she looked like the dog from his nightmare on the plane. At least her shape and coloring were similar.

He rubbed his eyes and wondered if he could find a decent cup of coffee before he started prepping for the mission. He was starting to lose his fucking mind.

Hale looked at him. "The guys really like her. She's good for morale."

"She's as good as dead if someone gets bit," Sam snapped. "As long as she leaves everyone alone and we do the same, I'll let it ride. First time I see someone feeding her, it's their ass and I'll double tap her right between the eyes."

Lewis spit into the dirt. "That's pretty fucked up, you know."

"Got it, but we're not in fucking Kansas anymore. The damn dog could have rabies, distemper. All kinds of good shit. We don't have the manpower to risk losing someone because they wanted to pet the rabid puppy."

Lewis held up both hands. "All right; Jesus. Did you not get laid when you were home or what?"

"Fuck off," Sam grumbled.

"Dude, what the hell is your problem?" Hale asked.

"Nothing. I just don't want anyone fucking with the damn dog. Is that too hard for you to comprehend?"

"Got it. Jeez," Hale said.

Lewis pulled his dog tags out of his shirt and unlocked the door to his trailer. "Go jerk off or something. Your mood sucks."

Sam flipped him off as he walked by. Hale ducked into his trailer a few minutes later. He walked into his own trailer, palming the phone card he'd left next to his bed. He had a few minutes; he wanted to try to sneak in a phone call to Faith before this mission. He wasn't superstitious, but he wanted to hear her voice.

He swung open his door and stopped dead.

Hale stood in the doorway, his hands stuffed in his pockets.

"Look, I know you're in a shitty mood and all, but..." Hale's weapon was slung across his chest, dangling from the three-point sling. He had a wad of dip in his lip and he spit around the corner of Sam's trailer. "So, ah, you got a sec?"

Sam rubbed his thumb over the cold plastic phone card. Regret cut him as he stuffed it into his pocket. Faith probably wouldn't answer anyway.

Sam stepped aside to let his team leader in. Hale was a good guy, but any time a conversation started with "Do you have a sec," bad things followed. The kind of bad things that when they were home in the States ended with Sam making sure Hale didn't choke on his own vomit. "What's up?"

Hale stood for a moment, looking around Sam's room. A thin coat of dust covered everything: the pillow on the bed, the frame. Sam's duffle bag sat in the corner where he'd thrown it the other night; he still hadn't unlocked his wall locker.

Sam had other things he wanted and needed to do. Instead, he stood and waited for Hale to figure out what the hell he was going to say.

He was not prepared for Hale to pull a business-sized envelope out of his cargo pocket and shove it at him.

Sam looked at it like it was dusted with white powder. "What's this?"

"I want you to make sure my mom gets this. And don't let them erase my computer, either."

Sam stuffed his hands in his pockets. "I'm not taking that."

Hale didn't budge. "Yes you are."

"No, I'm not because I'm not burying you." His throat thickened. He fucking hated this part of the deployment. The part where the guys started questioning whether or not their ticket would be punched. Whether they'd be the ones standing on the flight line or the ones being carried across it.

He didn't want to think about Hale or Lewis or any of his boys in that flag-draped coffin. He'd buried enough of his team this deployment. And the one before that. He wasn't sure how many more he could bury before he simply broke. "I'm not having this conversation," he said quietly.

"Good. Then take the damn envelope and make sure my computer gets home to my mom in one piece."

"Why are you doing this?" Sam asked.

Hale flushed and set the envelope on the top of the small table next to him when Sam refused to take it. "I just want to make sure. Cover all my bases, you know? Especially after we lost Bolowski and Tierney."

"We're not losing any more dudes."

Hale lifted a single shoulder. "I hope you're right. But in case it's me, just promise, okay?"

Sam sighed hard, breaking the tight knot in his chest. "Sure. Whatever. You couldn't give that to Lewis or something?"

"He'd probably send my mom a dick pic instead," Hale said dryly.

Sam laughed. "Yeah, you're probably right." He glanced at the envelope and felt the weight of it settle on his shoulders. One more thing not to screw up. One more mission. And the one after that. And the one after that. The pressure tightened on his heart.

"So you'll do it?" Hale asked.

This time, Sam didn't hesitate. There wasn't really any answer other than, "Sure."

He didn't touch Hale's letter. The white envelope stood out against the dusty surface, pristine in the dirt except for one corner that had a smudged fingerprint.

Sam sat on the edge of his bed, one leg bouncing as he tried to figure out why this mission was bothering him as much as it was. Something wasn't sitting right. Not at all. He was usually better at figuring these problems out but whenever he was stuck in the past, he'd bounce his thoughts off First Sarn't Gnash.

And Gnash was gone because he hadn't kissed the right ring.

So Sam sat and ran the mission through his head. Turned it around and looked at it from another angle. It was something about the location of the TAC. Why did it have to be so close to that building identified as having women and children in it? Why so close to that mosque?

Maybe he should get another look at the terrain. Maybe the commo guys knew something he didn't, but it didn't seem to make sense that they needed to be in that specific building in that specific neighborhood. There were always other options. Why not in this case?

His stomach rumbled, reminding him that he hadn't eaten since breakfast and it was closing in on dinner. If he missed dinner, he'd have nothing but an MRE until the mission was completed. It would be just his luck that it would end up being the MRE ham slice or the omelet. That would be nasty. If he were hungry enough, it would taste like a porterhouse. But on three previous deployments, he'd never gotten that hungry.

There was always a first time.

He glanced at that fucking envelope and wished that Hale had given it to someone else. He snatched it out of the dust and shoved it in the drawer and hoped he'd never have to take it out again.

He paused before shutting the door. A deep disquiet slithered across the base of his spine. He should call Faith. He suddenly wanted very much to hear her voice.

He glanced at his watch. He had time to swing through the call center on his way to chow. If he didn't get through to her, he'd have to wait until after the mission to try and call her again.

He closed the drawer and slapped his patrol cap on his head. He stuffed a Nutri-Grain bar in his pocket in case the chow hall was packed. He hated hanging out in the lines and the crowds. He hated listening to the Fobbits bitch and complain when the chow hall was out of their favorite food even more. They had no idea how good they had it. Fobbits never had to go out in sector, never had to risk their ass to get basic chow. They never left the damn base.

He headed back through the Jersey barrier maze that led past the company ops and back toward the call center. A massive armored vehicle rumbled past on the other side of the barrier. The new supposedly bombproof vehicles were still a rare sight. They were giant compared to the more familiar track vehicles, but according to the powers that be, they were more resilient when it came to withstanding blasts.

Sam hoped they'd get more. Soon. The last thing he wanted to do was die in the coffin of a Bradley, especially if another vehicle could withstand some of the massive blasts they'd been subjected to lately. The bomb makers were getting more skilled. Which meant that even if Sam thought this mission was the worst idea ever, he was going to figure it out. Clearing out the bomb makers might mean one more of his boys or someone else's troopers would get to go home in one piece.

He rounded a corner as the armored vehicle rumbled off. He glanced into one of the bunkers, then did a double take. The dog was there, lying in the shade. Her head was propped against the cement and her sides were heaving as she panted hard.

He wanted to keep walking. He wanted to ignore her obvious hunger. But he couldn't look away from the abject misery in her eyes. Her paws were too big for the rest of her body. She probably weighed thirty pounds when she should weigh fifty. Pity, far too familiar, rose inside him. Goddamned pity was going to get someone else killed. He couldn't stop the sympathy from overwhelming his good sense. He felt bad for the damn dog. If she was mousing, she was working damn hard for any meals she might manage to catch.

He pulled the Nutri-Grain bar out of his pocket. No one was around to see him break his own rule about feeding the stupid dog. He felt the weight of his own hypocrisy deep in his bones as he tore the thin foil wrapper open and shook the bar into his hand. It crumbled into his palm.

The dog lifted her head, watching him warily. She looked like she'd been kicked one too many times. He wasn't about to get close enough to hand her the bar, that was for damn sure. He'd never hear the end of it if he got bit after bitching at Lewis and Hale about the friggin' mutt.

She tensed as he crept a little closer. He wanted to toss it into the bunker to keep anyone from seeing it if she refused the meal. He was sure one of the mice would drag it off if she didn't eat it.

He hoped she didn't have any puppies. Starving puppies might send him over the edge of shit he couldn't deal with in this godforsaken war. It was a futile wish. She wouldn't have the empty sacs on her belly if she hadn't recently whelped. He inched closer until he was just at the edge of the bunker.

She rolled over and crouched on all fours, her head down. Her hackles rose slowly, one by one, until her back was rigid and stiff. Fear closed off Sam's throat. He'd never get his weapon raised in time to shoot her. Forcing himself to move, he tossed her the bar and held up his hands. He backed away as she crept forward until the bar was between her front paws. Her lips curled. Her growl rumbled deep in her throat.

He never took his eyes from her as he rounded the corner. He moved out at double time as soon as he was out of sight. He refused to look behind him, even as the back of his neck tingled with the primitive fear of being chased. His spine tingled as he ran, waiting for the sound of claws clicking on the gravel to announce his demise.

He kept running despite the shiver that ran down his back and clenched his balls. He knew, *knew*, that if he turned around he'd see her loping behind him, a predator toying with her prey, her jaws opening to snap on his neck.

He rounded a barrier and finally dared to look back. A shadow disappeared behind the cement, but he saw nothing else. No wild dog was chasing him. Nothing but shadows from the setting sun and dust dancing on the rays.

He was safe.

So why did he feel like he was still being watched?

———

"Hey, baby."

Faith's image froze on the screen, her smile warm and welcoming and frozen. Her voice, though, came through clear and filled with energy. It pushed away the ragged fear that swatted at him.

The air inside the call center was musty and stagnant. The air conditioner must have died hours ago. It reeked of balls and dirty socks, but none of that mattered now that he could finally see Faith on the line.

He closed his eyes, letting the sound of her voice clear away the unreasonable panic over that fucking dog. He almost wished the chow hall had been packed so he could have avoided it, but he'd gotten there during a lull. He'd stocked up on Pop-Tarts. Always a good substitute for real breakfast in a pinch.

"I miss you," she whispered as the video unfroze. She smiled and shifted so he could see her more clearly.

"I miss you, too. How are you feeling?"

She stood and showed him her belly. It hadn't been that long since he'd left her alone in the dark at the airport, but already her belly seemed a little rounder. Her hand slid over the gentle swell and Sam longed to cover her hand with his. He curled his fingers into his palms.

She sat back down and leaned forward, smiling into the webcam. "I'm good. Starting to feel less tired."

"That's good. Is Peanut being good?"

Her laugh chased away some of the darkness in his soul. "Yes, she's being good."

"Did you have the ultrasound already?"

"No." She laughed at him again. He didn't mind. It was a fleeting moment of normalcy in this hellish place, where dogs growled at you for trying to feed them. A sick metaphor for this entire fucking war. "It's not for two more weeks."

"Then why 'she'?"

She shrugged and cupped her face in one palm. "Why 'he'?"

"Touché."

She said nothing for a moment and he watched her eyes move over her screen, studying him. "You're not sleeping, are you?"

He lifted one shoulder, attempting a nonchalance he couldn't feel. "Not really. It'll be better soon enough. Jet lag is always rough." He shifted his weapon against his thigh. "Tell me something from home."

He wanted to be there. He didn't want to be where he was, looking at his fiancée's belly through a webcam. Wishing he could touch her, feel her breathing while he slept.

"A bird flew into the kitchen today."

"A bird?"

"Yeah. It scared the daylights out of me."

"What kind of bird? And were you hurt?" He didn't like the idea of a bird dying in the kitchen. Birds carried diseases and well, damn it, he wasn't there to take care of it for her. Not that Faith had any issues taking care of herself, but still.

"It was fine, but it was really nerve-wracking." She glanced over her shoulder, as though the corpse was still decomposing on the linoleum. "I think it was a sparrow? Not sure."

He smiled. "You screamed, didn't you?"

"You'd scream too if you opened the back door and a bird nearly took off your head." She did something on the keyboard. "It darted around the kitchen a little bit before it crashed into the mirror over the kitchen sink. It was so gross."

He'd seen birds do that before. Back in '04, the second year of the war and his first deployment, he'd seen a small black bird that looked like a miniature crow flying around inside a hangar bay. The commander had been adamant that they needed to get the wildlife out of the bay, not because it was a potential vector but because he insisted that the bird was an Iranian spy.

That commander had lasted a full 24 months in command, and had received a Bronze Star. Sam still couldn't believe that batshit crazy dude had lasted.

But he remembered the day the little bird had panicked and flown into the wall when Sam had been trying to shoo it outside. Its neck had crunched like a pretzel before it fell to the ground. He hadn't wanted to pick it up, but he'd only been a private then. Its head had lolled grotesquely when Sam moved it. He'd thrown it in a rusted-out trashcan. He'd managed not to throw up when it had twitched. Barely.

She smiled into the camera. "You're laughing at me, I can tell."

He matched her smile with his own. "I'm not. Really." But he was, because it felt good. Like sunshine pouring into the emptiest part of his soul.

"You are. You suck."

"You suck." He adjusted the headphones on his ears.

"And you like that."

Sam coughed out loud. His damn dick perked up at her words. "Don't." His voice thickened. "I'm in the middle of a public call center. I can't walk out of here with a hard-on."

Faith wasn't dissuaded. "I miss you inside me," she whispered.

"Jesus, Faith." It took everything he had not to adjust his pants. "Knock it off. You're going to make me look like a sex offender."

"Can I see it?"

"*No*, you can't see it. What part of 'public internet cafe' do you not understand?" But his lips curled into a smile. Goddamn, he missed her. "I've got to get ready to go."

She traced her bottom lip with the tip of her tongue. Sam was going to need to stop by a Porta-Potty on the way back to his bay. "You're killing me, babe. Please stop," he whispered.

"Tell me you love me." Her voice was low and husky. If he closed his eyes, he could almost feel her body beneath his, her breath on his skin. Clean sheets wrapped around them in the silence.

"I do. More than you'll ever know."

She leaned forward and pressed her lips to the camera. "I love you, too. Promise me you'll get some rest? You look exhausted."

"I'll do my best." The lie was smooth and easy, hiding the ugly truth.

"I guess that's as good as I'm going to get, huh?"

"Pretty much." He kissed his fingertips and held them up to the screen. "Miss you. Take care of Peanut, okay?"

"I'll talk to you soon?"

"I'll call again as soon as I can." His throat thickened.

"I love you," she whispered.

"I lov—" But the connection dropped, leaving dead silence on the line before he could answer.

He had to walk back through the barriers to get back to his trailer. Sam didn't think of himself as a coward, but he was damn sure considering taking the long way—a ten-mile walk around the perimeter of the base—back from the chow hall.

Fear mocked him as he stood on the edge of the cement barrier. He reached down and rested his palm on the pistol grip of his weapon. Comforted by the ever-present weapon, he palmed a magazine as he prepared to enter the labyrinthine nightmare.

The sun hung low in the sky. Dust danced in the sunset and reminded him of the deserts of Tattooine. The only things missing were the Evil Empire and the promising young farm boy. Sam was many things, but a naive farmer's son with delusions of grandeur was not one of them. No, the reality of the war was much, much worse than any teenage fantasy of glory.

The base was hustling with the noise of moving vehicles and barks of laughter as groups of soldiers moved to chow and back again.

Sam tapped the magazine against his thigh as he walked through the barriers and tried not to let his thoughts wander down the wormhole of what might be waiting around the next corner.

He hesitated as he approached the bunker where the dog had lurked. Cold shame slithered down his spine as he slid a magazine into the weapon and charged a round into the chamber. He would be prepared this time. Pathetic or not, he would shoot that fucking dog if she was still there.

Hate and fear did a twisted dance in his guts as he peered around the corner. He expected the starving mutt to charge at him, to attempt to rip his face off before he could fire off a single round.

But the bunker was empty. Cold relief trickled down his spine. He exhaled a shuddering breath and cleared his weapon, catching the round as it popped free and sliding it back into his magazine.

He didn't linger in the spot. It felt colder there, like something skulked in the shadows. The tiny hairs on the back of his neck stood on end as he moved through the cold spot and back toward the life support area where he and his boys lived.

He scrubbed his hand over his mouth, irritated that he'd allowed himself to get so tired that he was jumping at shadows. He needed to try and get some sleep before the mission. They were supposed to roll the TAC out in the middle of the night before the main body. A couple of staff weenies were going with them to establish the communications relay. All in all, they had two squads to secure an area that needed an entire platoon.

The weaknesses in the plan haunted him on the walk back to his trailer. They didn't have enough men, they were setting up near an orphanage, and the communications plan was about as weak as he'd ever seen. He felt the wrongness of the entire plan in his guts but the commander and everyone else were hell-bent that they were going to do this. The potential win—clearing the area of a major bomb maker and his associated minions—was too big to pass up.

He said nothing as he passed a few of his guys hanging out at the smoke point. The pungent smell of local cigarettes permeated the dusty air. He nodded in acknowledgment and walked past, needing a few minutes alone to maybe close his eyes. Or at least pretend he was going to.

Sam closed the door to his trailer behind him and sat for a moment on the grungy chair he'd stolen from some dickhead major's room when he'd first arrived. Man, one of the majors in the battalion ops had been pissed when he'd caught Sam taking off with it.

Cradling his head in his hands, he wrestled with the frustration that burned in him. He flipped his helmet over and pulled out a picture of Faith. Her smile reminded him that she was his reason for going home. It pushed away some of the fear that clutched at him.

He pulled out his banged-up green notebook. The empty page waited for him to fill it with words. Dared him to spill the fear, the uncertainty, the hatred of the war that wouldn't let him go.

He sat for a long moment, letting the words germinate in his brain. Then he started to write.

He wrote about how he'd wanted to be back here when he was home. He told her he was sorry for that. He wanted to be home with her more than anything and if he got the chance to come home, he'd make every single day worth it. He told her about the mission, broke all kinds of OPSEC rules and told her how screwed up the mission was. He told her about the bird that had died on his first rotation. Why he suddenly couldn't stop thinking about it. He confessed he worried about her and the baby. That he wouldn't be able to take care of her, but that he'd do his best. He told her about the school and the kids he'd seen. They were just like kids back home, full of life and hope in the middle of a hellish war. He left out the part he'd played in bringing that hell. He started to tell her about the dog. About the nightmare that seemed to be coming true.

But his ratty, Army-issued pen froze, as if it had run out of ink.

The word "dog" was half written, the "o" misshapen and empty. Incomplete, like his tale of this fucked-up war.

He set the pen down, unable to admit what the war had taken from him. He had no idea what to write about the dog. The only thing that seemed to make sense was that he was losing his mind. He wasn't ready to confess that. Not yet, anyway. Maybe if he really lost his shit, he'd find the courage to write it down and tell the woman who carried his child that the man she'd pledged her life with had completely gone off the deep end, tumbling into Nietzsche's abyss after the monster he'd sought to destroy.

He closed the notebook, unable to record every fucked-up thing he felt like writing. He stopped, feeling better now that he'd gotten at least some of it out. Even if he'd never send her the letter.

CHAPTER TEN

The middle of the night was never quiet on a base in Iraq. Missions were always going on, twenty-four/seven, except on major holidays like Christmas or the Super Bowl. Even then, the base was a constant hub of activity. Guards needed to be posted, chow needed to be served.

And on nights like tonight, when the base was ramping up for a major assault, the base was lit up like broad daylight. Generators pumped furious energy to a thousand lights. If the Iraqis didn't know they were coming, they were stupider than Sam sometimes thought they were.

Sam's headlamp hung around his neck, the bright LED lights illuminating the darkness already pierced by the floodlights of their staging area.

The Humvees felt small and incredibly fragile compared to the mighty Bradleys. He knew it made sense to take the Humvees even if it violated everything he'd learned as an infantryman who'd grown up around tanks and heavy units. The light fighters—crunchies, as the tankers called them—had no idea how good the concussion from the main gun of an Abrams felt when their asses were pinned down. That main gun could obliterate an enemy, leaving nothing but bloody dust behind.

It was therapeutic, sometimes, to watch the enemy die a violent death. Sam didn't feel bad about the death of the enemy. It helped that he didn't know their names or have to see their faces too often. The tank's guns blew them away before those memories had a chance to form, let alone burrow into his psyche.

The noise of the vehicles deafened everything around them. Merrick's squad was nowhere to be seen. The guys from the TAC had arrived about ten minutes earlier and Sam was lining them up in the formation as Lewis and Hale focused on making sure everyone had enough ammo and water. Hale lit into Jinx and Jinx argued for a hot second before slinking off to fix whatever Hale had found screwed up. Probably not enough water in his Camel-Bak. Jinx was worse than a chick about drinking water. He claimed to have gotten a bad infection in his dick from backsplash from a Porta-Potty one time and ever since, he was a pain in the ass about drinking enough water on missions if it involved him pissing in less than pristine conditions. He carried around an empty water bottle for just that reason.

Tick stalked out from between two vehicles, looking none too pleased to be up several hours before the ass-crack of dawn.

"Where the fuck is the second squad?" he barked. A huge wad of dip stuck out of his bottom lip.

"No idea," Sam shouted over the din. "But Merrick needs to get here soon or we'll have to roll without him."

Which was a horrible fucking idea, as horrible ideas went. It was a cardinal sin to move without a force big enough to secure itself. While the two-squad solution was less than ideal for the amount of area they were covering, it would be fucking suicide to roll with a single squad defending the TAC. They'd be writing for years at the Center for Lessons Learned about the catastrophic kill that took out 15–20 guys because they'd thought rolling out on time was more important than rolling out with enough men. Not exactly a comforting thought.

"I'll get our commander to find his commander and figure out what the hell is going on," Tick shouted.

Sam nodded and Tick stalked off. He almost felt sorry for Merrick if Tick got ahold of him. Tick was one mean son of a bitch when he got riled up, and Sam guessed he was about two notches down from fully pissed off.

He rounded the trail vehicle in time to see Lewis slap a skinny kid, who Sam instantly recognized as the Bible-thumping kid from the plane. His red hair was shaggier than Sam remembered, and he looked like he hadn't slept since they'd landed in country a few days prior. Sam knew the feeling. His eyes were wide with fear, his mouth gaped open. Lewis grabbed the kid by his body armor and shook him, shouting something in his face.

The kid looked one step away from pissing himself—if he hadn't already—but Sam didn't feel the least bit sorry for him. The commo guys who spent their entire careers on the base had this reaction all too frequently when they had to do their jobs outside the security of the concertina wire. Thankfully, there were more commo guys who loved life with the infantry and armor and were damn good at their jobs. He knew one sergeant first class who could jerry-rig an antenna with 550 cord, a gum wrapper, and a coat hanger.

If the kid didn't pull himself together, Sam would leave him in the truck guarding the radio. If he did, the kid would learn something today—with luck, something valuable that didn't involve life or limb.

Lewis shoved the kid toward one of the trucks. Sam did not interfere. He headed back up to his vehicle to do a comms check with Hellhound Main.

"Hellhound Main, Hellhound Main, this is Reaper Two Six. How copy, over?"

"Reaper Two Six, this is Hellhound Main. Roger out."

Which meant he was coming in loud and clear. Good. Clear, uncluttered comms made him happy. It was a good omen. It was when missions started out with shitty comms that Sam got edgy and started saying his prayers. Bad comms were pretty high up on the list of Not Good Things. Far too often, static had choked off the call of "MEDEVAC follows." He swallowed, shoving down too many memories of bad comms and failed missions.

He hooked the hand mic back into its rope and climbed out of the truck. He leaned up where Jinx was conducting weapons checks on the .50-cal.

Jinx looked down at him with a wicked grin and a thumbs-up. Good. His guys didn't think this was anything other than a normal mission. Headlights rolled around the Jersey barriers and crept to a halt fifteen yards from Sam's vehicle. Relief prickled his skin even as his palms slicked with sweat.

Merrick—the *de facto* NCOIC of the mission—had arrived.

———

"You're late."

"Seeing how you and your team were supposed to meet us at Gate Two across base an hour ago, I'd say you were the one who was late," Merrick snapped.

Behind him, Merrick's squad moved like shadows against the darkness. Thin, wiry shapes. Not a fat soldier anywhere on Merrick's squad. Not even a guy built like Lewis. Every one of his men was whip thin. He wondered if Merrick kept them that way on purpose.

"We were never supposed to meet at Gate Two. We settled on this as the exit because it was on the opposite side of the city."

"And the lookouts they've got watching the base won't notice anything different when the convoy leaves from this exit instead of the normal one."

Sam bristled. "Take it up with the commanders. This is where my commander told me we're leaving from."

Merrick stepped into Sam's space, close enough that Sam could smell the stale smoke on the other man's skin. It was a habit that was starting to get really fucking annoying. "Don't forget who is in charge of this mission, puppy," he hissed for Sam's ears only.

Anger sucked the air from Sam's lungs but he bit back his

sharp retort. It wouldn't do for the men to see him fighting with Merrick. They'd wonder what was going on. And then the rumors would start. He took a step back when all he really wanted to do was punch Merrick in the teeth.

"So are we leaving?" Major Whitman strode up, a cigar hanging from one corner of his mouth. He was easily the oldest major in the brigade, and he tried to hide it by looking way too eager for the upcoming mission. Sam had had more than one conversation with him where he'd confessed to wanting to go back to a line unit and lead soldiers, but Sam didn't believe his bullshit. He wondered how this man—the man excited about rolling off the base and into probable enemy contact—had become the same man who would bitch about a stolen couch.

He and Whitman didn't always see eye to eye on things, especially when Whitman's good idea fairies had Sam and his boys running a stupid mission to get their quotas up instead of caring about actual results from said missions. All so that some captain could say he ran x number of missions instead of what really mattered: ran x number of missions with y results.

Results mattered. At least, Sam thought they did.

Merrick straightened as Whitman approached. If Sam didn't know better, he'd have sworn Merrick had flinched away from Whitman. But that couldn't be right. Whitman was just a harmless pain in the ass. Merrick didn't strike Sam as the kind of guy who was intimidated by a gold oak leaf on someone's chest.

"Yes, sir. We're finishing up checks and we'll be ready to roll," Sam said. "Can you have your guys double-check the commo guys, sir? The last time we did this, they forgot some widget or some shit and we had to jerry-rig the antenna."

Whitman offered a mock salute, his jaw tensing in the shadows cast by the headlights from the rumbling Humvees. "Already done, chief. We're good."

Sam glanced at Merrick. "We're ready to roll. You're taking the lead to advance on the objective?"

Merrick nodded once and turned around, melting into the shadows toward his squad. It was more than a little creepy how he did that. His men reminded Sam of wolves. Sharp, hungry wolves coming up on the end of a long, hard winter. They only had a few days before they were all heading home. Sam tried not to be jealous. At the same time, he worried about how Merrick's eagerness to leave would affect his team's interaction with the locals.

Sam wondered if Merrick was ruthless and cold with the local nationals. He didn't give the impression of a man who would listen to a lot of excuses about why no one had reported the man who'd buried the last roadside bomb. Sam didn't have much compassion for the people who tried to blow him up on a regular basis. No, he wasn't a fan of the adult male population of Iraq, not by a long shot.

But the women? Yeah, he pitied the women. And the kids. Something inside him threatened to unlock, and he shut it down with a fierce violence. Too much pity got people killed.

He had no room for those thoughts as he locked and loaded his weapon and motioned for everyone to mount up. Merrick's trucks pulled in front of theirs and led the way out into the city. The convoy rolled out, heading toward the test fire pit. Something about the sound of the .50-cal going off over his head was beautiful, the reverb vibrating against his breastbone. It was the comforting sound of violent capability. The knowledge that if they needed to, they could unleash hell upon their enemies.

He hoped they didn't need to.

Theirs was not a clean job. It was a job that touched the most secure recesses of his soul. A soul that ended up tainted with darkness no matter how much he tried to shield it from the ugliness around it. Sam's hands had blood on them, and the blood was unclean.

He glanced down at the dirty green and leather gloves covering his hands as he lifted his weapon. The gloves did not protect him from the violence of his actions.

He fired a few rounds out of the window of the Humvee. Satisfied that his weapon would work when he needed it, he waited for the call from Merrick that they were moving.

They drove out of the protection of the Jersey barriers and concertina wire and guard posts. They rolled beyond the safety of the base and into the heart of the enemy's territory.

Sweat slicked Sam's palms in his gloves as he listened to the chatter on the radio. It warned them to watch the overpass as they wove beneath to make themselves more difficult to hit if some industrious soul was trying to throw something on them.

He lived in mortal fear of the RKG-III, Russian grenades that penetrated armor like a hot knife through butter. Their Humvees offered no defense against any explosion, but RKGs were particularly deadly. Launched with a tiny parachute, they floated down to their targets' vulnerable roofs.

He reached over and tugged on Jinx's leg, reminding him to duck at the overpass. The enemy had brought back a technique from Vietnam: a thin wire strung across an intersection or beneath a bridge.

Instant decapitation. A horrific way to die. Even worse to clean up. Sam had no idea how the mortuary affairs guys did their jobs and stayed sane.

Jinx crouched down behind the defilade until they were clear of the bridge.

The patrol moved quickly, following a familiar route. It was only at the last minute that they diverted from the normal and darted into the neighborhood.

The site occupation went down smooth, like a last shot of tequila. Merrick's squad emplaced the outer security while Sam's cleared the building. Up the stairs, room to empty room.

For once, intel had been right. They didn't encounter any resistance as they cleared the old building. The next closest building—the one alleged to be an orphanage—was buttoned up tight, no lights, no signs of life. Sam hoped the intel was wrong, that it wasn't an orphanage. So far, it looked as empty as the shell of the building they were actively clearing. He'd given up on praying a long time ago, but he prayed that it stayed that way.

The temporary TAC was cleared in under an hour. Sam emplaced the gunners on the roof, then went down to check the concertina wire while the commo guys lugged the heavy case holding the antenna onto the roof.

"Hellhound Main, Hellhound Main, this is Reaper Two Six Delta." Jinx swore and slammed the mic against the radio.

"That's probably not going to help." Sam leaned into the truck. "What's wrong?"

"I can't raise the TOC on the net."

"They don't have the antenna on the roof yet. The building is blocking you."

Jinx shook his head. "That's not it, Sarn't Brown. We lost comms before we entered the neighborhood."

"Show me." Jinx pulled out the map and pointed to the location, a hillside before they'd crossed the bridge and descended into the heart of the enemy, a location that should have had pristine communications.

Sam frowned. "This isn't showing as a communications dead zone."

"That's what I'm trying to tell you. It's really strange. We should have comms right now, but everything is coming in broken and unreadable."

Unease prickled at the back of Sam's neck. "It'll be fine once we get the antenna up on the roof."

Jinx looked at him, his eyes filled with disbelief in the complete and total bullshit Sam had just fed him. Concern creased the pale skin beneath his eyes. "Sure, Sarn't Brown. Whatever you say."

Sam gripped his shoulder. "It'll be fine. Just get back up on the guns. And don't forget to start the truck every hour to keep the radio from draining the batteries."

"Roger that, Sarn't."

Jinx climbed back up into the defilade.

Sam tried to ignore the fear curdling like acid in his stomach.

CHAPTER ELEVEN

"What the hell is that?"

The skinny kid stopped what he was doing and turned. "It's a coffee pot, Sarn't."

"A coffee pot," he repeated. Sam raised both eyebrows. It dawned on him that he didn't know the kid's name. He was a number on the mission. A butt to a seat. Not a name. Not a person. "And what generator are you going to use to power it?"

The kid's ruddy cheeks flushed. "I don't know. Major Whitman said to bring it."

Sam made up a few new creative ways to use profanity in a sentence. "Put that fucking coffee pot away until you've got the fucking radios working."

The kid's eyes widened quickly. "But Sarn't, Major Whitman…"

"I don't give a flying fuck what Major Whitman wants. Get the goddamned radios in system."

"Roger, Sergeant." The kid nodded and dropped the silver bullet coffee pot on a nearby table. His weapon bounced where it was slung across his back. Sam was honestly surprised the kid was even still carrying it. He'd lost count of the times he'd found commo guys setting up comms with their weapons stacked neatly and completely ineffectively in a corner.

He wondered where the kid had stashed his Bible. It felt wrong that he didn't know the kid's name. He shrugged off the feeling and headed up the narrow staircase, his shoulders nearly brushing each cement wall. He'd ask him in a little while. After the comms were up.

"What the hell is taking so long?" Sam barked as he came onto the roof to see two guys struggling to get the thin whip antenna erected.

Whitman slammed the hand mic against the radio. His face was a dark purple in the low light. "They forgot the connector."

"What connector?" Sam asked. He flexed his fingers to avoid bunching them into a fist.

"The connector that allows us to put these two hundred-foot cables together. We can't reach the truck without it."

Sam flushed with cold rage. "Are you fucking kidding me? You brought a goddamned coffee pot but you didn't check for fucking connectors?"

"Watch your mouth," Whitman snapped.

Sam was pushing his luck, but he was too fucking pissed to care. He flicked the good angel off his shoulder. "What the hell are you going to do about this?"

"I'm going to shit a connector, what the fuck do you think I'm going to do, Sergeant?" Whitman said. His use of Sam's rank was a cold reminder that Sam had crossed the line, a warning Sam ignored as the major continued. "You're going to move that truck to the bottom of this building so we can reach it with one cable instead of two."

Sam's mouth fell open. For a moment, he contemplated nailing the fat old bastard in his fleshy cheek. Faith would be thrilled by his court-martial. Instead, he snapped his mouth closed, stalked to the edge of the building and peered over the edge, smothering the pitch in his stomach as he approached the brink.

Still shrouded in darkness, a helo buzzed low overhead. It sounded more like a lawnmower than an instrument of airborne death. It distracted him, however briefly, from his fury. He glanced down the alley, briefly lit up by the lights overhead. Nothing but trash and shadows kept at bay by a lone vehicle.

"There is no way we can move that vehicle. It opens a massive gap in our perimeter," Sam said. "You were supposed to check the comms equipment, sir."

"And I said watch your fucking mouth, Sergeant. You'll move the fucking truck. Dismount the weapon and put the guard position down there. Problem solved."

Sam bristled. "Then your fucking commo guys are going to be the ones manning that position," he snarled.

"They're running the radios."

"Which any monkey with thumbs can do. And obviously, they don't do their job well if they forget the fucking connector."

Major Whitman glared, his jaw pulsing, his eyes lit with a terrible enmity that said Sam was in for it if they made it back to base. Pulling that truck back opened up a major hole in their perimeter. He hadn't been kidding about that. Whitman's fists were bunched at his sides and for a brief moment, Sam thought he was going to swing on him.

A burst of rapid fire echoed down the alley, bouncing off the walls like the inside of a kettledrum. They both ducked at the same time. Sam crept to the edge of the roof and lowered his night vision goggles, trying to get a glimpse of the source of the gunfire in the darkness. Two men rushed past the end of the alley but did not turn toward the first position in the outer cordon. The guards didn't move or otherwise give away their location.

"We can't move the truck," Sam said again, his voice calm.

"Then we need to find a new location, because these comms aren't going up without that truck coming closer to the building, or we're not talking," Whitman said.

Major Whitman knew his team had screwed up. They had made the entire mission vulnerable, and that grated on the old infantryman's nerves. He should be embarrassed, Sam thought. He should be goddamned ready to kill himself for screwing up something as basic as pre-combat checks.

Sam had to move the truck. He swore viciously as he headed down the narrow staircase. A smell like burned sulfur seared his nostrils as he descended the cement stairs. Fear mixed with unease. Heat coated the back of his neck. He turned around, fully expecting to see someone behind him, watching him from the vantage point at the top of the staircase.

But there was nothing but darkness leading to the roof. He was alone with the sounds of the distant battle. The primitive fear that something was coming slithered up his spine. And he could do nothing to stop it.

―――――

"I don't like this," Jinx said, shooting a glance at the skinny kid from the commo team. His hand rested on the butt of his personal weapon, mirroring Sam's stance.

"It won't be the first time we've been in a shitty spot because of commo," Sam said.

The skinny kid said nothing from his position in the prone. Flat on his belly behind a couple of cement blocks, he stared at the end of the alley, fear making his pale skin blanch almost translucent.

Sam hadn't been kidding when he'd told Major Whitman that the commo guys would pull duty. He gave less than a damn about the fucking coffee pot being unmanned. He felt like smashing the damn thing every time he looked at it.

"Yeah, I'll try to remember that if I'm pulling shrapnel out of my ass later," Jinx grumbled.

Sam grinned and slapped him once on the back. "Quit bitching. They got the antenna up, we've got comms back to the base. We'll be out of here in a few hours."

"Whatever you say, Sarn't Brown." Jinx hunkered down next to the commo kid.

Sam stood and kicked the commo kid's boot.

He twisted to look back at Sam. "Yes, Sergeant?"

"No sleeping on guard duty," Sam said. "Take all your orders from Jinx."

Sam had nicknamed him BK for Bible Kid. He was going to hell—either the one for sergeants who didn't take care of their soldiers, or the one for people who lost their faith. He wasn't sure which. But he couldn't bring himself to ask the kid his name.

BK looked at him, his eyes dark spots in his pale face. "He's a private. I'm a specialist. I should be in charge."

Sam wasn't in the mood to play nice. "I don't know whose dick you sucked to get promoted to specialist, but Jinx knows what he's doing. I'd just as soon not lose one of my guys because he took orders from you. Jinx is in charge."

Sam turned and headed back down the alley, but not before he heard Jinx whisper something to the kid that sound strangely like assault. Which was why Jinx was a PFC in the first place. He *might* have assaulted an MP at the chow hall. And his commander *might* have been trying to get some ass off the MP commander. So Jinx *might* have taken an Article 15 so that his commander could score.

Jinx took it on the chin, but that didn't mean he didn't rag on Captain Lehr relentlessly about taking his rank so he could get some ass.

But the skinny kid clutching his Bible didn't need to know that. It would probably violate his moral code.

Sam really needed to ask Bible Kid his name, but he couldn't summon the give-a-shit factor. He was just another face in the crowd.

Sam walked the edge of the concertina wire, checking the sectors of fire for each guard position. Checking to make sure everyone had water and bullets. Once the sun came up, they'd be more vulnerable. They couldn't be running around trying to fill their CamelBaks in the middle of the morning.

Their position was vulnerable. They were near an orphanage and too close to a mosque for Sam's comfort. He kept his eye on the mental prize: if the clearing operation succeeded in capturing the local bomb maker, it could drastically reduce the number of bombs both in their sector but also across the region.

It was worth it. Sam knew it, and yet the creeping feeling of something being *wrong* stuck with him. He rounded the corner to see the cable that had caused such controversy running up the side of the building. The antenna stood out against the light grey of the morning skyline.

His gaze drifted down to the empty vehicle at the bottom of the building.

No one was in the vehicle.

Swearing at the major, who was nestled safe in the building while his guys risked their asses to protect him, he cranked the truck to life. If it went too long without starting, the battery would die. When the plan had called for Jinx to man the big gun in the vehicle, that part of the comms plan had taken care of itself. Jinx would have never let the truck go too long without starting it.

Now? Now he needed to stick a boot in that major's ass to make sure the truck got started every half hour or so while Sam made his rounds to keep checking on their perimeter. If not, the radios could drain that sucker and they'd be stuck towing the vehicle back, which was never a good idea. Nothing screamed "attack me" more than towing a downed vehicle. If the shit hit the fan from this mission, the enemy was going to be crawling all over the city looking for a fight.

He remembered how, right after Sadr City blew up in '04, a unit from the Cav had lost a platoon out in sector, and they'd moved heaven and earth to get them back. He'd rolled through the city about a week after they'd unleashed hell. Angry men had stood on the sides of the road, their eyes filled with hatred. Sam would never forget one man who glared at him and drew his finger across his own throat.

He swallowed at the memory.

A butcher had stared at him as he'd sliced a goat from neck to balls. Entrails poured out onto the blistering pavement, and still the butcher had stared at Sam. It had been the first time Sam had been sure he was going to die in this war.

But he'd made it through that rotation and come back again and again and again. This was his fourth tour. He'd seen every-thing. Nothing surprised him anymore. That still didn't mean he wanted to limp back to base with a downed vehicle.

He killed the engine and headed into the building. A flicker of light caught his eye and he peered toward the growing light, near the edge of the building that intel said was an orphanage. A shadow slid along the low wall, shapeless and sharp all at once.

Sam gripped the butt of his weapon. His heart pounded in his throat. He waited, and then the shadow was gone.

Wishing he'd gotten some damn sleep before he'd rolled onto the mission, he turned away and ducked into the bombed-out building. It smelled like dust and—coffee.

He sprinted to the top floor. "You're fucking kidding me, right?"

Major Whitman held his mug to his lips as the radio chatter filled the background with static, punctuated by radio calls between the main base and the forward element. Distant gunfire crackled in the early morning light as the operation began.

And Major Whitman sipped his coffee.

CHAPTER TWELVE

"You're not hiding your emotions very well," Merrick said as Sam stalked onto the roof.

Merrick was pretty much the last person Sam wanted to see, but it was either sit with Merrick on the guard post or go back downstairs and punch Whitman in the face.

"The motherfucker better remember to start the truck," Sam muttered. He lowered himself with a muffled curse against the low concrete wall and cradled his weapon across his lap.

The *adhan* echoed across the skyline, the morning call to prayer a sound that Sam had long ago learned to hate. It was so frequently followed by violence that tensing up was practically a conditioned response.

He tapped his thumb against his thigh, waiting for the call to end. The last note echoed over the city, punctuated by a massive fireball that lit up the pre-dawn sky.

"Holy shit!" Sam flinched and ducked below the wall. The concussion of the blast followed the flash a moment later and reverberated against his ribcage. For a moment, his lungs didn't work. Just a moment, and then the feeling passed.

"Dump truck," Merrick said. "Probably six, seven thousand pounds of explosives."

"Or we could hope it was the cache they were using for the IEDs."

Merrick shrugged. "Could be."

"It would be nice if it was," Sam said, a strange need to fill the silence eating at him. "Make this whole clusterfuck worth it."

"It won't change anything," Merrick said, shifting to look out over the skyline.

Sam said nothing for a long moment. Merrick was right. "I know."

Nothing they did mattered. Even deeds cloaked in goodness and mercy backfired. Good men died when you acted and good men died when you did nothing. Sam knew that firsthand.

"There was nothing you could do, you know."

Sam glanced at him, fear clutching his throat. "About what?"

Merrick didn't know. He couldn't. Only Lewis and Hale knew the call that Sam had made, and they wouldn't betray him to a stranger.

"The major bringing the coffee pot."

Relief was cold on his skin.

"I know," Sam said. "It's shocking that he's an infantryman."

Merrick's grin was cold. Predatory. "Some men are more fit for life behind the lines of safety, directing others to do their evil for them."

Sam's stomach rumbled and he took a pull off his CamelBak, hoping the water would assuage the ache in his belly. "And some of us are meant to live in the muck and grime."

"Follow me." Merrick said the line from the infantry creed quietly.

A communion forged in fire and blood. A bond made of more than shared time in combat. A bond forged of having spilt enemy blood and lost more of their own.

"Yeah." Sam closed his eyes as the rapid fire of a machine gun echoed over the rooftops. A flight of doves cooed and took off in a flutter of sound.

He let his mind drift for a moment, needing to close his eyes and rest. His thoughts drifted a thousand miles away, to his fiancée and their unborn baby. How had she gotten the dead sparrow out of the kitchen? He suddenly wanted to know very badly what she'd done. How she'd done it. Had she nearly vomited, like he almost had, or had she been able to scoop it up and toss it in the trash as if it were nothing more than an old soda bottle?

"You've got someone special back home."

Sam was surprised by the lack of the question in Merrick's words. He glanced at his watch, not wanting to talk about Faith in the dirt and dust and smell of burning sulfur.

"I need to check on my guys and make sure the signal guys start the truck." He stood, his weapon bouncing against his thighs.

He felt Merrick's gaze on him as he descended the stairs. The exchange unnerved him, primarily because he and Merrick weren't exactly chummy. Why the sudden desire to talk about home?

Sam ran his hands along the walls, feeling the cold from the concrete penetrate his gloves. On the first floor below the roof, he found Hale checking on a few of the guys who'd taken up elevated positions above the alley where Jinx and the skinny kid with the Bible were stationed.

"Everyone's set," Hale said, stepping back from the open window.

"Any movement from the orphanage?"

"Not even the flicker of a candle. It's more like a morgue," Hale said. "It's creepy as fuck. There should be kids, right?"

Sam shrugged. "I would assume so. Who knows how things are done here."

Hale stuffed a wad of dip in his mouth, then tucked the green Copenhagen can into a pocket on his lower leg. "Did the commo guys really bring a coffee pot?"

Sam grunted, not wanting to pick that scab again so soon. Not when he'd just gotten over the urge to punch that fucking major on the face.

"Sore subject?"

"If I don't hear that truck start soon, someone's ass is going to be sore," Sam said mildly.

Hale motioned and one of the new privates skittered down the stairs, his boots thumping in retreat. A moment later, the Humvee rumbled to life.

"That's the major's responsibility," Sam said.

"Yeah, well sue me. I'd just as soon not get stranded here because he's too busy drinking his orange mocha Frappuccino to remember to start the truck."

Sam grinned. "Keep an ear on the comms. I want to know the second the order comes to get the fuck out of here."

"That makes two of us. This whole mission feels wrong."

Sam glanced at him sharply, surprised that Hale gave voice to the unease Sam felt. Of his two team leaders, Hale was more likely to question, to poke holes in the plan. Lewis was about as analytical as a UFC fighter doing heart surgery, but was able to see problems in the plan that were often glaringly obvious but tended to get written off as easy to mitigate.

"A couple more hours at most. We should be back on the base by lunch if we're lucky."

"Good, because shithead has already eaten his MRE."

A cold rage gripped Sam's guts. "Who?"

"The major and his crew of super geeks."

"They already ate? Are you fucking kidding me?"

"Yep." Hale rocked on his heels. "Here's hoping you're right and we're home by lunch."

Sam pinched the bridge of his nose and shook his head. What he really needed to do was hit something. It took everything he had to move down the stairs to the guard points outside the inner cordon instead of telling that fat fucking major what an idiot he was.

———

Sam did not do patience well. The sounds of the battle had shifted with the sun and echoed from a distant place across the river. Nothing had been as big as the earlier explosion, which felt like it had ripped out part of his guts.

He wanted to know what that explosion had been. He hoped and prayed that it wasn't going to result in a ramp ceremony. Those tore at his soul and ripped up his insides. He felt raw for days after. He never slept well after one, either.

But sleep was the least of his worries. As the battle shifted farther away, the communications that managed to come in were more broken up. Every so often, the truck would start, relieving Sam of at least the worry about whether they'd have to blow the vehicle in place or tow it back. Neither option would be on the table if they kept it running.

Sam made his rounds, periodically checking on all his boys as the sun climbed higher in the sky. Merrick did the same, and they did not cross paths again. Sam avoided him on purpose. He didn't trust that skinny fucker, and he didn't really care if Merrick knew it.

Merrick might have been in charge of the mission, but that only meant Sam was running on adrenaline and stress from checking behind everything they did. He didn't want Merrick's or his boys' eagerness to go home to result in a sloppy mistake that got someone hurt.

To him, Merrick's confidence seemed to border on arrogance, and Sam had been up close and personal with what arrogance could do in the middle of a firefight. It meant very bad things, and Sam was tired of very bad things.

He wanted to go home. He wanted to go home and really feel like he was home, instead of wishing for his leave to end so he could get back to the chaos and stink of war.

He was walking back into the building as an Apache buzzed overhead when he was damn near mowed down by the skinny kid he'd put on guard with Jinx. The kid's hands were wrapped around the silver bullet coffee pot.

"What are you doing?" Sam asked.

"They gave the call to break contact. We're packing up."

"So the first thing you pack is your coffee pot?" Sam ground his teeth to avoid ripping the fucking coffee pot out of the kid's hands. "Start the truck before you make another trip for the coffee filters."

"Roger, Sarn't." The kid scurried past and Sam waited for the rumble of the engine turning over.

Instead, he heard a click that made his heart stop.

He turned slowly back toward the truck.

Panic tore across the kid's freckles as he flicked the ignition switch once more. *Click. Click.* His eyes were filled with fear as he dared to meet Sam's gaze.

Red tinted the edge of Sam's vision. "Get the fuck out of my sight. Just fucking go."

Sam pounded up the stairs, past the positions his men were still manning, and stalked onto the floor just below the roof. Lewis was adjusting the sight on his weapon perched on the ledge of the window as Whitman listened to instructions coming over the hand mic.

Major Whitman looked at him, then keyed the mic.

"Hellhound Main. This is Hellhound TAC." But the lights were out on the radio. The truck was dead, and so was their radio. Which meant either that Whitman was too stupid to realize the radio had died, or that—Sam didn't know what else. He didn't care, either.

Sam waited for Whitman to drop the mic before he hit him. His gloved fist collided with Whitman's meaty jowl, exploding spit and chewing tobacco from his cheek.

Lewis pulled him off before Sam could hit the major again. "You stupid, ignorant prick. You and that fucking coffee pot just screwed us six ways from Sunday."

Merrick stood in the doorway, but Sam didn't care. He didn't care that he was the junior guy. He didn't care that Merrick outranked him and had just seen him assault a commissioned officer.

"What seems to be the problem here, gents?" Merrick said lightly.

"That coffee pot drained the truck's batteries," Lewis said, because Sam was still too pissed off to talk in anything other than creative profanity.

"Lovely. I hope the coffee was worth it," Merrick said. "Leave the vehicle."

Major Whitman's spit was flecked with blood. "We can't leave the vehicle. It's got sensitive items in it."

"And we'll be sure to mention that your coffee pot was the reason we had to blow up one-point-six million dollars' worth of equipment today," Sam said bitterly. "The initial plan was that we have to be at the rally point in thirty minutes after they call break contact. We're going to miss the link up with the patrol heading back to base."

"You're not blowing up the damn truck," Major Whitman growled.

"Fine, then you can stay with it until we can get a patrol coordinated to come out and properly recover it." Merrick's expression was merciless.

Panic flashed over the major's fleshy face. "There's no way."

Sam ignored him and turned to Merrick. "We have less than thirty minutes to be on the road."

Merrick nodded. "I'll get my driver to let the battalion ops know we're blowing the vehicle."

He slunk from the room like the wolf that he reminded Sam of, leaving Sam with Major Whitman and Lewis, who looked like he wasn't sure whether he was going to hold Sam back or join in.

"You better hope that your stupidity doesn't get anyone killed," Sam said quietly.

Then he went downstairs to figure out what he should salvage from the truck and what would be destroyed.

CHAPTER THIRTEEN

The thermite grenade was still burning when Merrick walked into the building.

"Settle in, boys. We're not going anywhere."

Sam leaned back from the window where he watched the wreckage of his truck smolder. They'd managed to push it into a wider space to avoid damage to any surrounding structures. Still, it hurt Sam's heart to burn his own truck.

It felt like surrender. Like defeat.

It felt like digging his own grave.

He didn't say any of that out loud. He looked over at Merrick, the heat from the burning vehicle warming the exposed side of his face. "What are you talking about?"

"The patrol is going to have to come back for us."

A cacophony of "Bullshit" and "What the hell?" rang up from the guys in the small room.

"That blast you just heard? It was a dump truck loaded down with explosives. They ran it through one of the guard points at the base and opened up a massive fucking hole in the perimeter. Our escort patrol was called back as part of the holy shit plan."

A rising fear squeezed Sam's guts. "How long before they come back for us?"

Merrick's eyes glittered in the midafternoon sun. "Unknown. In the meantime, we need to get that radio re-established."

Sam glanced out the window at the smoldering vehicle. "We're going to need another truck."

"They can't just leave us out here, can they?" Major Whitman's voice held an edge of something not quite panic.

Sam was unprepared for the violence of his own reaction. "You fucking coward," he spat.

"I'm in charge of this operation," Whitman said.

"And you've done an admirable job of fucking things up for us so far. How about you let the adults pick up and run with things now that you've broken all your toys?" Sam snapped.

"I don't appreciate your tone, Sergeant," Major Whitman said.

The attempt at pulling rank pushed Sam over the edge. He didn't think. Didn't consider the consequences. He lifted his weapon, thumbed the selector switch from "safe" to "semi" and fired.

It was quite possibly the dumbest thing he'd ever done. The round could have ricocheted off the walls, but instead it was absorbed by the soft metal of the coffee pot.

Everyone in the room hit the deck.

Sam fought the strongest urge to point his weapon at the major. It was all he could do to force himself to lower it. He wanted to drive the butt of his weapon into his fucking skull. Instead, he flicked his weapon onto "safe" as he lowered it. He jammed his index finger at the ruined silver bullet. "Your coffee pot cost me a truck. We could be heading back to base right now if it wasn't for your stupid officer tricks."

"I'll have your ass court-martialed over this."

"I think it'll take a hell of a lot more than killing a coffee pot to get me court-martialed." Sam stepped into the bigger major's face and prayed, *prayed*, the man would swing on him so he could bust his teeth in. "I've got a fiancée at home with a baby on the way. I want to go home to them and I'll be fucked if I'm going to sit back and let your coffee pot change that." He pivoted toward the stairs. "Get the fucking antenna back up and get a truck hooked up to it."

He walked out before he did anything else stupid.

Like actually shoot an officer.

————

"Pretty sure that was one of the top ten stupidest things I've seen in this war." Hale slid down the retaining wall next to Sam's position overlooking the alley.

Sam shot him a deadpan look. The sun blazed overhead, but the sky was empty of air support elements. The radios were eerily quiet. Every time they'd tried to call the base, their calls had been unanswered—just empty static filling the hand mic.

"I thought you were going to shoot him," Hale said when Sam said nothing.

"I thought about it," Sam admitted.

"Why didn't you?"

"Because I'm probably going to get my balls crushed over shooting his coffee pot. I'd just as soon that did not involve prison time."

"After everything we've done in this war, an accidental discharge that results in a soldier getting shot is the least of your sins."

Sam glanced at Hale. His willingness to lie for Sam—again—did not go unnoticed. "I appreciate that, but we've done enough harm on this tour." Sam looked back out over the city. Pyres of smoke filled the sky from the direction of the base.

That was not a good sign.

"You know I got married on midtour?" Hale's comment came out of nowhere.

"Oh yeah?" Sam's voice held genuine surprise. "Who's the lucky girl?"

"I've known her since I was six. We went to Sunday School together when we were kids."

"That's awesome, man. Congrats." He glanced at the younger sergeant. "Why didn't you say something before now?"

"Didn't want to listen to Lewis run his mouth." Hale grimaced. "And I didn't want to jinx it."

"Superstitious?"

"Yeah, well. You know how it is."

Sam didn't, but he didn't say so. Hale was beating around the bush. He'd get to his point soon enough. "So you gonna have kids?"

"Yeah, when I know I'll be around long enough to raise them. This fucking war isn't going to end any time soon." Hale paused, wiping his thumb over the lens of the optic on the top of his weapon. "How long before you think they'll come for us?" he asked.

There it was. The fear that everyone felt and no one wanted to admit. "I don't know. Once they get the base secured again, I assume."

"What if they don't come?"

That was not a question he'd expected from Hale. Maybe from Jinx, who was still on his first deployment and didn't realize that shit happened during combat. Maybe from the skinny kid who slept with his Bible as though it offered some protection from the banality of war's horror. But not from Hale, who'd been with Sam since his last deployment and who'd come through the fight for Najaf and Ramadi and Fallujah ready for more.

"They'll come. And if we don't hear anything by nightfall, we'll figure out what to do then." Sam cleared his throat and swiped his gloved finger beneath his eye to scratch an itch. "See who's running low on water."

"What about food?"

"If the poor bastards already ate their MREs, they can go hungry until we get back to base. Check ammo levels, too."

"Roger that, Sarn't."

Hale needed to be busy. The fear in his voice nagged at Sam, insinuating that his sergeant was fraying at the edges, but Sam ignored it. He'd focus on Hale when they all got back to the base. He didn't have time to lead a therapy session in the middle of the city, alone and unafraid in the middle of the battle space.

The silence on their end of the radio unnerved him the most. He'd tried Merrick's radio. He'd tried hooking the antenna up to every one of the remaining three vehicles.

Nothing. No updates on the fight on the base. No response when they tried to hail Hellhound Main. Only silence. Silence that whispered across Sam's neck that they really were alone. That they were going to die on this shitty outpost in the middle of the city.

"Fuck this." Sam pushed to his feet and went to find Merrick.

———

He found him on the bottom floor crouched next to a blown-out window frame. Merrick held his finger to his lips and motioned for Sam to approach.

Out the window, in a narrow space, a veiled woman led six small children away from their location. The kids couldn't have been more than five, all boys except for one little girl at the end of the human chain.

The woman hadn't seen them. They'd deliberately left the face of the building nearest the orphanage unmarked by concertina wire so as not to draw the kids' attention if they were in the street. Sam hadn't wanted to leave the building exposed but now, as the woman led the children away, none the wiser about their occupation or the vehicles hidden around back, he realized that the plan had had some wisdom after all. His skin prickled as he watched the children pick their way over broken pavement and trash.

The little girl stopped. Sam's heart stopped in his chest. She turned, her wide brown eyes looking right at him. As though she'd known exactly where to find him. Sam's heart caught in his throat. She looked exactly like another little girl from another town. Another fight.

Her lips parted, forming a perfect 'O' as her eyes met his. She stumbled when the boy ahead of her kept walking. Her feet had frozen.

They were caught. They were going to have to rush to the end of the street and secure the woman and the kids. Possibly blow their entire location.

It was a shit situation.

The little girl turned and watched where she was going because the little boy in front of her yanked on her arm. She gave a yelp of pain. Then they were gone, disappearing into a market filled with smoke and burned-out buildings instead of into a bomb-making factory.

The silence was sharp with relief.

"A little too close, that one," Merrick said, peering down the alley just to make sure they were alone.

Now that the kids were gone, taking with them the fear of having to do the horrific, Sam didn't mince words. "Look, I know you're waiting on your boys to come get us, but I think we need to try and get back to base."

Merrick's expression was sharp and hungry, as if he'd been waiting for Sam to make this very argument. "So you want to pack five vehicles' worth of people and equipment into four and hope we can make it back through a city where we're not exactly on friendly terms without getting blown up." He paused, his nearly black eyes darkening. "Did you even think that through?"

Sam crouched and drew a rough diamond-shaped sketch in the dust at Merrick's feet. "We could arrange the vehicles like this, with security in the front and rear, equipment packed tight into the middle two."

"And what happens when we get into a firefight, but can't dismount quickly because the team is packed into the trucks like sardines?"

"We hope we don't get hit," Sam said.

"In all my years in this line of work, I've never known hope to be a particularly effective technique." The censure in Merrick's voice should have embarrassed Sam, but he was worried about Hale. And Jinx. And Lewis.

And the major, for that matter. The fat bastard hadn't said anything since Sam had shot his coffee pot.

Sam probably was going to get court-martialed if he got back to base. Not if, *when*—Sam corrected his thinking.

"I just think if push comes to shove, we need to consider this as an option. We haven't gotten a single call from the base in almost five hours." Sam lowered his voice. "Some of the guys think they may have forgotten us."

Merrick shifted to avoid Sam's gaze. Even if he'd remained silent, Sam would have known the truth. "We have been left, haven't we?" The statement glittered darkly in the setting sun.

Night was falling fast, the sun obscured by so much smoke and dust.

"I think that's a safe supposition," Merrick said after a long moment.

Sam breathed out quietly. He supposed there were worse things. He wasn't going to panic. Not while he still had ammo and options.

"So what's the plan?" Sam asked quietly.

"Right now, we're waiting, because if they're still trying to secure the base, the worst thing we can do is try to approach. We're more likely to get blasted by friendly fire than not." He glanced at the cable strung up the side of the building. "I have no idea what's going on with the radio, but I'm hoping the problem is on our end and not theirs, if you get my drift."

Yeah, Sam got it. If the problem was with their radios, it was a significantly smaller problem than if they were looking at a major comms blowout at the main base. If the base comms were down, everything else probably wasn't doing too hot, either.

"So we wait until dark falls before we make a decision," Sam said. "If we have to move out, it's better to try to make it back to base in the dark."

"Right."

Sam wasn't really a fan of that plan, but it was the best option they had. They had the advantage of night vision goggles, which would give them some assistance should they need to maneuver. It was the least bad of all the terrible options.

"I'll go check the defenses," Sam said.

"Brown?"

Sam stopped and looked back at the skinny infantryman. "I'm surprised it took you so long," Merrick said.

"What's that?"

"Losing your cool on the major."

"You could have spoken up at any time," Sam said.

Merrick's smile was feral. "What's the fun in that?"

Sam walked away before he said anything else. The longer they stayed, the bigger the sense of dread bloomed inside him, like a poison flower. He didn't need to waste time or energy arguing with Merrick. He'd set the guard rotations, check on his guys, and hope the comms came back up soon.

CHAPTER FOURTEEN

Sam rested his head on his assault pack and attempted to close his eyes. They were heavy, too heavy. He only needed a few minutes of sleep and he'd be fit to fight again. He couldn't remember when he'd slept, really slept since he'd gotten in country. The jet lag had grabbed hold and refused to let go.

His eyes had barely closed when a boot scuffed on the floor near his head. He looked up to see Lewis hunkering down next to him.

"You're supposed to be sleeping," Sam muttered. "You've got guard in an hour."

"Are you honestly going to tell me you were sleeping just then?" Lewis asked.

"I was trying to," Sam said. "What's up?"

He was more than just the squad leader. Sometimes he was also the confessor or big brother. Or the father, putting boot to ass. Right now, he figured he just needed to listen. Lewis had been acting funny since they'd left on this mission. If his boy was reaching his breaking point—and everyone had one—Sam needed to pay attention.

"Hale isn't acting right," Lewis said, crouching down.

Sam said nothing for a long moment. "Did you know he got married?"

Lewis frowned. "Since when?"

Sam shrugged and sat up, popping the crick in his neck. "I guess he got married when he went home."

"Why didn't he say anything?"

"Apparently, he didn't want you fucking with him."

Lewis grinned wickedly. "What, is she a stripper or something?"

"I have no idea and I don't really care. Right now the bigger worry is what the hell is wrong with him?"

"He wants to go home," Lewis said.

Sam's irritation got the better of him. "We all want to go home."

"No, I mean like I think he'll do something stupid to get to go home," Lewis said quietly.

His words stoked Sam's irritation instantly. "Aw, fuck." Sam scrubbed his hand over his face. "Well, I would say we need to take him to the chaplain, but we're a little bit screwed right now."

"Tell me about it," Lewis said. He picked at the black beneath his nails with the edge of his Ka-bar knife. "What do I do? We can't take his weapon. I don't have the manpower to post a guard on him."

"We need to just keep him busy until we get back to base. Then we'll get him back to see the chaplain. Chaplain will talk to him. Hale's Catholic, Chaplain's Lutheran or something." Sam's words felt hollow, like he was grasping at straws.

"When will that be?" Lewis finally stopped picking at his nails and looked up. His eyes were tired, his mouth set. Sam had seen him in worse shape, but not recently.

"We're waiting until dark," Sam said. "If there's no word from the base by then, we're going to stuff everyone into the remaining vehicles and head back."

"Dark." Lewis glanced out the window. "Okay."

Sam frowned at Lewis' reaction. "It doesn't sit well with me, either."

"I didn't say anything." He slid the knife into its sheath. "I don't trust these fucks to do their jobs. I found a gaping hole in the perimeter a little while ago because one of Merrick's boys decided to go find a place to piss instead of keeping his position."

Sam ran his tongue over his teeth. "They're all we've got right now."

"I know. I don't have to like it." Lewis slapped his gloves on his thighs, then stood. "For what it's worth, we've all got our sworn statements ready for when we get back to base." At Sam's frown Lewis continued. "About the coffee pot incident."

Sam grinned and shook his head. "I don't even want to know."

"Let's just say you're going to be known as Mr. Coffee from here on out."

Sam laughed. It felt good. It was the first good emotion Sam had felt since he'd returned from midtour leave.

Lewis walked off, leaving Sam with the echo of the joke. He rolled onto his belly and looked out the window. The orphanage was empty and dark, the building blotting out the sun that had sunk below the edge of the city's buildings.

———

Their night vision goggles cut through the darkness. They owned the night, more so than any of the civilians around them and yet, with the approaching darkness, Sam's unease grew until it was a pulsing black thing inside him, a cancer that spread until fear was all he could feel.

He scanned the street but nothing moved, not even the air. It was hot and still. Stifling and silent as the shadows stretched across the street and consumed the remaining light.

The continued radio silence picked at his confidence that anyone was coming for them.

They had ammo. They still had the ability to roll back to base. Their situation was just significantly more vulnerable than Sam liked. He wasn't risk averse, but he preferred to avoid a suicide mission if he could.

He stood, frustrated by his own discontent. He picked up his gear and turned toward the door. A shadow caught his eye.

He turned back and looked out at the street once more.

A frail brown and white dog snuffled into view.

Sam blinked. "Can't be."

They were too far from the base for that fucking mutt to have followed them out here.

He rubbed his eyes, and when he looked again, she was gone.

Swearing at himself, he strode out of the room, his fatigue pushed away by irritation. He was just tired. He wasn't going to fail his team by losing his goddamned mind. He was getting them home, damn it.

All of them.

No matter what.

He found Hale on the roof, manning the .50-cal and squirting cheese onto the cracker from his MRE. It was a running joke that no one could eat that cracker dry in less than two minutes and not choke to death. The cheese made it marginally more palatable.

Sam's stomach chose that moment to rumble its discontent. Still he avoided eating. He wasn't sure that he wouldn't puke if they ended up convoying out of there alone.

"You realize that cheese is going to keep you from shitting right for a week, right?" Sam said. He sat, right on something that poked him in the soft part of his ass.

Hale shrugged. "Occupational hazard."

"Yeah, well, so's death but I'm not in a rush for that, either." He tried to shift and move the rock under him into a less pointy position.

"Lewis talked to you, didn't he?" Hale said.

"Does it matter?"

Hale sighed and bunched up the cracker wrapper, throwing it on the ground. "I'm not crazy, you know."

"I know that. No one said you were."

"Except Lewis. He's always busting my balls."

Sam sniffed and shifted, trying to get the rock out from under his ass. He felt around beneath him and found the source of his pain. It wasn't a rock but a spent shell casing. "Will you two cut the shit?"

Hale snorted then took a pull off his CamelBak. "I have two brothers. I don't fight with them like I fight with Lewis."

"Yeah, well, your brothers don't have your back when the shit and the fan decide to make a porno, either," Sam said.

Hale wiped his mouth and shifted to lift his head from his sight to look at Sam. "I know. I'm just not sleeping well, that's all."

"When's the last time you got any sleep?"

"Couple nights ago. Fits and starts. I'm just edgy, that's all." He glanced up at Sam. "I'm not going to blow my brains out or anything. You can count on me, okay?"

Sam gripped his shoulder. "I know that, man. I'm just checking on you, that's all."

"Thanks. But I think you should be more worried about that kid with the Bible. He hasn't moved from his corner since you shot the major's coffee pot."

Sam sighed. He was never going to live down the coffee pot. "He's not in my squad. I've got other problems to worry about. Let the major do something for once that doesn't involve crashing comms."

Hale grinned and turned his gaze back to his sector. "Did you ever watch *The Exorcist?*"

"Now that's a random question. Yeah. Everyone has, haven't they?"

"I hadn't. 'Til last week. You know they filmed part of that movie up north of here? Some place called al Hadr."

Sam frowned and glanced up at the falling darkness. Stars fought through the haze and the smoke to carpet the night sky. "Let me guess. You watched it and that's why you can't sleep?"

"Every time I close my eyes, I see the air shifting in front of my face. Shadows dancing. It's creepy as hell."

Sam squeezed and released Hale's shoulder as relief washed over him. He shouldn't be relieved that his guy was scared from a movie, but it was so much better than the alternative of Hale possibly blowing his head off because he wasn't sleeping. A fake demon? Yeah, Sam could deal with that. "Dude, you brought this shit on yourself," he said with a chuckle.

"Thanks for the sympathy, dick face," Hale grumbled. "I thought it would be like any other horror movie. I've seen every *Saw* movie and, dude, nothing has ever scared me like that movie."

"The scene when her head spins around do it for you?"

"No, actually, it's the fact that the devil gets the priest in the end."

Sam frowned. "Huh?"

"Yeah, the devil wins. He gets the priest." Hale wiped his hand off on his uniform. "The good guy loses."

Sam watched as another star valiantly fought for its place in the night sky. "Yeah, but the good guy sacrificed himself so the little girl could live."

"Pretty shitty way for the girl to live. Why couldn't the devil just be defeated without the good guy having to give up his soul to save the little girl?"

Sam shrugged, not liking the direction this conversation was taking. They'd never talked about what happened that day. Sam still saw her face in his nightmares. Her face, judging him for making the call he'd made. "I don't know, man. Maybe you need to ask the chaplain that." He scrubbed his hand over his jaw. He needed to shave. "It's just a movie."

"Yeah. Maybe I will."

Silence settled over them in the darkness. *The Exorcist* was bullshit, Sam thought. It made for good storytelling, that was all. Even if the priest had killed himself to save the little girl, nothing kept that demon from going back after her.

The priest's sacrifice was futile. Just like half the decisions made in this damn war.

But he couldn't tell Hale that. Not right now, when he was a snail inching along the razor's edge.

"A little kid lived because of a good man's sacrifice," Sam said after a while.

Hale's answer penetrated the fear that had been Sam's constant companion since that day two months earlier. "That doesn't mean the good man's soul was worth it."

"No," Sam said, his voice thick. "No, it doesn't."

———

Night in the middle of the city, far from any support and without communications, was a chilling place to be. This sector of the city had no power, so the silence was heavy and absolute. It hung on, accenting every sound. Strange how the world went so eerily quiet with no electricity humming in the background.

The silence was screwing with him. Sam gave up trying to catch a ten-minute nap. He wasn't a fan of lying to himself, but he'd fed himself a complete line of bullshit by believing he was going to get any sleep.

Instead, as the night crept on, he made his rounds, pulling guys off guard who looked like they were half dead on their feet so they could catch a fifteen-minute nap or so. Just a quick few minutes to close their eyes, then he'd get them back in the fight.

He stepped into the command post, where he tried not to notice the major toying with the pieces of his silver bullet coffeepot. Sam paused when the radio crackled, but nothing was there. Just unreadable static across the 'net. No comms crossing the distance between their location and the main base.

Hope died in his chest.

He kept going, heading down to the bottom floor. He paused at the entrance to one of the rooms. Peering in, he saw Merrick talking with Hale, his hand on Hale's shoulder.

Sam was about to go on, about to ignore the fact that his team leader looked like he was confessing his sins, when Merrick looked right at him. Sam blinked and could have sworn that Merrick's eyes gleamed in the darkness.

He stepped into the room. "Everything okay in here?"

Hale turned, his cheeks flushing. "Yeah. I was just telling Sarn't Merrick that one of his guys got caught sleeping on guard duty."

Sam recognized the lie as soon as Hale spoke, but he wasn't about to call him out in front of Merrick. The lie, though—the lie nagged at the back of his mind. Still, he let it go. He had more important things to worry about than what Merrick was talking to Hale about.

Hale would be okay. If Sam said so often enough, it would be true.

Merrick clapped him on the shoulder as he slipped past, out into the stairwell and into the darkness.

Sam said nothing, waiting for Hale to come clean.

Hale looked away, avoiding Sam's gaze. "I wasn't lying, Sarn't Brown," Hale said.

"But you weren't telling the whole truth, either."

Hale met his eyes. Sam had never seen more naked fear in his soldier's eyes. "I won't let you down, Sarn't Brown. Whatever it takes. I'm going to make sure we get home."

Sam crossed the small space, his weapon bouncing against his chest from the three-point sling. He gripped Hale's shoulder and spoke very quietly, so that if Merrick was still in the hall, lurking in the darkness and shadows, he wouldn't hear Sam's next words.

"I don't know what's on your mind, but we're going to get through this."

Hale smiled thinly. "I know we will."

The certainty in Hale's voice sent a chill down Sam's spine. "Hale…"

"I'm fine, Sarn't Brown." His gaze didn't waver. "Really. I'm going to go check on Jinx."

He brushed past Sam without another word, leaving Sam with the disquieting realization that Hale was not doing okay, and that there wasn't dick he could do about it until they got back to the base.

Frustration clawed at him as he moved through the building, checking on the guard positions. He found Lewis flicking a wad of dip into the dirt, watching the alley near the orphanage.

"Hale is not okay," Sam said.

"No shit, Sherlock. What clued you in?"

"I'm not really in the mood for fucking jokes," Sam said in a low voice. "Get ready to pack out of here ASAP. I'm going to find Merrick. We've waited long enough."

"No argument there," Lewis muttered. He stopped Sam with a palm on his chest. Sam looked down at the hand from the junior man, then up into his eyes. "Hale's going to be okay, right?"

Sam took a deep breath before he answered. The evening call to prayer echoed over the city's rooftops, haunting and beautiful. Sam hated it. Hated the war, hated this place. Hated all of it in that one moment.

Lewis dropped his palm.

Sam gripped the other man's shoulder. "I'll move heaven and earth to make sure of it."

CHAPTER FIFTEEN

"There's still no communication from the main base," Sam said as Merrick hunkered down next to him. The major was slumped in a corner, his chin resting on his chest. A fleck of spittle dribbled from his open mouth as he snored softly. "We've waited long enough."

Sam pulled the antenna cable off, turning the connector to look at the pins.

Merrick sat, scuffing his boot against the dust-covered floor, leaving one leg bent so he could prop his elbow on it. "I've done all of that."

Sam flicked his gaze toward Merrick, then back to the cable in his hand. "I'm not saying you didn't," Sam said as he blew into the connector on the hand mic, then wet the inside with his pinky before attempting to reconnect it. "Doesn't hurt to double-check everything." He keyed the mic. "Hellhound Main, Hellhound Main, this is Reaper Two Six, over."

Nothing but static came back over the net. Not even a dead space where the distant end might have tried to key the mic.

It was as if a bubble enveloped them. No communications. No overflights. Just a pitch-black night, layered in dust and sand and the sound of spent ammunition casings skittering along the concrete floor. It was like the world around them had come to a grinding halt, and they were the only ones left.

It was a deeply unsettling thought. Sam slammed the mic down and stood, pacing to the window to peer out into the darkened street. He didn't want to be here anymore. Not this building, not this mission, not this fucking country. He was trapped, the walls squeezing in on him as he kept racing around the hamster wheel. Running his ass off and going nowhere fast.

"I've been stranded before," Merrick said, fiddling with the knob on the radio.

Sam rocked back on his heels, tapping his thumb against the butt of his weapon. "I don't actually care. When are we leaving?"

Merrick ignored his comment but said nothing else. The silence stretched between them, cold and uncomfortable.

Finally, Merrick spoke. "I'd been arguing with the boss about this little goody two-shoes lieutenant. My boss didn't appreciate my point of view."

"What was the argument?" Sam still didn't care. Not in the least. But maybe if he humored Merrick, he'd get around to answering the frigging question about when they were going to leave. He fought the urge to kick the major's boot to wake him up.

"That the lieutenant wasn't as good as he thought he was." Merrick spit into the dust. "Then I got left out in sector, and lo and behold who comes to rescue me? The kiss-ass lieutenant. Who the boss then rewarded with even greater responsibility."

"So why does it sound like you're not happy about being picked up when you were alone in the enemy territory?" Sam watched the thin man out of the corner of his eye.

Merrick shifted his weight onto his heels as he traced the antenna to the back of the radio. "I think I'd rather have died than be indebted to that sycophantic little fuck," Merrick said. "And the worst part is that he's so goddamned *nice*."

"These are not bad things," Sam said mildly.

"In our line of work? Yes they are." Merrick looked up at him, his eyes razor sharp. "There is no room for *nice* in what we do. Nice gets you killed. Nice gets your men killed."

Sam flinched and turned away, he hoped before Merrick saw his reaction. Nice did get good men killed. Sam knew that firsthand. He'd have to live with that guilt for the rest of his life. He would get no absolution for his sins. Not in this life, not even if he lived to be one hundred.

"Made hard choices during this war, huh, Brown?" Merrick asked.

"Haven't we all?" He didn't want to have this conversation. Not here. Not now. Not when he needed to get back to the base to get Hale checked out and there wasn't jack shit he could do to speed up the process. "It's full dark now. When are we leaving?"

"What's the worst thing you've seen during the war?" Merrick asked, ignoring Sam's question a second time.

He could answer. Or he could insist on the answer to his own question first. Somehow, he didn't think he was going to get that.

Sam leaned his back against the low wall and tipped his head back to look out over the city. Smoke shadows blotted out the night sky.

The memory came unbidden and unwelcome on the pixie dust swirling in the sparse lights.

"There was this little girl once. She was probably about five. Maybe older, but she was so little. She was walking through raw sewage barefoot, picking through the trash. I think she was looking for something to eat." If he closed his eyes, he'd see her clearly again. Brown eyes too big for her face. Hair dark and stringy around cheeks that should have been chubby and bent with laughter. Clothes tattered and torn, her shirt barely hanging onto one shoulder.

The problem was, he wanted to forget her. He didn't want to think of these people as people. He wanted to be able to shoot the engine block of a car or blow up a building without feeling guilty. Without feeling like the war was going to permanently stain his hands and blacken his soul.

He wanted to be able to go home to Faith in a few months and hold their son or their daughter and not wonder what the war had done to him. Would he be able to go home and be the same again? Or would he always wonder whether the war had permanently twisted something up inside him, because of one bad decision with a kid no one had cared enough about to keep out of the middle of a firefight?

That little girl haunted him. She kept him up at night, making him think about things he wanted to forget, making him feel guilty for making the wrong choice. Why were there so many fucking children in the middle of a war zone?

"You don't like thinking about her." It was not a question.

"Not really. I mean, what if that had been my kid wandering around in the shit and the piss?" Hungry and lost. Jesus, his heart ached just thinking about what this war had done to her. "I'd do anything to keep my kid from having to live like that."

The words left a fleeting hypocrisy in his heart. He'd protect his own child, but a child alone in a foreign country? No, he couldn't have done anything to protect her.

He'd turned his back on her and tried to forget he'd ever seen her. He was the worst kind of coward.

He rubbed his chest and flicked his night vision goggles down to check the street, penetrating the darkness with a light green haze.

At the end of the alley, a flicker of movement caught his eye. He stilled, watching the shadows twist and writhe along the wall.

The dog plodded back into the street. Her head was low, her movements quick and stealthy. Her nose was to the ground, her tail down. Shallow grooves hung between her ribs. Her hip bones protruded grotesquely from her body.

It couldn't be the dog from the base. This far away? She couldn't possibly have had the energy to make it this far. And yet, as she skulked into the alley, Sam knew. It was the same dog. She had the same torn ear as the dog from the base.

It couldn't be a coincidence. Sam swallowed and wished the

green tinge had never illuminated the pathetic mutt. "Fuck." She looked miserable. How long had that stupid breakfast bar prolonged her misery?

He should shoot her. It would be a kindness, rather than to let her continue to scavenge and starve.

Merrick moved to the other window, his own night vision goggles down to illuminate the night. He'd barely glanced down the street when he leaned back, lifting the goggles away from his eyes. "I see you've met Anu."

Sam couldn't have been more surprised if Merrick had said he'd helped all of her puppies find good homes. Merrick did not strike him as the kind-to-animals type. "You've named her?"

Merrick moved away from the window, dropping his NVGs. "She named herself."

"What the hell does that even mean?" Sam snapped. He couldn't look away from the bedraggled dog. Didn't notice that Merrick once again ignored his question.

The dog shuffled closer. Sam's breath caught in his chest as he watched her. Anticipation clutched at his throat as she scratched at a pile of debris. Victory leapt inside him as she procured something edible. She ate hungrily, the tip of her tail wagging ever so slightly at the sparse meal.

And then the hunt was on again.

As she slunk down the alley, Sam held his breath. The closer she came, the harder it was for him to fill his lungs. Panic slithered in and took hold. Air. He needed air. He forced himself to slow his breathing. To accept what little oxygen his lungs could hold.

The skinny dog lifted her head. In the pale green light of the night vision goggles, her dark eyes met his.

———

Sam dropped his head back against the concrete. His helmet tinked off the edge of the broken window frame, jarring his brain. Black stars floated in front of his vision.

He held his silence even as the panic fled and his lungs filled. *What the hell just happened?*

He sat for a long moment, just breathing, Merrick's words echoing in the dull emptiness of his brain. *She named herself.*

He was losing his fucking mind.

He closed his eyes and again saw the pale dog, her ribs bathed in green shadows as she slunk down the trash-strewn streets.

Sam flicked off his night vision goggles and blinked, waiting for his eyes to adjust and decided that Merrick was going to answer his fucking question. "You don't strike me as the type for all that mystical woo-woo stuff."

"It's not. She guards us. Lets us know when the enemy are coming. She's always around. I credit her for helping me get every day closer to home." Merrick pulled out a packet of MRE crackers and tore the package open. The plastic crinkled loudly in the silence. "So tell me, Sam Brown. What would you do to go home? Would you listen to a stray dog if it meant the difference between life and death?"

Sam rubbed his eyes with one hand, the other resting on the butt of his weapon. The cool steel penetrated his gloves, seeking his skin. "Kind of a pointless conversation, isn't it?"

"It's never pointless to have something you're living for." Merrick turned to look at him, his face bathed in the pale green light from the radio display. "What are you living for, Sam Brown?"

Sam thought for a long moment about simply closing his eyes and drifting to sleep for a few minutes, ignoring the question. If he did, he'd mark himself a coward for running from something as innocuous as a question about going home.

He could answer that without selling his soul to the devil, right?

The problem was, he didn't want to get to know Merrick. He didn't want to swap stories of home or of sad-faced women crying when they told them they loved them. He didn't want common ground with the sharp-faced platoon sergeant who looked like he was one bad explosion away from committing the next Haditha.

He closed his eyes. "I want to go home and try to be a good man," he said softly.

"You're not a good man over here?" Merrick's voice held a mocking lightness that belied the heaviness of his question.

"You've been here long enough. You tell me if it's possible to go to war and stay a good man." The question annoyed him. He was too tired to wax philosophical about the war, even if he was the one who'd answered the question in the first place. He could have just said his future wife and child, but for some perverse reason, he wanted to hide them from Merrick.

Despite having spent the last few hours with Merrick, Sam's apprehension remained. An edginess to the man's movements made Sam uneasy. The man's eyes had a shadow Sam didn't trust.

Merrick was shifty. That's what it was. The man rarely sat still. Even when he wasn't moving, Sam could practically see the gears in motion. Strategizing. Plotting. Scheming. Asking questions that made Sam think of home. Questions that drew thoughts up out of the dark place where he kept those thoughts safe and clean, untainted by the war. He didn't want to think of home, or of Faith, or of their baby on the way.

He needed to focus on this war, this mission, this moment.

"What do I think?" Merrick parroted. "I think good men go to war and rarely ever return."

His words sounded ominous. A portent of doom, if Sam believed in those.

"When are we leaving?" Sam asked for the third time.

"The longer we sit here, the more I realize that they really have forgotten us," Merrick said. His voice held no bullshit, just resignation. "Either that or shit is really fucking bad back on the base."

"We'd talked about waiting until darkness. It's dark now."

"And there's quiet in the city."

Sam scrubbed his hand over his face, not liking that response one bit. "This means any movement will attract attention."

"From an angry group of Iraqis who are tired of having their neighborhood blown all to hell every time the American's decide to go hunting for bad guys." Merrick sounded like a man who'd just been told he was going to die.

"We've got two courses of action," Sam said. "We stay, we could get hit. We try to make it back to base, we could get hit."

Merrick's gaze fell on him. Sam felt exposed. Vulnerable. "This position is already fortified."

Sam rubbed his hand across his jaw and popped his neck until it cracked. "Okay, then."

"Look, whatever is going on back at the base will be cleaned up by dawn. They'll get themselves unfucked and then figure out we're out here." Merrick's voice took on a calming tone that instantly grated on Sam's last nerve.

"You're remarkably calm for being in the middle of a clusterfuck."

"When you've done the things I've done this year, waiting until morning isn't that big a deal." Merrick started to head for the door. He stopped and patted Sam's shoulder. "A year is a long time to spend on a walk through hell."

"I know. This isn't my first rodeo."

Merrick offered a thin smile. "Then you should already know the way this ends."

CHAPTER SIXTEEN

The explosion happened without warning. It could have been at the end of the block or right outside. The *whoompf* of the blast followed the flash and knocked the air from Sam's lungs. The explosion sent the dust around Sam flaring into the air and sprinkling down like fresh snow.

The silence that followed the blast lasted for an eternity, ringing in Sam's ears and blocking out all sound.

"Everyone okay?"

He was sure he'd spoken. He'd felt his lips move. Lewis lifted his head from his arms. His mouth moved.

Sam heard nothing. It felt like there was cotton stuffed in his ears, a thick, fluffy feeling that made his head feel full.

He gripped the outside of his ear and wiggled. Sound rushed back, crashing over him in a cascade of noise.

"Is everyone okay?"

Lewis gave him a quick thumbs-up before heading out to check the perimeter. Attacks usually followed a blast like that.

But once Sam finished checking the guys on the roof and no attack had begun, a deep unease settled in his gut.

"Is this normal?" Sam asked Merrick. He kicked at the wreckage of the coffee pot.

Merrick's gaze dropped to Sam's foot. "What?"

"Blasts with no follow-on attack?"

Merrick pulled his helmet off and started fiddling with his helmet light. "Depends. Blast like that probably shouldn't have been wasted. But they've been getting more erratic. Trying to screw up the guys looking for patterns, you know?"

Sam crouched down, scrubbing his hand over his face. A high-pitched squeal rang in his ears. "They're that complex?"

"Sometimes. Depends."

Sam rubbed his ear. "Any luck on the radio?"

Merrick shook his head. "Nothing but static."

"We've still got five hours until dawn."

"Yep. Gonna be a bad night, if that blast is any indicator."

"You think they're hitting the base?"

"They'd be stupid not to, especially since where that earlier blast hit the base, too."

Sam leaned back against the wall. "Fuck. I just want to go home," he muttered.

He sensed a subtle shift. Something in the air, something in the way Merrick stood.

"You've got a lot waiting for you?" Despite asking the question, Merrick's words were certain.

"Yeah." It must have been the bone-crushing fatigue that had burned away Sam's defenses.

"How pregnant is your fiancée?"

"A little over four months." Wistfulness, completely out of place, flushed over Sam's skin. "She got pregnant right before I left this time. We think it was my last night in the States."

"No chance it could be someone else's?"

Merrick's words slapped at him, clawing at the fear every soldier faced when he kissed his girl good-bye and headed off to war. Sam didn't open his eyes. "No. Faith doesn't cheat."

"You sound so sure." Merrick's voice picked at the wound he'd just inflicted.

"Are you trying to fuck with me right now?" Sam asked, keeping his voice mild.

"Just asking a question."

Sam finally opened his eyes and looked at Merrick. Shadows sliced across the other man's sharp features. His eyes were pitiless black holes in his face. "What's your point?"

"What would you do to know with absolute certainty that you could go home to her?"

Sam pushed to his feet, irrational anger driving him away from the man in the shadows. "I'm not playing fucking games, Merrick."

"It's not a game, Sam. What we put out into the world is what we make happen."

The use of Sam's first name paused the anger inside him. Only for a moment and then it resumed. "I'm not doing this. I'm going to go check on my guys."

Merrick shifted, kicking his feet up on the blown-out window frame. He pulled a toothpick from a pack and stuck it between his teeth. "Suit yourself." He looked out over the city cast in shadows and obsidian darkness.

Sam hesitated. "What game are you playing?"

"You spend fifteen months over here. Getting blown up day after day. You start spending a lot of time thinking about home. What you'll do after that first kiss. After that first hour, that first day." Merrick turned his head slowly back toward Sam. His eyes glinted in the shadows, reflecting a light that Sam couldn't see. "What would you do? To go home, right now, and place your hand on her belly? Feel that baby move. What's that worth to you?"

Sam closed his eyes. The fingers of his right hand twitched, remembering the feel of that small bump. He looked up, remembering how she'd smiled and looked down at him, running her hand through his hair as he kissed her belly. "Anything," Sam whispered. "I'd give anything to be home with her right now."

Merrick shifted so quickly Sam almost missed it. One minute

his feet were kicked up on the windowsill, the next Merrick stood right in his face. His teeth gleamed white in the shadows. "Are you sure? Because 'anything' encompasses a whole lot of options. Especially in combat."

"No shit."

"You ever think about what 'anything' entails, Sam? Really think about what you would do?"

Sam looked away, down toward the remains of the coffee pot and the radio that offered nothing but static. The men around them were silent. Almost specters. They might as well have been alone. "No." The lie was cold on his tongue.

"Do you always lie to yourself?"

"Fuck off, Merrick." Sam turned to go.

"The Memorial Day attack."

Sam's breath lodged in his throat. "What do you know about that?" he whispered.

"More than you think." Merrick smiled. "You could have sacrificed yourself to save your men. Instead, that little girl died so that you could live." Sam froze, his hand on the doorframe. Ice slithered over his skin. "Two of your boys went home in flag-draped coffins despite everything." A scuff of boot on the floor. Merrick's words whispered over the back of Sam's neck. "How does that feel, young Sam Brown?"

Sam whirled and slammed Merrick against the wall. "How do you know about that?" There was no force in his words. Only shame.

Merrick smiled, holding both hands up. "Small war. Rumors get around."

"That's not how it went down."

"Really?"

"No." Sam turned away, needing to put distance between himself and Merrick before he did something else he regretted. It had been an accident. He hadn't meant to shoot her.

She wasn't supposed to be there, goddamn it.

"Then the war has done its worst to you?" Merrick asked.

"I've done enough," Sam whispered, his voice ragged.

"Really? What would you really do to go home to Faith? If shooting that kid would guarantee you a trip home, would you do it?"

Sam cocked his fist back. Paused. Then shoved Merrick away.

"Your game of 'what if' sucks. Stay the hell away from me."

***

Sam climbed the stairs to the radio room. The truck below rumbled in the darkness. He was making the major put a guy in the truck and start that son of a bitch on a timer. He wasn't going to lose another truck. Not again.

He was going to have his face ripped off by Captain Lehr if —*when*—they made it back to base. Sam wasn't going to hesitate to name the major and his shitbag soldiers as the cause of the damage. He had no reason to hide the truth.

He walked into the radio room and saw Lewis screwing with the radio. Lewis glanced up at Sam as he walked in and shot him a quick thumbs-up.

Hope soared inside him and prickled across his skin as Lewis spoke into the black hand mic.

"Roger that, Hellhound Main. Tracking link up location."

Sam kicked the kid curled in the corner, where his face was resting on the shattered remains of the coffee pot. He blinked and looked up slowly, his eyes fogged with sleep. "Huh?"

"Get up. We're going home," Sam said.

The kid's eyes got wide as realization dawned. He scrambled to his feet. He slung his weapon over his shoulder and started tossing things into the deformed silver bullet. His feet were scuffs on the stairs.

Sam watched him go then turned back to Lewis. "I've never seen anyone move so fast in my—"

A pop pierced the silence. The crack of a rifle retort off the dusty alley walls. Sam froze.

Lewis' eyes widened. A dark pool formed beneath his left arm where he was still holding the hand mic. It fell from his hand as Lewis dropped to his knees.

"Lewis!"

The world exploded in fire and violence, but it all sounded very far away as Sam crawled through the dust toward Lewis. He ripped open Lewis' body armor, looking for the source of the blood.

Lewis tried to talk, but his words gurgled in his throat. A fine red mist spread across his lips.

"Don't talk," Sam said. His fingers searched Lewis' ribs and found a tiny entrance wound beneath his right armpit. Blood gushed from the exit wound beneath his left. Sam ripped the first aid kit open and screamed for help as he tried to apply pressure to stop the bleeding. He held the plastic from the pressure dressing over the larger of the wounds.

Lewis' eyes rolled back in his head. He coughed, trying to breathe. Sam heard only fluid where there should have been air.

"Stay with me, buddy. Lewis, open your eyes, goddamn it." He pressed his knee and a second plastic wrap to the entrance wound.

Lewis gripped his calf. Then his grip went limp.

Sam lowered his head to Lewis' mouth. The war raged around them but Sam heard nothing, felt nothing. Focused only on Lewis. He slammed his fist into Lewis' still chest.

And then the rage came.

———

Sam scurried across his position on the roof. The gunner was dead; someone from Merrick's squad, a kid he didn't know and didn't take time to mourn. He focused on getting the big gun firing again, sending steel on target. Below him, shadows ran in the darkness. Sam flicked on his optics and looked to identify friend from foe.

One by one, he picked off the enemy, keeping them from

approaching the undermanned fighting position halfway down the alley.

"Jinx! Get down there to Hale!" he shouted from the roof.

Sam kept firing, talking with one of the heavy weapons from a lower floor.

"Well, how's this for a morning wake-up call?" Merrick asked, slamming into the sandbags next to him.

A whistle flew by Sam's head and he ducked instinctively. The building reported to have been full of kids before sunset exploded. Bits of concrete rained down on them and a piece skidded between his body armor and his neck. He swatted at it as the concrete rain continued. As soon as it stopped, he lifted his head and started firing again.

Merrick leaned over the edge of the building with his optics. "Well now, this is truly fucked," he said.

Sam glanced at him on a pause from firing. "That's not helping."

Merrick's eyes were wide from the flashes of light from the weapons fire. "Who said I'm here to help?"

"You could start shooting at something," Sam snapped, focusing his attention on the advancing forces down the alley. "I've pulled our security in closer to us. We've got three down and five wounded. I think that fat fucking major got a paper cut, but he's applying pressure like it needs a tourniquet." He looked over at Merrick. "We need to consolidate the — fuck!"

Hot lead skittered down his neck. His flesh bubbled beneath the shell casing. He tried to slap it away, but the casing was melted to his flesh. Grinding his teeth, he yanked it free. Skin peeled off with it and the exposed meat protested the kiss of hot, dirty air on the open wound.

"Fuck fuck fuck." Sam started shooting again. "Are you going to do any fucking thing?"

"Seven dead, Sam." Merrick's smile was blank. Empty. "How bad do you want to go home?"

The war fell away in that moment. Sam squeezed the trigger of his weapon but felt nothing. Heard nothing. The concrete in front of Sam's face exploded between them, but neither of them moved. "What are you talking about?"

"You said you'd do anything to go home." Merrick tipped his chin.

"Now isn't really the fucking—" Sam ducked as a piece of concrete flew by his head—"time!"

"It's never a good time," Merrick said.

"Fuck this, man. I'm pulling our guys in the rest of the way. You can sit here if you want."

Merrick blocked him from leaving. It was only then that Sam noticed the blood on Merrick's uniform. The whites of his eyes seemed too stark against his skin.

"You want to go home to your baby girl?" Merrick asked. His voice was soft, eerily soft. And yet, Sam heard him perfectly.

"Baby girl?" Sam whispered. A thousand emotions swelled inside him, picturing Faith holding a tiny bundle of little girl. A miniature version of Faith. Safe. Secure. "How do you know that?"

Merrick smiled and held out his hand. "I'll take away all the fear, Sam. All the sadness. You can go home to your precious Faith." His hand was skeletal in the shadows. It gleamed like bone.

Sam looked back up at Merrick. "We need to get off the roof before we get blown up," Sam said, grasping at reality in the fog.

"Just take my hand. I'll make sure you get home." Merrick lifted his hand just a little bit. "It's a small price. After all, you did promise *anything*."

The building exploded beneath them, the concussion from the blast throwing them off their feet.

Sam shook off the haze from the explosion. Merrick stood over him, holding out his hand.

Thinking he had to have been losing his mind, he gripped the other man's hand.

And went back to war.

———

The sniper had only been the beginning. The enemy had funneled down the street. Where there had once been a crew-served weapon was now an area manned by only a couple of dudes with smaller caliber M4s.

"Jinx, get a 240 on this street!" Sam shouted.

"Busy right now, Sarn't Brown." The 240 was rocking down the second avenue of approach. No second gun was answering Jinx's bursts—because the second gunner would have been with Lewis.

Sam went to find the missing weapons system. The skinny Bible Kid was curled up beneath the truck, his hands cupped over his ears, tears streaming down his face. His weapon lay in the dirt, unused. Useless.

Sam dragged the kid to his position a few feet away. Concrete exploded over Sam's head as the enemy tried to gain ground in the alley.

"Get on the fucking weapon and kill anything that fucking moves," Sam said.

The kid opened his mouth and Sam didn't think. He slapped him on the back of the head and pointed down the alley. "Start shooting. Time fucking now."

It was goddamned chaos. Merrick was nowhere to be seen. The .50-cal was dismounted on the ground and essentially unusable. They were trapped.

And the enemy kept coming, stepping over the bodies that piled up in front of them. They kept coming.

Sam grabbed a grenade and lobbed it over the defensive position where Hale was busy trying to jerry-rig a mount for the .50-cal. "Frag out!"

Everyone ducked as the grenade went off. Rounds flew again, as if the enemy hadn't even blinked.

Inside the truck, the radio chattered constantly. It took Sam a minute to realize what he was hearing.

"Reaper Two Six, this is Thrasher Seven. Looks like you guys could use a hand down there."

"Thrasher Seven, your timing is fucking perfect." Air support. Sam had never been so fucking happy for air support in his entire life. "We'll mark our position with red illum," Sam said into the hand mic. "Weapons free to the north of our position."

"Roger that, Reaper Two Six."

The sound of the helo opening up on the enemy was the sweetest sound.

———

There was relative silence after the gun run was complete. As though the world had stopped, and all the violence and death had stopped with it.

The patrol that had been coming to get them pulled up to the end of the alley.

Captain Lehr strode down through the bodies and the death toward Sam, whose boots were suddenly welded to the ground.

Lehr grabbed Sam by the back of the neck. "Fuck, dude, you okay?"

Sam said nothing. No, he was not okay. His guts twisted and threatened to release. "We need to get the medics down here," he said when he could finally talk.

Lewis was already dead. Hale was bleeding from a cut somewhere on his face. Jinx's hand was bloody.

And the Bible Kid?

Not a scratch or spot on him.

Sam fought the urge to kick him where he sat next to the tire of the Humvee. It would have been like kicking a puppy who'd just gotten whooped for shitting on the floor. As the rage peeled back in layers, Sam realized he didn't want to be the kind of man who kicked puppies.

The medics trotted down the alley. Overhead the helos guarded their position, keeping any more enemy from approaching.

Sam started toward the stairs.

Captain Lehr stopped him. "Let them do it, Sam," he said quietly.

"Sir —"

"Don't. Trust me, the nightmares aren't worth it."

They finished packing up the gear. Sam tossed the antenna from the roof and the radio—now splattered with Lewis' blood—into the back of the truck.

The medics came down the stairs with Lewis between them on a stretcher. He was covered with a poncho. Sam looked at his commander.

"They're out of body bags at the base," Lehr said quietly.

"It was that bad?"

Lehr nodded. "I'm sorry we couldn't get to you until now, Sam." He rubbed his hand over his mouth. "So fucking sorry."

Sam said nothing, unable to speak beyond the lump in his throat. As the adrenaline faded, the anger rose up, dancing and twisting with a raw sadness that sliced at his guts.

He climbed into the truck. Jinx guided it down the alley, over the bodies they'd shoved to one side.

Sam didn't care about the enemy dead. He wanted to kill them all over again. Hate clawed at him.

And on the ride back to the base, Sam grieved.

CHAPTER SEVENTEEN

Sam supposed he should be used to what stress could do to people. But two hours after they finally made it back to base, he walked into the TOC and found Captain Lehr and Captain Tarsis screaming at each other. The skinny kid stood between the two captains, holding a hand mic and looking like he'd rather be anywhere else than right there, on radio detail.

Sam looked away from him. He felt the shame of not knowing that kid's name but now, with Lewis' death burning in his heart, he had no fucks to give. Instead, he folded his arms across his chest and waited for the two captains to either come to blows or back off into separate corners.

"I don't give a flying fuck, Ross. Your fucking guy was responsible for making sure they made the rally point."

Tarsis was a mean little bastard, apparently, because he shoved Lehr back a step. "And your fucking people are the ones who blew a goddamned truck, remember? Don't you stand there and fucking blame my goddamned squad who knows that fucking sector better than your goddamned fucking cowboys." Spittle flew from his mouth as he shouted.

Lehr had taken a single step in his direction, fist half-cocked to strike, when Sam interrupted their fight.

"If you ladies are about done, I need to work on one of the computers," Sam said quietly. He wondered where Tick and Merrick were, and why anyone was allowing these two captains to fight in the TOC in the first place.

Lehr took a step back, his chest moving violently as his breath sliced in and out of his lungs. He said nothing, jerking his thumb over his shoulder toward his office and then stalking out of the TOC.

The skinny kid slithered out of Lehr's way, then slowly set the hand mic down. He looked like he'd rather melt into the shadows than sit in the TOC in the dark and listen to the radio chatter — chatter that was clear as the night sky now that they were back on the base.

"I'm sorry about your boys, Sarn't Brown," Tarsis said roughly.

Sam's throat thickened. "Thanks, sir," he said after a moment. "Sir?" He flexed his hand, trying to shake off an unfamiliar tightness in his tendons. "Is Merrick around? I need to catch him before you guys head out and make sure I've got the paperwork right."

Tarsis' face darkened to a deep shade of puce. His jaw tightened. "Fuck you, Brown. I offer sympathy and you ask me about fucking paperwork?"

"Sir?"

"Merrick's dead, you fucking asshole. You're just like your goddamned commander. Fuck you, you little prick."

Sam looked at the blank space where the angry captain had just been, his words echoing on the back of Sam's skull. *Dead?* When the fuck had Merrick died?

Sam rubbed his hands over his face and closed his eyes, trying to think back to the firefight. The last thing he remembered was taking Merrick's hand after the building had gotten blown up.

That had been real, right? His fucking hand hurt as if it had been in a death grip. Why couldn't he remember?

"You okay, Sarn't?"

Sam glanced toward the door and fought to keep his expression blank. The Bible Kid stood in the doorway, framed by the two-by-fours that made up the door in the first place.

"Fine, why?" He frowned. "Why are you on radio guard instead of racked out?"

The kid lifted one shoulder. "I volunteered. Figured I was too keyed up to sleep anyway." He folded his hands behind his back. "I'm sorry about your team leader," he said after a moment.

Sam ground his teeth. "Yeah. We all are."

"I know you're not big on faith and all, but Ecclesiastes 3:1 says 'To every thing there is a season, and a time to every purpose under the heaven'."

Sam's breath came short and quick, blocked by a spike of inchoate rage. "Don't. Don't fucking quote me scripture right now and tell me that there's a reason for my guy to be cold in the fucking morgue right now."

The kid's eyes went wide. "Sarn't, I just meant—"

"Not one more fucking word," Sam snapped.

"Sarn't."

Sam's fist exploded on the desk. Paper shot out from the pressure of the blow. "Shut. The Fuck. Up!" he screamed. "I don't want to fucking hear about a purpose. I don't believe in your fucking God. I want my fucking soldiers back!"

The kid pressed his mouth into a tight line and backed slowly out of the office.

The echo of Sam's scream rang against his skull as he started filling out the paperwork for a soldier killed in action.

———

Sam's hand burned. He sat in the middle of the trailers in the life support area with his guys, smoking a cigar and trying to ignore the fire that seemed to pulse beneath his skin.

They sat together, all the remaining men of Sam's team. They sat together beneath the metal awning between the trailers that protected them from the blistering heat and punishing sun, and swapped stories about the dead. Laughing about the time Hale had t-bagged Lewis and posted the picture on Facebook. About the time that Lewis had damn near died trying to eat an MRE cracker in less than two minutes. Sam laughed because he couldn't show his boys the grief that ripped at his guts. He laughed for Lewis. For the crazy bastards on Merrick's team whom he hadn't really known, but now mourned as some of their own.

He cradled the cigar and listened to the guys reminisce about Lewis. About the time he'd pranced around the middle of the life support area wearing a thong made out of Smarties. Or the time they'd gone and Party-Boyed the Iraqis and damn near got shot in the process. Apparently the Iraqis didn't think a bunch of dudes running through their trailers wearing thongs and grinding on them behind their backs was nearly as funny as the Americans did.

Sam looked around the small cluster of his squad, flexing his hand. A couple of the guys had wandered down to the call center to try and get a line back home. There were long waits. It wasn't every day that a ten thousand-pound bomb went and blew a hole in the base defenses. People would be worried back home, prob- ably because some asshole had already posted about the attack on Facebook.

He wanted to call Faith, but figured he'd wait until the lines were a little less than six hours long. Besides, he wasn't sure what to say to her. He had no words that would adequately explain the sadness cutting at his heart.

He looked around the small group, ignoring the water bottle passed around. Sam was willing to bet it didn't have water in it. He didn't see Hale. Come to think of it, he hadn't seen him since they'd rolled back on base and cleared their weapons at the clearing barrel.

He stood and hiked his pants up higher on his hips. He remembered he needed a new belt, but he didn't feel like walking two miles to the shoppette to get one. He could jerry-rig his pants for now with 550 cord. He'd go tomorrow, maybe.

He walked down the corridor between the trailers, his flip-flops scuffing on the dusty wooden walkway, and pounded on Hale's door.

Silence. He leaned closer to the door and listened for the sound of a bedspring or a chair creaking.

Nothing.

He pounded again, then turned the handle.

The door slid open. It was dark inside Hale's room. Lewis' bed was empty; his blankets and equipment already inventoried and packed out to be sent home to Lewis' mom and dad. Sam hoped they wouldn't fight over Lewis' stuff. It wasn't much, and Sam knew how much Lewis hated it when his parents fought. They'd been divorced for twenty years, but they still fought like they were married. He wondered who'd tell Lewis' ex-wife.

He stepped into the trailer and flicked on the light.

Hale was lying in bed, his face cradled on one bent arm. His mouth was slack, his breath slow and even.

He hadn't even taken his boots off. Sam double-checked Hale's weapon and found it had been cleared.

He wanted to wake up his team leader but figured if he was asleep it was probably for the best. The rest of the guys were going to get shit-faced tonight. Sam was going to make sure every one of them found their way back to their own beds and keep trouble, in the form of the company commander or any other officer, away. The boys needed to process their grief, especially before they went back out in sector.

Sam pulled a blanket over Hale and clicked off the lights as he left.

Hale would sleep it off. So would the boys.

And Sam? Sam would sit up tonight and smoke a cigar, hoping the lines would clear up so he could call Faith.

He collapsed into the ragged camping chair outside his trailer while the boys drank and Sam smoked. He leaned his head against the wall and tried to remember why he was here and what the good fight really was.

And his hand? It continued to burn.

CHAPTER EIGHTEEN

It was dark but the stars and the moon were blurred by dust. Two days after returning to base, alone in the darkness, he felt empty. Wrung out.

Hollow.

Pieces of him were missing, settled inside a fucking coffin across the goddamned base inside mortuary affairs. Lewis' death had crushed a vital piece of Sam's heart.

But Merrick's death?

It haunted Sam.

The end of the firefight was a goddamned blur. When the hell had Merrick gotten hit?

The news of Merrick's demise did something to Sam's insides. For a man Sam hadn't particularly liked, he found the news of his death...unsettling.

He headed across the base, unable to sleep, unable to sit up all hours of the night and listen to the remnants of the mourning that had gotten too melancholy. He'd left the guys and grabbed his gear, heading across the base, through the midnight silence and swirling dust, to the call center.

Silence was relative. Generators rumbled wherever he walked

through the barriers. The test fire pit popped off every so often as the next patrol rolled outside the wire, hunting the high-value targets who'd planned and executed the attack on the base. Seventeen soldiers were dead and dozens wounded. The background noise ground on, but the noise of soldiers? That silence was eerie.

Sam trudged through the darkness, listening to the sounds behind him. Waiting for a scrape of claws against gravel or the sound of a snuffling snout against the dust.

He was losing his shit in the dark and the dust. He needed a good night's sleep. That would fix everything. But every time he'd tried to close his eyes since they'd gotten back, his thoughts started racing. Instead of sleeping, they spun and spun and spun.

He rounded the last corner where the damn dog had been last time. He stutter-stepped, flicking on his flashlight and scanning the area before he proceeded.

He fully expected to see the dog behind him.

But he was alone.

At least, he thought he was.

The last time he'd seen her, she'd been out in the town, snuffling along the wall, miles away from the relative sanctuary of the base. He had no idea how she'd gotten that far from the base in the first place. There was no way she could already be back, but enough strangeness had happened that Sam wasn't taking chances.

He moved only when he was damn sure the bunker didn't have a dog hiding in the shadows.

He walked past, refusing to admit that he might have skittered past the opening, just in case…well, just in case. The shadows didn't normally freak him out, but tonight, on the walk to the call center, he didn't have his night vision goggles. The darkness was absolute and terrifying.

He walked on in silence, the tiny hairs on the back of his neck shivering in the evening wind as he left the silence of the concrete pathways and reentered civilization. Or at least what passed as civilization on the base. He walked past a group of soldiers smoking near the entrance of the morale tent. Someone was calling bullshit on the last round of spades.

Sam smiled sadly. Lewis and Hale always argued about spades. He wondered if he should ask Hale to play a game. Once Hale woke up. He needed to stop back by Hale's trailer and check on him before he crashed tonight.

Assuming he slept. Sam didn't count on it. He was starting to think he would never sleep right again. He rubbed his face as he walked past the network ops cell. Maybe he'd take that last sleeping pill he had been saving for the flight home. Maybe he'd get that good night's sleep tonight and hope he could bum another pill off the doc before the flight home in a few months. He didn't want to start taking them on a regular basis. He wasn't going to become another fucking statistic, some pussy-ass soldier who couldn't cut it.

But maybe just this once. Just to reset. He could do that, right?

He rounded the last barrier and approached the call center. Relief prickled over his skin that the line was only two soldiers deep.

He drummed his fingers on the butt of his weapon, shaking his hand and hoping the burning sensation would stop. He hoped Faith would answer the phone. Goddamn, he needed to hear her voice. To be reminded of some good in the world. That he had a reason for fighting the good fight, which right now felt so fucking pointless.

He sucked in a deep breath and shoved the grief that threatened to escape its confines back down into the box where it needed to stay.

He wasn't going to break. Not here. Not now. Not ever. He had a job to do. He needed to stay strong, especially if Hale was breaking down on him.

He waited in line, rubbing his hand against his thigh, hoping to wipe the sensation from his skin. Nothing he did made the burning stop.

His turn came before he lost his mind to the insanity of

standing still. He moved to the phone. It was slick and warm from the other soldier's hand, but Sam didn't care. It was a chance to hear Faith's voice. *Please let her answer.*

He punched in the numbers, held the receiver to his ear and waited.

The trill of the ring purred against his ear. The silence between the rings stretched until forever.

Then there was a click.

"This is Faith. Leave me your name and number and I'll call you back."

His heart sank in his chest. The grief, bound until that moment, started to break free from its bonds.

"Hey—" He cleared his throat. "Just wanted to tell you I love you and that I'm okay. I'll try to call again soon." He hung up, having no idea when he might make the trek across post to make the call again.

———

He collapsed onto his cot, not bothering to kick off his shower shoes or hang his towel up to dry. He'd regret that tomorrow. Or maybe the day after that, when the stink of mildew transferred to his skin.

But he didn't have the energy to get up. He kicked the towel onto the edge of the bed and threw his arm over his eyes. They felt gritty and dry. He tried blinking, but nothing brought relief. His eye sockets felt as dry as the desert.

He fell into sleep. It was a strange sensation, marked by the feeling of his body rising into the air above him. Or maybe he was sinking away from it.

He wished he had more fucking Ambien.

He blinked and looked around him. He was in the alley. Hale was to his left, standing still, facing down one of the dark alleys. Lewis was to his right, weapon raised, pointing into the dark.

Sam frowned. This had to be a dream.

It was a shitty dream.

But he lifted his weapon and scanned the sector in front of him, sweeping side to side as they advanced, shoulder to shoulder, down the alley.

Sam's foot squished into something wet and solid. He stole a glance and immediately wished he hadn't.

It was a foot, still strapped in a decaying sandal. He shuddered and jumped away from it.

Neither Hale nor Lewis acknowledged his reaction. Sam breathed in through his mouth, trying to block the smell from the death and decay as they advanced down the alley to the next intersection.

The squad was behind them. He could hear booted feet sloshing through the water, along with muffled curses.

The edge of the alley approached. Sam held up his hand, and Lewis halted, taking a knee.

Sam eased up to the edge of the building. Taking a deep breath, he held it as he inched around the corner, slowly.

A flash of teeth. The swipe of a claw against his face.

The putrid stench of death blowing up his nostrils.

Sam bolted upright in his bed, sweat running down his body. He swiped at his forehead, his lungs heaving. His cheek burned as something hot dripped down his face.

He slid his finger over the spot, and was stunned when his finger came away wet and red.

He blinked. Panic took hold, squeezing his already struggling lungs.

He shoved the damp towel out of the way, swaying when he stood. The nightmare still pulsed through his veins and blurred his vision. He stumbled toward his shaving kit and pulled out the cheap mirror.

His cheek was unmarked. He scowled and turned the mirror to a different angle, looking at his face in the red emergency light. He flicked on the light.

Nothing.

He set the mirror down, killed the lights and shuffled back toward his bed.

Grief leaked out from its bonds. Sam sat awake and let it come.

CHAPTER NINETEEN

The sun rose over the base. Sam stood on the roof of the battalion headquarters, beneath the field of radio antennas, listening to the morning call to prayer. He thought about smoking a cigarette. He hadn't slept. Oh, he'd lain in the dark and listened to the sound of boots crunching on the gravel outside of his trailer, but he hadn't actually succumbed to anything remotely capable of being called sleep.

His hands shook. He thought about that cigarette again. He'd smoked, once upon a time. He'd never wanted a smoke as bad as he did right then. He wanted to skip the ramp ceremony, but he couldn't. Not with the rest of the platoon showing up—at least everyone who wasn't on guard duty.

Sam wanted to punch Tick in the throat for refusing to change the duty roster. He and Sam had gone toe to toe, but Tick hadn't budged. Sam's squad was pulling duty on the southeast guard tower.

Hale had volunteered to pull guard duty instead of going to the ramp ceremony. He looked like shit. Sam was worried, but short of dragging Hale to the aid station, he couldn't do much. The only thing he could do was keep an eye on him. And the dead last thing he wanted to do was let Hale head across the base to the guard tower alone.

Fucking shit, this dilemma sucked balls.

And when Hale had volunteered, Sam knew it was the wrong decision. Hale, more than anyone, needed to say his final farewells to Lewis. Goddamn Tick for not making this easier.

"You sure?" Sam had asked.

"Yeah, I'm good, Sarn't Brown." He'd looked away, his eyes darting toward the darkness. "I just—I'm not ready to say good-bye."

Hale couldn't say Lewis' name. Sam understood that. He'd said nothing as Hale had slung his weapon across his chest and started off toward the guard tower.

Sam stood on the roof and felt his skin crawl as the final notes of the call to prayer echoed across the city. He hated that fucking sound. It boiled inside him, simmering with a dark and twisted rage. Prayers to a God that did not exist, an empty stupid gesture. Hatred burned hot and deep inside him, overshadowing the burning sensation on his hand. When was his hand going to stop fucking hurting? He seriously considered taking a lighter and holding it over his hand to see if the sensation was real or imagined.

Instead he stood, hands clenched by his sides, and tried to find the strength to climb down and go say good-bye to one of his best friends.

He wished Faith had answered the phone. Maybe if he'd gotten to talk to her, he wouldn't feel so anchorless right now. So lost. Maybe he could have slept instead of lying in the dark, staring at the dust swirling before the faint green lights on the air conditioner.

The last note from the call to prayer hung on the dawn. Sam took a deep breath, clenching his fists once more. He turned away from the beauty of the sunrise. Away from the red and gold and orange piercing the darkness and driving it away. He didn't want to see something beautiful. He didn't want to see anything good. All the goodness in the world was dead.

He climbed down, stepping into the shadows and the cool predawn shade. The cold kissed his skin, damp and wet. He pressed his hand to the concrete. The rough surface of the rock bit into his skin and did nothing to alleviate the burning sensation.

He adjusted his weapon and headed down the hill toward the airfield where the C-130 waited, its back gaping and waiting for its precious cargo.

The crowd had already formed on the edges of the barriers. Soldiers milled around, talking and bitching and joking. Sam felt out of place until he spotted a couple of familiar faces from his squad. He wove through the bodies and the bullshit toward his team.

"Sarn't Brown, did you talk to Hale?" Jinx asked, spitting onto the concrete. The blob of liquid nicotine spread like a dark stain.

Sam nodded. "Yeah."

"He's having a hard time."

"I know. I'm going to walk over and check on him after this." He jerked his head toward the waiting aircraft. "Think they got Lewis into the box?"

Jinx grinned. "Yeah, they probably had to stuff him into it. He'd been getting kind of fat from eating all the ice cream in the chow hall."

Sam grinned back, drumming his fingers on the butt of his weapon and fought back tears. It felt good to joke. Lewis would want them to. He'd be pissed if he knew they were taking his death seriously and moping around the post. "He'll have all the ice cream he wants now."

Except that Sam didn't believe in heaven. But it felt weird to think Lewis was just gone.

Jinx stuffed his hands into his pockets and scuffed the toe of his boot on the ground. "Yeah. Probably. His mom is going to be pissed."

Sam said nothing for a long moment. "Yeah."

He was saved from saying more as a sergeant major started herding them toward the airfield. They slipped through the barriers and lined up. The engines screamed as the jet ramped up for its preflight inspections. The ambulance hadn't arrived, but their battalion sergeant major had a thing for pushing people to hurry up and get where they were going, then making them wait.

Sam didn't mind. He didn't have anywhere else to be. Not really. He stuffed his patrol cap in his cargo pocket on his thigh and folded his arms over his chest, standing silent, surrounded by brothers and a few sisters from his fellow companies.

The engines crashed to silence, shutting down abruptly. The sudden shift fell over them like a physical wave. There was a heavy pause before the talking started up again—more actual conversation, less shouting in each other's ears.

And then it appeared. Escorted by two gun trucks—one to the front and one to the rear—the woodland green camouflaged ambulance stood out in stark relief against the desert sand around them. Silence rolled over the company of men. Everyone snapped to parade rest while the vehicles maneuvered into place.

The sergeant major stepped onto the ramp of the aircraft. "Group, atten-*tion!*"

As one, the formation snapped to attention. No one looked, but everyone knew the ritual as the honor guard carried the coffins, each covered in the American flag—pinned to it to prevent it from flying off—out of the back of the ambulance and into the back of the waiting aircraft.

As they walked slowly by, Sam lifted his burning hand in a final salute. His throat closed off. He couldn't think of his friend, his team chief, in that box. Nothing of his friend was left beneath that flag. It was just an honor. A tradition that he had to uphold, no matter how much he wanted to run from the airfield and drown his sorrows in rage.

Sam didn't run. He didn't drop his salute. His hand burned along with the tears he refused to shed.

———

He detoured back, turning down the long road by the osmosis pit, which sucked all the bad shit out of the water and turned it back into plain water that would be sprayed on the roads to keep the dust down. Disgusting, when you thought about it, but Sam figured it had to go somewhere. He just hoped some industrious entrepreneur wasn't out there bottling it for soldiers to drink and selling it back to the Army.

He rested one hand on the butt of his weapon as he walked, ignoring the pain in his fingers. For the moment, it seemed to have subsided.

He let his mind drift while he walked, barely hearing the rhythmic crunch of his boots over the dust and gravel as the sounds of the base faded behind him. The guard tower was a short distance away from their sector of the base, but a long walk because of the way the barriers had been set up. Sam walked along the perimeter for nearly four kilometers; in reality, the tower was only a kilometer away if he had been able to walk a straight line.

The next two guys should have relieved Hale already, and Sam needed some time away from everyone to clear his head. The memory of that flag-draped coffin had burned into his eyes, blocking his vision with blurry red, white and blue.

He kept walking, because that's what guys like him did. They kept going, stayed strong. Brought their boys home.

He didn't want to dwell on the fact that he'd just lost another soldier. He couldn't. He kicked a rock in front of him, watching as it skittered over the dust and down the slope away from the path. He turned toward the guard tower, then kicked the bottom rung before climbing up a sketchy-looking ladder made out of two-by-fours and plywood. Not exactly confidence-building. But hey, if his troops could climb it, it couldn't be that bad.

As it shifted and groaned beneath his weight, Sam made a mental note to get a better ladder. If he survived this climb.

Reaching the platform, he adjusted his weapon. His boots scuffed over the dusty wood.

No one had relieved Hale. He still stood behind the weapons system, his skin pale, his eyes red. He glanced at Sam and there was no hiding the raw grief flooding down the man's cheeks.

"I can't stop thinking about it," Hale whispered, his voice breaking. "Every time I look down the sight of the weapon, I see Lewis standing there in front of me." He offered a watery grin. "He flipped me off at least twice."

Sam put his hand on the other man's shoulder. It burned on contact, a quick flash of heat that made him pause. He squeezed Hale's shoulder tight and was shocked to find the other man felt frail, as if he'd lost a dramatic amount of weight almost overnight.

"I think we're all having a hard time," Sam said.

Hale stepped away from him. Folded his arms over his chest, rocking back and forth on the balls of his feet. Sam said nothing, letting the silence hang between them while whatever Hale needed to say took shape.

"I want to go home, Sarn't Brown," he finally whispered. "Do you know what I'd do to go home?"

Sam swallowed the lump that blocked his throat. "I can guess."

Hale looked at him. In a flash, Sam thought he saw Merrick standing there instead of his long-time friend. When he blinked, the vision was gone. Just like Merrick. Just like Lewis.

"When we were out there…I would have done anything for all of us to make it back." Hale scrubbed his hand over his jaw. "I would have sold my soul just for the chance, the fucking chance to go home to Crystal."

Sam froze, a thousand pinpricks of ice dancing over his skin. "Don't say stuff like that."

For a man that didn't believe in God, that was…that was too much tempting fate. Or some shit.

"Why not? It's true. I told Merrick as much."

The cold slithered down Sam's spine. Hale's eyes looked wild.

"When was the last time you slept?" Sam asked. He'd seen him sleeping. He'd pulled a blanket over him. But had Hale really been asleep? Heaven knew what lack of sleep could do to a mind.

Hale shrugged. "I guess yesterday."

"You need to head back. I'll stay here until your relief comes."

Hale opened his mouth to argue, but Sam cut him off. "This isn't up for debate. Go. And I expect to see your ass in your cot, getting a solid twelve hours of rest. You move your ass before then and I'm dragging it to the mental health docs."

Hale pursed his lips, his expression sour. "I'm not fucking nuts. I'm pissed. Why aren't you pissed, man? They killed Lewis."

"I am pissed. And it fucking hurts. But we've got to do our goddamned jobs," Sam nearly shouted. Going off on Hale wasn't the solution.

"Don't give me that politically correct officer bullshit answer." Hale ripped his helmet off and threw it against the wall. "Do you know what I wanted to fucking do?" he screamed. "I wanted to un-fucking-load on those bastards. Use the main guns and level this fucking city. I wanted to kill everything that fucking moved. Kids. Dogs. Cats. Fucking everything about this place fucking sucks and you're just standing there? Telling me to get some rest? Fucking Lewis is dead." Tears streaked his cheeks, smearing the dust on his face.

"I know. I got it. I was there, remember?" Sam fought the lump rising in his throat. He didn't know what to do with his hands. "But this?" He motioned at Hale's agitation. "Go to sleep. The boys need you with your head in the fucking game tomorrow when we roll back out on the next mission." He paused, gripping Hale's shoulders and looking him dead in the eye, hoping to see his team chief still in there. "*I* need you."

Hale jerked away. "Don't tell me to go to sleep. Let me go fucking kill something. I want to make someone bleed. Someone needs to pay."

Sam backed him against the wall, his hands on either side of Hale's neck, holding him steady. "Stop. Right fucking now. Just stop. You're not going to kill anyone. You're going to go get some goddamned sleep and you're going to get your head back in the game." Sam ground his teeth, searching for a way to reach Hale behind the rage and the grief. "We lost Lewis. And it fucking sucks." His voice cracked. "But we've still got to get through this thing. We've still got to get home. I need you in order to do that."

Hale looked away, his jaw tense and tight. The fight sagged out of him and once again he felt frail. Hollow. "Sure, Sarn't Brown. Whatever you say."

He left Sam there without another word. The silence stretched out in front of him, over the rooftops of the city a click away. After a quick functions check on the .50-cal, Sam leaned against the low wall, scanning the sector of the city that had taken his best friend.

Hale's words taunted him.

CHAPTER TWENTY

The sun rose higher in the sky, bringing with it brightness and dust and lung-searing heat. Sweat soaked through Sam's uniform. His tongue stuck to the roof of his mouth as all the moisture drained from his body and through his skin. He'd figured the guys spelling Hale would be here shortly. "Shortly" had turned into an hour without water, and Sam was deeply regretting his decision to take Hale's place.

At least he had MRE cheese and crackers in his pocket if he got really hungry. Even though that cracker was going to be a motherfucker to eat without any water.

He leaned on the sandbags next to the .50-cal, his hands clasped in front of him, watching a bongo truck in the distance. The Jersey barriers stood in stoic formation, a single line of sentries demarcating the space where Iraq ended and America began. At least, that was what they told themselves. The truth was they were vulnerable. The barriers had been breached, destroying in one massive explosion any sense of safety they'd had on their bases.

Sam thought it was highly ironic that the people who'd been the safest on the base were now skittish and jumpy. They didn't have any problems sending troopers out to live on unprotected

CPs in the middle of the city. No, that plan only sucked when it was their ass on the line.

He shook his hand when his palm started tingling. He pulled his gloves off and looked at it. He saw no marks on his palm. Nothing visible that made his skin feel like a thousand burning needles were puncturing his skin and massaging his nerve endings with raw fire.

He turned his hand over, looking at the veins standing out on the back. Nothing there either, but his skin felt like he was holding it over an open flame. And the pain was getting worse as he looked at it. His fingers trembled and spasmed, twitching like an electric current. The fire crawled up his forearm, twisting through his veins. He shook his hand, banging his knuckles against the wood beneath the sandbag. Pain shot through his bones, but the fire still burned.

Something caught his eye. He glanced over the edge of the sandbag.

"No fucking way," he mumbled.

The dog slipped onto the base, appearing from nowhere down the line of Jersey barriers. There had to be a hole in the perimeter. That was bad. If she could get through it, a small kid could get through it. The last thing they needed was a kid running around the base. That little girl from the street could fit through same as something the size of that dog. He never wanted to see another little kid in the middle of a firefight again. Ever.

The pain in his hand subsided as he watched the dog slink down the line of the barriers, her body hugging the concrete. He could have sworn he saw the bone white of her ribs against her fur. Her snout was to the ground, her tail tucked between her legs. Her ears, though—her ears were perked up, one twitching one way, the other straight forward. She was alert even if she was pathetic.

How the fuck was this dog still alive? There was no reason for her to live. She was suffering in the heat and the drought and the lack of food. It was a goddamned shame to leave her alive. Sam lifted his weapon, drawing a bead on her ribs, just over her front leg.

He flicked his selector switch from "safe" to "semi".

It would be a mercy to put her out of her misery.

He shifted and the packet of crackers in his pocket crinkled.

He could feed her. But it would only prolong her misery. Better to shoot her and keep any puppies from being born and dying in the dry, hungry heat.

He bent his knee. The package crinkled again.

He paused, then flicked the selector switch back to "safe" and slung his weapon across his chest. He pulled out his knife and tore the cheese packet open from end to end. The cheese oozed like glue as he peeled the package apart, opening it to give her easy access to the yellow gold goo.

He looked down as she approached the guard tower. If he dropped the cheese, it could land face down in the dirt. It felt wrong to feed her the cheese coated with dirt and sand.

His stomach rumbled as he looked down at the cheese. The guard shift should end soon. He could get more food at the chow hall. When would she eat next?

He swallowed and his tongue stuck to the roof of his mouth. He sighed as he reached for his weapon. Technically he wasn't abandoning his post. He was just going to climb down, set the damn cheese down and let the dog eat, then climb back up and hope someone showed up to relieve him before he died from lack of water.

He felt like a dumb shit for not having his CamelBak. He should have known better. It wasn't like this was his first deployment.

He folded the cheese closed, then awkwardly climbed down the wobbly ladder.

His boot hit the ground and he damn near jumped out of his skin. The dog was right beneath the guard tower, less than five feet from him. He dropped the cheese, fumbling for his weapon as her hackles rose like spikes along her back. Her teeth were pristine white, and glistened with the only moisture around. One paw hung suspended in the air as she growled, the sound low in her throat. Mud matted her fur along the prominent bone of her hip.

Sam's hands shook as he raised the weapon, charging a round into the chamber and flicking it to "semi" in a single gesture.

He slipped his finger over the trigger, sighting in on her forehead. He couldn't believe he'd come down to feed the fucking mutt and she was about to attack him.

He shifted his weight, balancing with his feet shoulder-width apart.

Her paw connected with the ground and she lowered her body into a crouch. Her body trembled. His finger tightened on the trigger.

She lifted her paw.

The report of his rifle echoed off the barriers, mixed with her pain-filled yelp.

And that was how the nightmare began.

———

"What the fuck are you doing?" Tick's voice came from very far away, echoing from the end of a long tunnel.

A hand moved slowly into Sam's field of vision, dragging his weapon down off his shoulder then farther, out of his hand. He reached for it, but was too slow.

Tick braced one hand on his shoulder, keeping him still. "Answer me, Brown. What the fuck are you doing shooting inside the perimeter?"

Sam twisted, looking at the spot where the dog had been.

Shock, like tiny bolts of lightning, prickled over his skin.

Nothing was there. Oh Jesus, there was nothing there.

He looked back at Tick. His mouth opened but nothing came out.

This was. . .

He looked back where the dog had been, then shrugged off Tick's hand. He lunged toward the spot.

It was a small dust-blown depression beneath the tower. No paw prints. No sign of blood.

Nothing to indicate that a feral dog had just been about to attack him for fucking feeding her.

He turned slowly back to Tick and the two soldiers standing behind him.

Three people had seen him fire his weapon.

Inside the perimeter.

Holy fuck, he'd had a negligent discharge.

Reality was a bitch and she'd slapped him in the face, hard.

His guts twisted. His fingers twitched for a weapon no longer in his hands.

"I need you to come with me to the TOC."

———

Sam didn't say anything for the majority of the walk. He trudged quietly behind his first sergeant, shame and embarrassment wrestling for supremacy inside his colon. He'd thought he was going to shit himself when he realized he'd fired at nothing.

But she'd been there. He'd heard her. He'd seen her.

Tick stopped. They were nowhere near the TOC. Alone. And Sam's weapon was in Tick's hand. Shame burned in him.

"What happened?" A quiet condemnation for breaking their rules.

"There was a dog." He managed to meet Tick's dispassionate eyes.

"What dog?" Tick hadn't seen her. He'd seen Sam fire his weapon but he hadn't seen the skinny, miserable bitch that had come out of nowhere. He didn't believe Sam.

Hell, Sam didn't know if he believed Sam.

"She was walking toward the guard tower. I didn't have a good shot at her from up there, so I climbed down."

"Why?"

"Why what?"

"Why did you climb down?"

The cheese. He'd forgotten about the cheese. He must have dropped it at some point, because it was no longer in his hands.

But he couldn't admit to that. Add in feeding the damn dog to firing his weapon inside the perimeter, and he was either going to be declared fucking nuts or worse. He'd simply cement the record against him.

"I needed a better shot." The lie slid easily along his tongue, but left a bitter aftertaste. Something fetid and sour. "I didn't want to wound her."

"You shoot dogs for fun?" There was judgment in Tick's voice. Funny, Sam had never thought of him as an animal lover.

"We're supposed to shoot them, right?"

"You're supposed to call vector control."

Sam shrugged and stuffed his hands in his pockets. He couldn't look Tick in the eye. Not when he was lying his ass off. A cloud of shame hung over his head, thick and heavy. Worse, it clung to his skin.

"Too far away." *I just want to go to sleep.* But he didn't say that out loud.

Tick sighed and started walking again, clearly expecting Sam to fall into step with him. Sam obeyed, falling in on Tick's left because Tick outranked him.

"I'll do what I can," Tick said after a long moment. "But I've got to tell the commander. And now is not a good time for an negligent discharge. We've had six in the brigade. The brigade commander is thinking about withholding punishment to his level."

Sam's stomach flipped. Withholding punishment to the O6 level? That meant Sam could kiss any hope of a career in the military good-bye. His record would be flagged. He'd get a negative evaluation report.

He was finished.

He had no idea what to say in the aching silence so he marched on. At some point he realized he'd hunched his shoulders. He'd given up on some fundamental level, and he hadn't even been judged yet. Or at least, he hadn't been convicted yet.

He wanted to straighten his back, to show the fucking war that it hadn't beaten him yet. But his shoulders were heavy. His boots dragged with every step. His thighs protested every single step that took him closer to the commander and the reckoning he faced in the command cell.

The wind picked up. It blew tiny bits of sand into his skin, sanding off the layer of shame and disappointment and leaving him raw and ragged and teetering on the edge of an abyss.

CHAPTER TWENTY-ONE

Sam was alone in his trailer. The air conditioner hummed over his head. He stared at the smeared dust on the bottom of it, evidence of someone's failed attempt to clean it.

He hadn't taken his boots off. His feet rested on the dusty black bed frame, his hands were folded behind his head. His body was covered with a thin sheen of dirt and sweat, but he couldn't find the energy to get up and move to the shower.

He needed to do something. Soon. The longer he lay there, the harder it would be to break free from the miasma that pulled him down into the darkness, the crushing sadness that had been nipping at his heels for days since he'd shot the dog.

His mind refused to accept that he'd fired at nothing. Over and over it repeated the events that led up to him firing his weapon. Over and over, he saw the whites in her eyes, the glistening pallor of her canines. He'd lifted his weapon. Taken aim.

He wondered now if he could have backed away slowly. Climbed the ladder and gotten away from her.

But then she'd still be walking around the base. And she was dangerous. A threat to his soldiers and every soldier on the base. He'd done the right thing.

Except that now his weapon was back in the ops tent. And the commander had given him a direct order to stay away from work for the next 48 hours.

What the hell was Sam supposed to do for 48 hours, trapped in his trailer? He couldn't go anywhere on the base without his weapon except the shitter and the shower. Any place that had people was bound to have a sergeant major who would kick his ass for not having his weapon on him. Which meant he couldn't call Faith. He couldn't get on a computer and check his email for a note from her.

He felt trapped and helpless and bitter. That fucking dog had been there. He had nothing to do but wait it out, while the bitterness clawed at him. It was an ugly thing to be trapped with one's thoughts, wondering if you were going crazy. Had he seen the dog? Had she really been there?

Why didn't he fucking know anymore?

He closed his eyes, shutting out the smear of dirt on the bottom of the air conditioner. His eyes felt gritty and dirty. Dry. He wanted to sleep. So fucking badly. But every time he closed his eyes, he felt his rifle in his shoulder pocket again. Saw that fucking mutt with her too white teeth.

Nothing about her had said "hallucination". Maybe if she'd had saber tooth tiger teeth, he'd have realized she wasn't real. Maybe if she'd been larger than a real dog, he might have thought twice about shooting at a figment of his imagination.

But he couldn't deny the truth of it. He'd shot at a shadow, something only he could see. And now, their company was short a key leader because his first sergeant and commander hadn't made up their minds what to do about the negligent discharge.

Frustration was a stink on his skin. He sat up with a muffled curse and dragged his hand over the sweat on his face.

He'd shot that fucking dog. He wasn't goddamned crazy.

He grabbed his headgear and stomped out of his trailer. There was one place he could go on this base that didn't involve getting his ass handed to him.

He headed out through the barriers beyond the latrines and

the showers and down the dusty trail that led away from civilization to that guard tower.

It was a long walk, unnerving in the swirling dust that blocked out the sun with a grey haze. The heat was oppressive, like standing in a hair dryer on full blast and adding sandpaper to his exposed skin.

He dropped his head down and walked. Something had to have been there. Even though two days had passed, he couldn't have lost his mind. That dog had been there. Maybe he'd winged her and she'd taken off before any blood had hit the ground. Maybe the wind had blown away her footprints before he'd walked over.

There had to be a rational fucking explanation other than Sam was losing his mind. Because that reality wasn't something he wanted to consider. That reality would keep him from going home to Faith. It would keep him from holding his baby or making another one with the woman who meant more than life to him.

He was going home, damn it.

He stuffed his hands into his pockets as he walked along the t-walls toward the guard tower. He looked up and saw two shadows, who looked like they were doing anything but guard duty. Fucking in the guard tower. Some people would do anything for a piece of ass.

Knowing he wouldn't be seen as long as they were distracted, he made his way beneath the tower. He could still see the depression beneath the tower. Deeper now, blown by the wind. He ran his hand over the smooth sand. It tickled his palm, reminding him of the time he'd taken Faith to Sand Beach in Bar Harbor. It had been the middle of the winter. The wind had blown in cold off the North Atlantic, but they'd sat on the beach and let the wind pound against the blanket that covered them while Sam's hands had wandered over her body.

He remembered the whisper of her breath against his cheek. The feel of her body moving sweet and silky against his fingers.

He swallowed and jerked himself back to the present. He

wasn't going to find what he needed wandering down Memory Lane. He looked up as the tower over his head creaked and groaned. Or maybe that was one of the tower's occupants.

His gaze traveled down the wooden beams, hoping to see a splatter of blood. A tuft of fur.

Goddamn it, he wanted to find something that proved he wasn't fucking nuts.

He looked down the line of t-walls. A shadow slipped against the grey concrete and his blood quickened in his throat. That was where she'd come from the other day.

He didn't realize he was holding his breath until his lungs ached and his hands shook.

He walked down the line of barriers, running his fingers down the burning concrete.

There, in the shadowed space between the two barriers: a tiny gap. And on the edge of that gap was a smear of blood that reminded him of the smear of dust on the bottom of his air conditioner. A haphazard streak.

Something had run away.

It should have been relief that washed over his dirty skin. It should have been something cold, refreshing. Reassurance that no, he wasn't losing his mind.

Instead, he felt a sick guilt twist around his heart.

———

He'd stayed too long, looking at that smear of blood and the validation it offered his sanity.

He stayed until the sun sank behind the Jersey barriers and shadows crawled along the concrete.

It was only the nightly call to prayer that jerked him out of his reverie. Jolting him that he'd been gone too long and that his commander and first sergeant might be looking for him. No one wanted the crazy kid wandering around the base at night unsupervised.

But the blood. Proof was in the blood on that barrier.

He shoved aside the guilt and headed toward the TOC, walking quickly through the dark shadows between the barriers.

With the shadows came the silence. With the silence came the fear. A creepy presence trickling down his spine told him that he was being followed. That some whispering death was sliding its fingers over the back of his neck.

He stopped. A claw. He had heard a claw scraping over concrete, a screeching, cutting sound.

Sam whirled, his blood pounding as he reached for his weapon.

It wasn't there.

Fear danced over his spine and dried the spit in his mouth. His bladder clenched tight.

The shadows behind him didn't move. Stillness answered his questioning look. He breathed deeply and turned away, running from one darkness into another. The feeling was something primitive and wild and deeply unsettling.

He was unarmed against the night.

He picked up his pace, running his hands along the barriers as night fell suddenly and completely, wiping out any daylight.

In the distance, at the edge of the barrier maze, lights beckoned like a savior. Offering warmth and safety. Offering shelter from the night.

He fought the urge to run. Then he heard it again. Closer this time. Near his ear. Above his hand on the wall.

He spun.

"Who's there?" His voice broke over the fear, crackling like a splintered cracker falling out of its sleeve.

The wind swooped down over the top of the barrier, spitting sand over his face and neck. Sam closed his eyes and felt like *something* had just stolen a piece of his soul.

He froze as the sound sliced by his face. He spun.

"What the fuck?" He sucked in a deep breath, felt the air trapped in his lungs. He needed to move but couldn't shake the feeling that he was surrounded. Trapped. His breath came in quick, frozen huffs. His fingers scraped along the barrier, reminding him that he was real. That this wasn't something out of a twisted fucking nightmare.

He bolted, racing through the darkness, fleeing the shadows that hunted him, that made him feel like fucking prey.

He burst out of the edge of the maze and crashed into a mass of people and noise and *light*.

The buzz of activity had never been so fucking welcome in his life. He stood for a moment, letting the feeling of people wash over him and chase away the hunted feeling.

Tick stepped out of the company ops, scanning, always scanning the faces and people around him.

He could show Tick the blood. Tick would believe him.

He could get his weapon back. He could prove to Tick, to his commander, *to himself*, that he wasn't crazy.

He crossed the wide-open space and moved toward his company ops. Tick's eyes widened. Just enough that Sam noticed.

And his excitement ebbed. Just a little. But it was enough.

"What are you doing out, Brown?" Tick said roughly.

Sam took a deep breath, determined not to let the manic feelings rushing through his veins come out in his words.

"I went for a walk."

"You didn't sign out."

Sam shook his head. "Forgot. Needed some space." If they were going to make a big deal out of his failure to sign out, Sam couldn't do a damn thing about it. Arguing or lying about it would only make it worse.

"Where did you go?"

"Guard tower." Tick's expression flickered briefly and Sam knew he had him. "I went looking for the dog. There's blood on the wall, Top." Tick said nothing for a long moment. "I swear to you, Top. It's there. Go look." Sam barely kept the edge of panic out of his voice. If Tick didn't believe him—if he wouldn't even go look—

Sam shook the thought off. There was no way Tick wouldn't at least look. He'd give Sam that much benefit of the doubt, right?

Tick sighed heavily. "When's the last time you slept?"

"I'm good." The lie was easy and smooth and didn't even leave a bad taste in Sam's mouth.

"I'm worried about you, Brown. You've been through a lot the last few days. Losing Lewis and all that."

Sam swallowed, his tongue swollen in his mouth. "I'm good. I—I just need you to believe me about the dog."

"I do." The hesitation was gone. "I wrote a sworn statement. You need to go inside and get your weapon back. I can't afford to have you go down, son. I need you to get some sleep and get ready to roll again." Tick gripped his shoulder, near the juncture of his neck. "You don't do anyone any good if you go down. Get some sleep. Your boys need you in the fight."

Sam nodded and this time, the relief was warm and wet over his sticky skin. A cleansing.

Tick believed him.

Sam wasn't crazy.

He breathed out a hard, shaky breath.

It was going to be okay.

CHAPTER TWENTY-TWO

A pounding pulled Sam from any hint of sleep he might have achieved.

It echoed on the walls of the aluminum container and bounced around his head. Sam stumbled to the door, tripping over the sling of his weapon.

Jinx stood in the pool of light from the spotlight overhead. His eyes were wide, his nostrils flaring with each breath. "Hale's gone."

Sam frowned and glanced at his watch. Just past midnight. "What do you mean, Hale's gone?"

"No one can find him. He signed out to go to the morale tent, but that was hours ago. The commander just initiated a recall."

Alarm pushed away the last remnant of sleep. "Have we checked the call trailers?"

"Yeah. Everywhere he normally hangs out."

"Give me five minutes to get my boots on."

They were on in less than 30 seconds. "Where have we looked?"

"Everywhere. They're searching trailers now and if we can't find him, they're going to call a base-wide alert," Jinx said. As a rule, Jinx wasn't prone to panic but a wildness to his movements made Sam worry.

"Has anyone checked the migrant workers?" Third country nationals. Brought in for cheap labor by the big contractor companies looking to suck off the war effort for profit.

Jinx looked at him funny. "Why the fuck would Hale be there?" No one went there. Americans didn't hang out with the workers and the workers avoided the Americans except when their jobs brought them into contact.

"I don't know." Sam's voice sounded funny to his own ears. "But I've got a bad feeling about this."

"No shit." Jinx drummed his fingers on the butt of his weapon.

They walked together toward the migrant workers' living quarters.

Sam had thought GIs lived bad on his last deployment; stacked into tiny trailers on bunk beds living assholes to elbows. This? This was fucking inhuman. Twenty men were living in a space for maybe five, packed into tiny spaces. The top bunk was barely a foot from the ceiling in most of the trailers they walked by.

Toward the end of the slum was a bevy of rusted-out shipping containers, shrouded in shadows and reeking of old metal and mildew. A graveyard.

Clouds moved and the containers were illuminated in eerie soft light.

He tapped Jinx on the shoulder.

A flash of movement caught his eyes. A quick flash of light. The thud of a body hitting the ground.

Sam got there first.

Jinx took one look and whirled away, violently throwing up anything that had been in his stomach.

Sam's own guts threatened revolt at the carnage within.

Hale's eyes were white against the blood on his face. His lips were curled in a feral smile as he ran his hands over the walls with manic fury. Blood smeared beneath his hands.

"Jesus Christ, Hale!"

Hale didn't react to the sound of Sam's voice. Sam felt rather than saw Jinx come in next to him, his weapon raised. He reeked of fresh vomit. Sam's stomach threatened to spin.

Hale turned slowly, lifting his weapon where it had been stacked against the wall.

"This is the price, Sam." Hale's voice sounded different: warped and twisted, like metal grating on metal.

"What. The fuck. Are you talking about?" Sam growled, holding his own weapon low and ready.

At least three bodies were lying at Hale's feet. Three dead men, slashed and bloodied by a man Sam had called brother. Blood was smeared on the walls of the shipping container and seeped into the wooden floor.

"Jesus," Jinx whispered next to him.

"We were all supposed to die out there," Hale whispered. His eyes gleamed as the moon shifted free of the clouds again. "I saw it."

"Saw what, you fucking psycho?" Jinx asked.

"Stop it," Sam whispered. "Saw what, Hale?"

"Saw our deaths. It started with Lewis. And then they were going to blow the trucks. You'd die. Jinx. All of us were supposed to die." He rubbed his hand lovingly down the handgrip of his M4. "But I made a bargain. I wanted you to get home, Sam. To Faith. To your kid. Jinx, your mom would have been so pissed if something happened to you."

"My mom's going to be pissed if she finds out about this," Jinx whispered.

"Shut it, Jinx." The coppery smell of blood burned Sam's nostrils, coated his tongue. "This is really fucking bad, Hale."

Hale shrugged. The man who'd been like Sam's little brother lifted shoulders covered in blood. "It's the price. You'll get to go home now. You'll get to see Faith again." His thumb flicked over the selector switch, but he didn't flip it.

"Put the weapon down, Hale." Sam didn't panic. At least not any more than he already was.

"I don't want it to be like this," Hale whispered. "But it's the price we had to pay."

He moved before Sam realized what he was doing. Sam lunged for Hale's weapon, but slipped in a puddle of blood and piss.

The flash of Hale's weapon was the last thing he saw before his skull exploded in pain and the darkness pulled him under.

———

Promise me, Sam. Promise me you'll do whatever it takes to come home to me.

Sam looked down at Faith, her breasts heaving as her body moved beneath his. Her fingers dug into his shoulders and dragged him down, drawing her mouth to his. "Promise me," she whispered.

Sam's balls tightened and he lifted her hips, driving deeper into her warm wet heat.

"I promise."

Sam opened his eyes, the sound of his own voice pulling him out of the dream and into a fucked up reality.

The first thing he noticed was that he was not in his trailer. He opened his eyes, seeing a blinking, bouncing light on a heart monitor. The end of that monitor was stuck to a shaved spot on his chest just above his nipple. The beeps grated on his ears in time with his heartbeat.

He swallowed and his tongue protested the movement.

He blinked. His eyes felt gritty and the bright lights burned.

Then he tried to move. His entire body was weighted down. The blanket might as well have been made with lead.

He blinked, wishing he could rub his eyes. Why couldn't he rub his eyes? He tried to lift his hands but they were heavy. So heavy.

He hadn't felt this way since the first time he'd smoked a joint with Tommy. Tommy had laughed his ass off, but Sam had just lain back on the hay bale and let the world spin around him. Tommy had sounded very far away, and Sam? Sam had floated.

That was how he felt now: heavy. Stoned. He tried to lift one hand. Just one hand. His arm moved slowly, weighted down as if it was coated in lead armor.

His hand moved toward his face. Slowly, slowly it filled his field of vision, getting bigger and clearer as he continued to blink.

Then it stopped. Halfway between his face and the bed, it stopped. Something tugged at his wrist, like a band pressing on his skin. It was heavy. It was thick.

His vision cleared. His wrists were bound with thick leather straps. Dark brown leather bit into his skin.

Holy fuck. He'd gone crazy. This was what they did to crazy people. He knew that. He'd taken one too many soldiers to the funny farm. This was what they did to people who tried to hurt themselves. Jesus, had he cut his wrists? Why couldn't he remember what he'd done?

Why was he even in the hospital?

Oh God, what had he done? What had he done?

He heard someone screaming from miles away, an echo over the pounding of his heartbeat, the steady beat of the heart monitor.

A skinny, bald, black-skinned nurse rushed into the room.

And Sam realized the screaming came from him.

———

The next time he awoke, he felt the bindings on his wrists. They were heavy and reminded him of the crazy he'd embraced.

Something fierce and wild burned into his lungs. He couldn't breathe, he couldn't think. The pressure on his wrists seared up his arms, wrapping around his lungs like a constrictor.

"You don't have to be afraid."

The voice penetrated the fear. It was soft and soothing and way too familiar. Sam frowned and blinked and opened his eyes.

The skinny Bible Kid lay in the bed next to his. His eyes were the deepest blue and utterly calm.

"I never asked you what your name was." Sam's voice was broken, cracked from disuse.

The skinny kid smiled. "My name is Bill." He shifted beneath his blanket and Sam caught a glimpse of white gauze against the translucence of his skin.

"Sam."

The skinny kid smiled. "I know."

Sam swallowed and tried to find any moisture in his mouth. His bottom lip was split down the center. He bit down, needing the pain to prove that this was real.

Warm blood coated his tongue.

"Why are you here, Sam?" the kid—Bill—asked.

Sam ignored his question. "When you were on the plane, where did you go?"

Bill tipped his chin, his eyes dancing in the bright hospital lights. "What do you mean?"

"When we landed. You weren't on the plane. I never saw you in Kuwait." At least, he didn't think he had. It was only now that it was dawning on him that the kid had disappeared until that fire-fight. "Where did you go?"

Bill smiled. When he did, his lips pulled apart, exposing a dark hole where his tongue should have been. His smile was simple; his words, not so much. "To and fro and back again."

Sam frowned. "I've heard that before."

"I thought you said you knew your scripture, Sam?" Bill licked his lips, his tongue reminding him of a snake. "Have you figured it out yet?"

Sam rolled onto his back, trying to ignore the bindings on his wrists that protested the movement. "Figured what out?" He wasn't in the mood for word games. And even though he felt bad for never asking the kid's name, he still wasn't in the mood to listen to him preach.

"The game of souls."

Sam closed his eyes hard and tried to ignore the whisper along the back of his neck that said he'd lost his mind. Or worse, the one that said nothing had ever been clearer.

"You can deny it all day long," Bill said. "But that doesn't make it less true. The lie doesn't become the truth so long as you repeat it often enough." He paused. "Just because it's believed doesn't make it true."

Sam opened his eyes and looked past the heart monitor to the kid lying in the bed next to his. There was a distant crash, a boom that rattled the walls around them. But Sam said nothing.

"It's all a game," Bill said. "He who has the most souls wins."

"That's not in the scripture you claim to love so much," Sam said. "That's not how it's supposed to go. We're supposed to be the good guys."

"Really?" Bill asked, his eyes narrowing into hard slits. "You think there's a greater good that comes out of this war? Out of any war? The only thing that comes from war is death. Death of humanity. Death of souls. Death of good men who should have gone home to their wives and mothers. You think it's some noble cause, some good fight?" He leaned up on one arm and Sam saw it: his arm, bound in thick white gauze.

Bill kept talking, ignoring Sam's scrutiny. "There are no good fights, no just wars. You strike a bargain, you shake a hand, one promise and that's all she wrote." Bill pinned him with a hard look. "You made your promise," Bill whispered. "Now you have to live with the cost." He smiled thinly. "Can you live with the promise you made, Sam?"

"I didn't make any promises," Sam said softly. But the drugs washed over him in an unexpected wave and pulled him back down into sleep, the word "promise" echoing in his ears in time with his heartbeat.

Promise me.

Promise me you'll do anything you have to. Just come home to me.

Faith's whispered plea bounced from puffy cloud to puffy cloud. Sam wanted to go running after it, but the cloud wrapped around him and held him warm in its embrace.

Promise me.

So what if he'd promised Faith he'd come home to her? That couldn't be what Bill was talking about. It couldn't be. A promise to his future wife couldn't be wrong. Certainly not evil. That wasn't a deal with the devil. How could a simple promise be evil?

He turned in the bed, but it was dark. No sound came from the other bed, just a quiet rise and fall of the lump. Bill must have been sleeping. At least, Sam thought he must have been sleeping. If that was what you could call it when the drugs burned through your veins. Sam didn't really think so. Not without stretching the truth something fierce.

He shifted again. His hand burned hot and he rubbed it against the sheet, trying to make it stop. It was the first real thing he'd felt since he'd woken up in the hospital.

He almost didn't want it to stop.

He wanted the reminder of what was real. Could anything be real if he was high?

And what did it say about his mental state if he was feeling a fire that wasn't there? He rubbed his hand again, hard enough for friction to heat his skin.

He froze.

Burn. His hand burned. He'd taken Merrick's hand.

A thousand images flashed through his memory.

What would you do to go home, Sam?

Anything.

Anything? Anything is a lot when you're at war.

Cold flooded his veins and he shivered violently. He'd told Merrick he would do anything to go home to Faith. Denial rolled through him and he curled into a ball, ignoring the bindings on his wrists.

He closed his eyes again, shaking his head and mumbling it was a lie. He hadn't done anything wrong.

He was vaguely aware of someone coming into the room. Bill hadn't moved.

And then the puffy white clouds were back. Merrick sat on one, his lips curled in a feral smile, his sharp bones spearing the clouds and tainting them with darkness. His arms were wrapped tight around Faith, dragging her farther and farther from Sam. No matter how hard he struggled, Sam couldn't reach her.

He couldn't save her.

All the promises in the world, and she was still out of reach. Forever out of reach.

When he woke the next time, Chaplain Cloud was sitting next to his bed. Sam wasn't sure how he knew that, but as his vision cleared and the effects of the drugs faded, he knew.

He didn't question how he knew. But he was damn glad to see him. He tried to smile but the split in the center of his lip opened up again, tearing the thin scab from the fragile skin.

"Sam." Chaplain Cloud's eyes were calm. The lack of judgment or fear was a balm to Sam's frayed nerves.

"It's..." Sam's voice cracked and he cleared his throat weakly. "It's been a rough couple of days, huh, Chaplain?"

Chaplain Cloud's smile was warm. "Indeed it has." He swallowed and patted Sam's forearm briefly. As though the contact wasn't allowed. "How are you feeling?"

"High?"

Chaplain laughed quietly. "That's to be expected. You've been having nightmares."

Sam frowned and the muscles of his face were tight from lack of use. "Oh." He wanted to deny it, but what was the point? Everyone was going to know he was crazy. He'd probably be evacuated out of theater, sent home in disgrace.

"No one is judging you."

Sam looked away. "I'm judging me. I fell apart."

"Under the weight of a very heavy trial." He reached forward and patted Sam's lips with a towel, wiping away the blood.

Silence hung on for an hour, maybe more. Chaplain didn't leave and Sam didn't speak. He couldn't. The thoughts racing around his head were legion, unmoored. Violent and angry. Sad and crushing. But they all circled around one question.

He cleared his throat. Chaplain Cloud looked up at him from his book. "Do you believe in the devil, Chaplain?"

Chaplain sighed and rubbed his eyes beneath his glasses. "Yes, Sam. I believe in the devil."

"Like a real devil. A real evil, not a TV demon."

"I know what you mean, Sam. And yes, I believe in real evil." He closed his book. "No, that doesn't make me crazy," he said.

"Really?" Hope. Hope that maybe he wasn't crazy. Hope that maybe he wasn't slipping off the edge of reality and into a world made up of padded rooms and fuzzy walls. "Does the devil whisper in your ear, too?" The question danced on the edge of madness.

"The devil can only work on you if you've given him the opportunity," Chaplain said. "We must always be on guard against the temptation of this world. The devil is always trying to lure us from righteousness."

A wave of puffy clouds washed over him, threatening to pull him under once more. "If the devil is real, does that mean the things we do are not our fault?"

"Sam, we are responsible for our own actions," Chaplain said. "The devil may tempt us but we have the freedom to choose."

"So if we fail? If we choose wrong?"

"Then we have to ask for forgiveness for our sins. For our weakness." He paused. "Our God is a loving God. We must simply seek repentance and sin no more."

"It doesn't sound that easy. Why does God forgive us over and over again?"

Chaplain smiled. "Because He loves us."

Sam closed his eyes, surrendering to the warm puffy clouds once more. The chaplain's words were little comfort.

He was certain that God, if He existed, would have no forgiveness for a man who'd sinned as Sam had sinned. A child was dead because of Sam. All so his men could go home again.

Maybe it had been done in the heat of battle. Maybe he wasn't a murderer. But he felt it. The wrongness of taking that shot.

A dog bayed in the distance; a sad, mournful sound. It haunted his sleep, tormenting him. Whispering that his choice, his sin, would come for him. Soon. Soon the debt would be paid.

Why him?

He knew.

The bed next to him was empty. The empty space was the first thing Sam saw when he opened his eyes, the first thing his brain registered.

The second thing he realized was that his thoughts were clear and empty, not puffed up, swollen caricatures.

He blinked and looked at the bed. The plastic mattress was exposed and glistening with cleaner. The sterile smell penetrated Sam's sinuses.

A motion near the door caught his eye. Tick stood there. Watching. Waiting. Judging.

But Sam didn't say that. He couldn't force the harsh condemning word out of his mouth. So he said nothing as Tick approached.

"You ready to bring your lazy ass back to work?" Tick asked. His eyes were wary, betraying the fear he tried to hide. The fear that maybe Sam had really lost his shit.

"You gonna let me go back to work?" Sam asked. He shifted and his hand moved freely. He looked down. His wrists were unbound. He pushed upright.

"Depends on whether or not you want to go crazy again. Docs

said you've been sleeping better the last few nights." Tick folded his arms over his chest. "Why didn't you tell anyone you hadn't slept?"

Sam frowned. "What are you talking about?"

"You lost your shit when we found Hale. Scared the living shit out of Jinx. I think you gave him PTSD, man. Seriously fucked that kid up, seeing you screaming like that."

Sam sucked in a shuddering breath. "So that wasn't a nightmare. What Hale did—it was real?"

Tick nodded once. "Yes. I wish it wasn't true, but it was."

Sam sniffed and sat up. "Fuck."

"Yeah." Tick swallowed. "So you'll have to pull duty in the TOC for a little while, 'til the commander and everyone are sure you're okay. But we'd like you to come back, Sam. If you're up for it."

He looked over at the empty, naked bed. "What happened to him?"

"Bill?" It struck him that Tick knew his name. "He pulled the sutures out. Bled out before the orderly knew what happened."

Sam scrubbed his hands over his face. A strange grief twisted inside him. Something not quite sadness. Not quite raw.

"So now what?" Sam says.

"The commander is arguing to get any actions against you dropped. So long as you keep taking care of yourself and get enough sleep." Tick coughed into his hand. "We need you back, Sam. We're down too many men."

Sam nodded. He wanted out of the hospital, but not to go back on patrol. No, he wasn't sure he could ever roll back on patrol. Not yet. Not until he convinced himself that the dog had been real, that he'd really shot her.

It was suddenly the most important thing in the world that the dog was fucking real and not a ghost.

That he wasn't fucking crazy.

Sam stood and started pulling on the clean uniform that Tick had thrown onto the foot of his bed. It was something so simple and yet for a moment, Sam just sat, wearing his pants, feeling the cold metal of his dog tags bounce against his chest.

With each piece of his uniform, a piece of his soul fell back into place.

Finally he stood. "I'm ready."

"I know you are." Tick gripped his shoulder. "I believe you about the dog."

Sam looked at him quickly. He blinked. Had Tick told him this before? "What?"

Tick nodded. "Yeah, man. I believe you. For what it's worth, I don't think you're crazy, either."

Sam said nothing, his throat blocked, his heart pounding in his ears. If Tick believed him, maybe that meant he wasn't crazy. Maybe he'd just forgotten to sleep, forgotten to take a knee.

He glanced back at the empty hospital bed. He felt nothing for the kid who'd died there. Nothing other than the vague sadness he felt when any soldier died. Maybe that said something about the kind of person he was.

The walk out of the hospital was quiet. Sobering. Sam followed his first sergeant from the hospital and a thought whispered against the back of his neck that maybe, just maybe, he wasn't crazy.

Tick wasn't normally a man of many words but today the silence felt comforting.

Nothing but the sound of boots crunching on gravel interrupted his thoughts.

And the uncertain feeling he was being watched.

CHAPTER TWENTY-THREE

Sam walked into the company ops and felt every pair of eyes turn in his direction. A hush, awkward and heavy, settled over the soldiers in front of him. Jinx was behind the ops desk, his face cut with shadows from pale light and not enough sleep. The kid looked like he'd aged five years in a week.

His eyes, though—his eyes flashed with surprise, but only for a moment. Then his face broke into a wide smile and he came around the desk. Too fast, he crashed into Sam and hugged him close.

"Damn but it's good to see you, Sarn't Brown."

Sam breathed deeply, the smell of dust and familiar dirt. The ops wasn't much, but it was as close to home as he'd felt in a long, long time.

"Sorry, man. Sorry for leaving you alone." Sam's throat was tight, his lungs hard to fill.

"Nah. It's all good. You had a rough time." Jinx slapped Sam on the back of the neck. "But you're back now, right?"

"Yeah, man, I'm back. I promise not to freak out anymore, either."

Jinx laughed at the faint joke and went back to the weapons rack. He reappeared a moment later. "I think this is yours," he said, with a glance at Tick. Tick nodded once and Sam slipped the sling over his shoulder.

Sam slid his hands over the barrel, over the smooth stock. He released a deep breath. His hand shook a little bit as he cleared his weapon, then flipped the ejection port cover closed.

Another piece of something that had been missing slipped back into place.

Tick slapped him on the shoulder. "Keep your head up. As soon as the investigation is closed, we'll let you know. Got the commander to agree to give you your weapon back until its finished."

Sam looked up sharply. "I'm still being investigated?" His fingers tightened on the butt of his weapon. Fear slithered up his spine and whispered that they were going to take it from him again. That his wrists would be bound and the puffy clouds would come and carry him away again.

"Yeah." Tick dropped his hand. "We tried, but they won't drop it."

"But you believed me. About the dog?"

Tick nodded. "I believe you. The battalion commander, though, is another ballgame."

Sam swallowed. He nodded back, and felt the weight settle on his shoulders. It wasn't an easy feeling. Reality shifted in front of him and for a moment, he was back, back in the hospital. Back in that trailer.

"I'm going to head back to my trailer," he said, looking at Tick.

"Yeah. Get some sleep." Tick watched him carefully, his eyes searching, seeking.

He wasn't sure Tick would have given him back his weapon so soon after being released from the hospital, but as he slipped away from the company ops and between the Jersey barriers, he counted his blessings that Tick trusted him.

Either that or Tick was an idiot. But it felt damn good to have his weapon against his stomach and chest once more. Comforting.

He rested his hand on the butt as he walked, felt the sway of it bump against his sternum.

There was only one place he was headed. He was being investigated. Which meant that if he didn't find the dog or proof that she'd been real, he was toast, his military career ended by what was either a negligent discharge or a fucking hallucination. Either way, Sam's elbow scraped against the cement as he slid through a narrow space. Breaking away, heading toward the source of his damnation or salvation.

Either way, he'd know.

It felt good to be outside, in the heat and the sand and the dust. His blood pounded against his ears, but he kept on toward his path. His head was clear. He knew what he needed to see. Even if it proved he'd lost his damn mind, he needed to see. Just once more.

The tower loomed in front of him, a lone sentry on an empty part of the base. The city was there, just on the other side of the wall. But it was the tower, pitch black against the afternoon sky, that drew him.

"Hey!"

Sam stood at the base of the tower and looked up. A skinny black kid looked down at him.

"That's 'hey, Sergeant,' soldier," Sam said. The kid wouldn't know whether Sam was supposed to be there or not.

"Sorry, Sarn't. I wasn't expecting anyone."

"Go back to guarding your post. I'm walking the perimeter." As good a lie as any. The kid wouldn't care and Sam…Sam needed to check beneath the tower. He didn't want to do it with an audience.

The kid stuck his head back in the tower. Sam took a deep breath. Hesitated.

Then stepped beneath the tower.

The sand had blown into tiny dunes, drifts formed by the wind. Undisturbed by a dying dog. Or a living one, for that matter. There was no hint that anything other than a spider had walked there recently.

A dog certainly hadn't died there.

Hope sank in his chest. He thought he'd known. Damn it, he'd been so certain. He stayed there, crouched beneath the guard tower. Above him, the kid took a step and dust sprinkled down on Sam's head and neck.

It was a long moment before he straightened and dusted himself off.

He sighed and headed back toward the main base, dipping through one of the barriers to take the long way home. He needed to clear his head. To wrap his brain around what he'd done.

He'd shot at a figment of his imagination. A hallucination. There was no dog. And since there was no dog, that meant Sam was one cracker short of a sleeve.

He'd never guessed this would be what crazy felt like. That questioning of his own memory, wondering what had happened and what parts his mind had filled in.

He walked away slowly, fighting the dejection that threatened to crush his soul with each step. It hadn't happened. It hadn't been real.

Which meant he'd really lost his shit.

He let his mind wander, listening to the crunch beneath his boots. Wondering if the sound was real or if he was hearing things.

Funny thing, this insanity stuff.

He rounded one of the barriers and damn near tripped over a far too familiar dog. He froze, shock crawling over his skin when she looked up at him. Her body went rigid. She was too close. Close enough that he could see her whiskers tremble. Close enough that he would never get his weapon raised in time if she lunged.

He held his breath, afraid to break eye contact. Afraid to exhale.

Her lip trembled. A quiet *whuff* blew past the lips of her muzzle.

Sam blinked, unsure of what he'd just seen. But then she whuffed again. The tip of her tail twitched. Just enough. Just enough for Sam to be nearly certain he'd officially gone off the deep end. Now a dog who'd threatened him a few days ago was wagging her tail at him. Jesus, insanity was a wild fucking ride.

"I shot you," he said. His voice croaked in his throat.

She whuffed low in her throat at him and turned away, pausing to look back at him.

"Holy fuck, I'm in a demonic version of *Lassie*." She wagged her tail. Sam sighed. "What the hell, I've already lost my mind anyway."

He followed her, his hand on his weapon. The sun sank behind the barriers, casting cold shadows. He knew where he was heading. His palms became slicked with sweat the moment it dawned on him. Farther from the American side of the base than a lone GI needed to be. His bowels threatened to turn to water.

Every step became harder and harder to take. And then it was there, a looming hulk in the shadows: LEVIATHAN SHIPPING written in big block red letters.

Sam's breath caught in his throat. She stopped at the entrance of the container, her tail brushing against the yellow crime scene tape that blocked most of the entrance.

He was shocked when she slipped beneath the tape and into the darkness. No one had locked the damn door.

He heard her claws scrape against the wood floor. Imagined bloody paw prints in the darkness.

He didn't want to follow her. He didn't want to step into the madness inside that container. That much he knew was real. Hale had cracked. Had slaughtered those people.

For what? What the hell had Sam missed? How had his friend, his fucking brother, become a goddamned psycho?

There was nothing like the fear that turned his guts sour, that made his sweat stink.

He didn't want to do it. His mind revolted, urging his feet to cooperate, to take him the hell away from the terror and the madness inside.

Instead, his feet carried him closer. One step. Then another. Until he ducked beneath the thin yellow tape and entered the darkness.

———

Cold crawled over his skin, descending on him like a bucket of snow. Thick and heavy and wet, it numbed him and wrapped around him. His heartbeat slowed. His movements were heavy.

He groped in the darkness for his flashlight and pulled it from the pouch on his hip.

Light flooded the inside of the container and he wished he didn't see it: blood, too much blood. He heard the echo of the screams in that blood, felt the sound of Hale's knife as it sliced into men's flesh.

"What the hell happened?" he whispered to the dog. The idea that he was talking to a dog – the very dog Merrick said had named herself – no longer seemed fucking nuts.

She sat at the end of the container, her back against the farthest wall, in a clean spot among the splattered streaks and handprints.

This was what violence looked like. It reeked of shit and piss and death.

The dog sat silently now. No more friendly wags of her tail. No more whuffs. Silent. Stoic.

Watching.

Sam had the uncomfortable thought that she'd lured him here to his death. Standing in the middle of that trailer, surrounded by the end of life, he felt his will to live slipping. The fear clung to him, seeping into his pores, whispering that he was already dead, he just didn't know it yet.

The insanity taunted him, plagued him. Whispered that he

was well and truly crazy and he should just give up. Give up wanting to go home. Give up wanting to go back to Faith.

He didn't deserve any of that.

He'd been lying to himself.

There was no hope for someone like him. No forgiveness.

He had allowed this to happen. He'd been so focused on other things; he'd missed all the signs that Hale was slipping into madness.

Guilt, sick and twisted, writhed in his soul. For the rest of his life, he would remember the feeling of standing in that container, the stink of death clinging to his skin, burning into his nostrils.

He would never get the stain off. It would always be there: permanent, haunting his sleep. Reminding him of what he'd failed to stop.

Blood streaked across the rivets. Splattered and smeared, it stained the walls. It would never come out. It was seared into the metal. The ghosts of the dead haunted it.

"They should burn this," he mumbled, scanning the walls with his light. The light flickered, and fear skittered down Sam's spine.

"What am I supposed to see?" But the dog didn't answer him. Funny, he thought; in this version of reality, the dog should talk to him.

His light flickered again. "Oh, shit no." He had the sudden, clenching fear that if the light went out, he'd never find his way out of the darkness and back to sanity.

He shifted and turned slowly, the light illuminating his path down the opposite wall. Bloody, ugly words, written in harsh letters, stopped him short.

You were bought with a price.

Sam read the sentence, again and again, until it was branded onto his memory. He glanced at the dog as his light flickered once more, fading this time to complete darkness before sputtering on again.

"Was that why you brought me here?" he asked her. She didn't move. Sam shook his head. "I must be losing my mind if I think a damn dog is going to answer me," he mumbled.

He looked back at Hale's last words. Sadness bloomed inside of him, spilling like ink onto a page. Threatening to blind him with tears in the already tenuous light.

"She will answer you, you know."

CHAPTER TWENTY-FOUR

Sam spun at an all-too-familiar voice.

Merrick.

Merrick stood in the entrance to the container, his body silhouetted against the fading light outside. He stepped into the beam of Sam's flashlight. His skin was tight and translucent, cast in harsh shadows and black contours.

Sam's lungs panicked. "You're dead."

Merrick *tsk*ed and took another step closer. His boot made no sound when it touched the wood.

"I feel pretty good for a dead man," Merrick said with an arrogant smile. "You, however, look like you've had a rough couple of days." He tucked his hands into the pockets of his uniform. "Sleep recently?"

Sam lifted his weapon, his flashlight cupped beneath the barrel of his M4. "Don't come any closer."

The light flickered. Merrick snapped his fingers and it flared brighter, brighter than any battery was capable of. The brilliant flash painted the picture on the back of Sam's eyes when he blinked.

"So have you figured it out yet?" Merrick asked.

"Figured what out?"

"What Anu brought you here for."

"What are you talking about?"

Merrick nodded toward the dog. "Anu. She brought you here. She'll answer you, too; just not how you think."

Sam's flashlight flickered as Merrick took another step closer.

"Who are you?" Sam demanded. He took another step backward. "*What* are you?"

Merrick's smile widened and reminded Sam of a smooth-talking lawyer. "You already know the answer to that," he said softly, his voice filled with the hissing of a thousand snakes. "I have so many names," he said. "The gatherer of souls. The adversary. Old Scratch." He smiled. "I am every thing to every body."

He took another step toward Sam and finally, Sam moved. Backward. Away from the stench of sulfur and the reeking darkness that pulsed off Merrick in black, stinking waves.

"I'm what you needed me to be," he hissed. He took another step, his palms open, his hands empty.

"I never needed you," Sam said. His voice broke and sounded far, far away.

"Oh, but you did," Merrick said. His smile flattened. His eyes glittered like black diamonds, hard and merciless. "You needed me to get back to your precious Faith. You called me. You opened the door wide for me to walk right through." Another step closer. "You made a promise to do anything to get back to her. Anything. You lied!" Merrick hissed.

"What are you talking about?"

"The little girl. Remember the little girl?" Merrick's smile was cold and hard. "You killed her to protect your men. You failed." A harsh whisper.

Sam stumbled and nearly fell. He struggled to hold his weapon higher. "That's not true!" Sam shouted. His shoulders bumped the wall behind him first, then his buttocks. He was trapped. Trapped in a container of death with…his brain rejected the truth.

It couldn't be.

Merrick's smile was back, filled with charm and malice. "Even after all we've been through, you still don't believe?" He folded his hands over his heart. "I'm wounded, Sam." He lowered his hands. "What's it going to take for me to make you believe? Do you want to know what Lewis and Hale are doing right now?"

"Liar!"

"They're burning. In the cold fire, they're burning. Do you know why?" He held up one hand and an echo of a scream filled the container. "Because they failed to see the truth, too. There is no way to come home from this the same." His voice took on a mocking tone. "You think you can go to war and not do unthinkable things? You think you can go to war and go home the same loving man you were before?" His eyes narrowed to slits. "Your men are dead because you failed to do what you were supposed to do. You were supposed to sacrifice yourself to save them. Instead you were a coward. A miserable, stinking coward who kills little kids." He paused, tipping his head to look at Sam with benign curiosity. "I think I shall enjoy making you burn." He held up his hand. "I want you to hear the truth. For once in your life. *Listen.*"

Sam? Sam?

The voice. A voice he knew well. A voice he heard in his sleep. A voice he woke to. The voice of his love. His Faith. It bounced off the walls and then it twisted, rising, getting louder and louder until it was a continuous agony-filled scream.

"Faith!"

He fell to his knees. His weapon banged against his kneecap. His hands fell limp by his sides. The flashlight rolled a foot away, bumping into Anu's paw. He'd forgotten she was there. "That's not true. She's not—"

"Oh, but she is." Merrick's voice was gleeful. "How long has it been since you talked to her, Sam?" Merrick trailed his fingers down the wall of the container. Metal on metal screeched into the darkness. "She died from an infection from your precious Peanut. The baby killed her, Sam. Your baby killed her."

"No! That's impossible!"

"Is it? Or is it just that you destroy everything good you touch?

You could have saved your men, Sam. But that one little girl was too much for you." The screeching grew louder, drowning out everything but the hissing sound of Merrick's voice. "You're a selfish man, Sam Brown."

"That's not true!"

"Just because you don't want it to be true doesn't mean it's not."

Sam's flashlight flickered, sputtering one final time before it gave up. Darkness fell, sucking all the light into the macabre darkness behind Merrick. The blackest night, the blackest depths. It was an absence of everything. A perfect evil.

He could still see Merrick, despite the lack of light. Somehow the darkness illuminated him. His eyes glowed red, piercing the abyss behind him.

"Do you believe me now?" Merrick asked. "Your precious Faith is dead. And you killed her." Merrick crouched down in front of Sam. He looked over at Anu and patted his thigh. The dog didn't budge.

A lightning rage flashed across Merrick's face. Just an instant, but Sam saw. In that instant, he saw through Merrick's lies, through his own fear to a faint glimmer of hope.

"Your precious puppy not obeying anymore?" Sam asked.

Merrick's jaw twisted. "She can disobey all she wants. She knows who she works for."

"You said she told you when the enemy was coming." Sam didn't look away. "Maybe she switched sides."

Merrick shook his head slowly, his eyes glittering dangerously. It dawned on Sam that it might not be a bright idea to taunt the man in front of him.

"Anu doesn't have a side," Merrick said. Those blood red eyes focused back on him, and Sam's soul cowered. "Not everything is black and white. You promised you'd do anything you could to get back to your Faith. But she's gone now, Sam." He paused. "And you killed her."

———

"You're lying." Sam's voice was weak. He trembled with fear. The glimmer of hope died, wilting in the dark.

"You think so?" He reached out, touching the spot over Sam's heart with one clawed fingernail. Sam's skin burned beneath his fingertip. "Your precious Faith is dead. Everything you did to go home to her was for nothing."

Sam felt the tapping against his breastbone, a hollow echo above his empty heart. *Tap. Tap. Tap.*

"It's time. You need to come with me." Merrick reached out to tap Sam's chest once more.

The idea of him touching Sam made his skin crawl, his soul retreat. He grabbed Merrick's wrist. Surprise lit the cold red eyes.

"You lie. Everything you say is a lie," Sam snarled. "Faith is fine. She was fine the last time I talked to her."

"Did she tell you about the bird, Sam?"

Sam froze. He hadn't told anyone about the bird.

Merrick's smile was cold in the shadows. "Yes, Sam, I know about the bird. Who do you think sent it? She was crying and screaming and cursing you for not being there while she swatted at it with a broom." Merrick inhaled as though savoring a delicate aroma. "The scent of her fear is a beautiful thing. She died alone in the hospital room, the baby inside her poisoning her blood. It was a terrible way to die."

Sam lunged, his hands going for Merrick's throat.

Merrick laughed. With one simple move, he wrenched Sam's arms behind him, pinning him against Merrick's chest. Sam was shocked to find Merrick was nothing but bone. Unbreakable, solid bone. "You're so naive. You think you can beat me? You think you can win? Your pitiful lives are so short, so pointless." Merrick's voice hissed in his ear, his breath hot against Sam's skin.

His palm slipped up, forcing Sam's chin higher until Sam thought his neck would snap. He tried to slam his head back, but Merrick dodged and slipped his arm around Sam's throat.

Like a patient constrictor, Merrick squeezed, slowly pushing the air from Sam's lungs. Refusing to allow his throat to expand.

Sam's vision faded to white stars against the blackness, then Merrick yanked him back, throwing Sam off balance.

The dark expanded and Sam realized he wasn't passing out. He was being dragged into the night beyond the container. A sinking hole in the center of the blood. Not his body. His soul. It felt like it was being sucked out of his skin, pulled toward a vacuum that didn't exist in this world.

"Your death will be mourned as just another tragic non-combat-inflicted injury," Merrick whispered. "And your Faith will die alone."

Sam stiffened. "You said she was dead," he managed.

Merrick's lips brushed his ear. "I lied."

Sam's mind raced, trying to figure out a way to break the hold, but Merrick was too strong. With every step, he felt darkness swirling up, pulling him under.

If he passed out, he was a dead man.

He had just one chance.

He dropped all of his weight, letting his legs go slack. The sudden shift in his load unbalanced Merrick and a sudden rush of air filled Sam's lungs as Sam was thrown away. He landed hard on his knees, hard enough that he thought he would shatter bone. Bright pain exploded through his body. His palms scraped against the dried blood smoothed over the wooden floor, and splinters cut into his flesh.

He turned and tried to crawl away but the container tipped up. He scrambled, trying to find a hold, anything to stop his slow, tormenting slide toward the blackness below.

Anu growled low in her throat as Sam's fingers unexpectedly found a tiny hole, a hook for a cargo strap. The metal sliced into his fingers as he dug into it, held on with everything he was.

Anu. She had Merrick's leg, dragging him away from Sam, toward the opening of the container.

Nothing but darkness was down there now but somehow Sam

could clearly see shadows and shapes and writhing things reaching up out of the depths.

His foot jerked. Merrick's clawed fingers curled around his ankle. "You're mine," he hissed.

Sam's fingers nearly snapped with the added weight. He swung his foot violently, trying to kick Merrick away.

"Your soul is mine."

"She's not dead!"

Sam's free foot connected. Blood exploded out of Merrick's mouth. His lip burst like a bloody grape. He spit and a tooth tinked against the wooden floor, bouncing down, down, like a pebble skittering against a cliff wall.

Merrick looked up at him. His bloody smile was black and cold. "You think you've won? You think this is freedom?" His laugh grated, a harsh echo against the container walls. "Your God doesn't care about you. He abandoned you the moment you were formed in your mother's womb." His other hand swung up, gripping higher on Sam's leg. "You let me in once, Sam. I'll never let you go."

Sam kicked. And kicked and kicked until the face smiling up at him was bloody pulp. Until Merrick's fingers released. Until Anu dragged Merrick away.

And the macabre abyss swallowed him.

CHAPTER TWENTY-FIVE

The quiet told him he was still alive.

No puffy white clouds. No drug-induced visions.

Just quiet beneath the sound of his own heartbeat. He felt the weight of Merrick's hand still on his ankle, but he opened his eyes, shifted and looked. There was nothing there.

His palm no longer burned.

He pushed up to his hands and knees, his bones protesting the movement, his muscles creaking and groaning as if he was an old man.

For a moment, he simply rested there on his hands and knees. Then he moved to sit on his ass at the opening of the bloody container. The crime scene tape flapped in the light breeze above his head.

He sat for a long time, listening to the world as it went on around him. The distant echo of the test fire pit. The rumble and squeal of an armored vehicle as it rolled by. Distant shouts in languages he couldn't understand.

And beneath it all, the sound of boots on gravel. Crunching closer, getting louder with each step.

Tick stepped into the faint light. He said nothing for a long time.

Sam, too, remained silent. He wasn't in a hurry to explain why he was there. He didn't know if he was in trouble or not. But funny, he didn't care anymore. He'd wanted to find the dog's body, find some proof that he hadn't lost his mind.

His brain still hadn't come to grips with what had happened. There were too many questions he was afraid to answer.

Tick reached up and pulled a cigar out of his chest pocket. His lighter flared bright as he sucked on the end. Smoke puffed out around it. He took a deep, slow breath, then wrapped his finger around the cigar. "Been a rough few days," he said.

He'd been saying that a lot recently.

Sam pressed his lips together and nodded, unsure of how his voice would sound if he spoke.

Overhead, the moon drifted from behind a heavy cloud. Pale silver light flooded the alcove. Made even the darkness around them look shimmery and pretty. Less violent and ugly. Everything looked better in the moonlight, Sam supposed.

"So this is where she died, eh?"

Sam looked away from the moon and over at Tick. "Huh?"

Tick pointed with his cigar to the side of the container. Sam stood and walked. His foot rolled on a rock and he stumbled.

Flies buzzed at the side of the container. There, hidden in the shadows, half in a hole in the dirt, was the body of a dog. Her carcass was bloated and reeked of decaying flesh where the flies had feasted on her.

Sam's breath trembled in his lungs and for a moment, insanity dashed up at him. A wild, mad laughter twisted up against his lips but he mashed them shut, refusing to reveal to Tick and the world at large that he was well and truly fucking nuts.

"Well, shit, son," Tick said roughly. When had he stepped so close to Sam? He could smell the thick scent of cheap underarm deodorant. It was a fake, heavy clean that clashed with the stench of death and Tick's cigar. "Looks like you found the body." He slapped Sam on the shoulder. "Congratulations. You're not fucking crazy."

Sam thought about telling Tick he wasn't so sure of that, but thought better of it. Why bother? If he'd really lost his mind, well then, it wouldn't take long before something else tripped the alarm.

He felt bad that he'd actually shot the dog. Whether she had really been there or had been a shared figment of his imagination, he no longer knew nor cared. He thought again about laughing, but mashed his lips together and said nothing.

Really, why bother?

————

The haze that surrounded his brain made his thoughts slow, his actions slower. Tick thought he was just adjusting to everything, but Sam knew the truth.

There was no adjusting to the life he lived now. Knowing that evil was real made walking back through the concrete barriers at night that much harder.

But he kept that to himself. He needed to call home. The memory of Merrick's words whispered across the back of Sam's neck. Maybe he hadn't been lying. As soon as Tick had shown the commander the body, Sam broke free, walking as quickly as he could toward the call center.

He didn't care how long he had to wait in line. He didn't care if it was the middle of the day or the middle of the night back home. He needed to know that Faith was okay. Needed to know that Merrick had lied to him. Needed to chase away the insidious whisper that there was something behind him, following him through the barriers, nipping at his heels and chasing him toward the crazy.

As he emerged from the barriers, his heart jumped. No line snaked out the door of the call center.

It was a good omen. It had to be.

He approached the stairs that led up into the trailer and saw a sign hanging on the door:

Closed until further notice.

His heart went into a spiral of sadness and doubt. He didn't know why it was closed. He didn't care. It was closed.

He couldn't call home.

His steps were heavy as he started back through the maze toward his trailer. Maybe it would be open in the morning.

He tried not to let the sadness and the doubt worm their way into his mind, but by the time he made it back to his trailer, he was tired. Worn down by the war, the loss, by the uncertainty of what was real and what was not.

He opened the door, the lock turning with a muted click, and climbed the two steps into the dim and dusty trailer that was his space.

He stood there and felt the familiar solitude. This time, he knew that Hale wouldn't be knocking on his door. Lewis wouldn't be showing up, ragging on Hale.

A massive hole gaped in the center of his heart. Around its edges danced a lingering fear that maybe Merrick hadn't lied.

Maybe Faith was…he covered his mouth with his hand. No. No, he wouldn't believe the lie. He would call home soon.

Besides, if she was…gone, his parents would have sent a Red Cross message.

He would know right away if something was wrong, because that was how the system worked. He didn't have to wait months to send a letter home and receive a response.

He just had to find a working phone line.

He lifted his weapon over his head and for a moment, sat on the edge of his unmade bed.

A flash of silver caught his eye. He lifted the edge of a t-shirt he'd left crumpled on the bed.

The medallion his mother had snuck into his pack. He coiled the chain in the palm of his hand. The metal was cold and gritty with dust.

His hand no longer burned.

He stared for a long time at the medallion: St. Michael the Archangel.

Battling the dragon.

Protect us.

He swallowed, his mouth dry.

He didn't believe.

Except that now…His hands shook as he lifted the chain around his neck. It was cold and unfamiliar against his skin, pressing into the base of his throat.

It couldn't hurt to wear it.

What did it say about him that he turned back to a God he'd abandoned just because things had gotten a whole lot of sideways?

He looked at his palms. He could still feel the echo of Merrick's hooked finger tapping on his chest. *Tap. Tap. Tap.*

He rubbed the spot, felt the dry skin of his fingers catch on his uniform.

He rubbed until his fingers burned and the cotton felt hot beneath his touch.

And then the tapping was on his door.

In the middle of the night, the tapping was at his door.

CHAPTER TWENTY-SIX

Seven Months Later

Sam was the only soldier on the bus, so far as he could tell. He rode the Greyhound north on I-95. The closer he got to Bangor, the tighter his guts twisted.

He had no words to describe the fear inside him. No sound that could release the anguish he'd held within for the last seven months.

Hope, that strongest of emotions, had abandoned him. He had felt nothing for the last seven months. No happiness. No sadness. He'd walked around in a haze of endless numbness.

Even the transitioning with the incoming unit hadn't lifted his spirits.

The tapping on his door that night all those months ago had crushed the tiniest bit of hope he'd clung to.

And now, riding north, through the trees and the flashes of civilization, he felt something.

It was fear. Curdled in his guts, it worked its way through his skin until he was slick with sweat.

The heat on the bus didn't help. It was May in Maine, still

frigid by Georgia standards and downright subarctic by Iraqi. Still, the heat smothered him, coating his skin and making his clothes stick to his body as the miles rolled by.

He could do little but wait and stare out the window. An ancient, rusted-out Blazer that should have been scrapped long ago rumbled past the bus, going far faster than was probably a good idea.

No thoughts tumbled inside his head. He felt no racing anticipation, only dread at what he knew was waiting for him at that bus stop in Bangor.

The sun set into the wet Maine treetops. The winter had been hard, which meant that mud season was harder. Wetter and muddier, with a few floods along the miles of streams and rivers that ran through Maine's interior.

The trees glistened in the twilight, their boughs heavy and damp. The road was slick with sheen as they pulled into the bus stop.

Sam waited, unable to summon the energy to be excited. It was only when the last person left the bus that he stood, shouldering his assault pack before he took that first step to face the thing he'd been dreading since that awful tapping on his trailer door.

He stopped by the doorway. Light reflected on the wet bottom step. The cement too was wet. Fresh and clean. Free of the mud from the rest of the state.

He took that first step. Down, down, then off the bus.

The crowd had dispersed. A few stragglers here and there. A pair of lovers locked in an embrace beneath a shimmering streetlight. Something romantic and timeless.

That would never be Sam. Not for as long as he lived did he think he would ever feel that lust pounding through his veins again. Something had died inside him.

He might not have given up his soul. But then again, maybe he had.

He scanned the faces in the bus station.

He'd have to wait for his ride. He wondered if Tommy had gotten his message.

The clear glass door opened.

Faith stepped out of the darkness and into the light of a solitary street lamp.

Her hair was shorter than when he'd left, twisted at the back of her neck. Her cheeks were hollowed out from weight loss.

She had no bump beneath her belly, no baby on her hip.

He'd known what to expect after that dreadful tapping had destroyed his hope for the world.

But now, seeing her, seeing her real and whole and safe standing in front of him…for the first time in months, his soul leapt in his chest. Swelled with emotion and feelings he'd thought had died the night he'd learned their child had been born without a breath.

Tears filled his eyes, but his boots were rooted to the spot. She clutched her arms tighter around her belly. Her eyes showed fear. Uncertainty.

And then she was in his arms, her thin body pressed to his, and everything he'd thought had died in him was alive. He breathed in the clean, Coppertone smell of her hair, felt the soft warmth of her skin. He buried his face in her neck and he knew, he knew that Merrick hadn't won.

Faith was alive. He'd made it home from war, from the hell that he'd lived through.

"You're home. You're home." Her words were a watery chant in his ear, against his neck.

He buried his face in her hair and wept.

He was home.

Jessica Scott is an Iraq war veteran, an active duty army officer and the USA Today bestselling author of novels set in the heart of America's Army. She is the mother of two daughters, too many animals, and wife to a retired NCO. She and her family are currently wherever the Army has sent her.

She's also written for the New York Times At War Blog, PBS Point of View Regarding War, and IAVA. She deployed to Iraq in 2009 as part of Operation Iraqi Freedom (OIF)/New Dawn and has had the honor of serving as a company commander at Fort Hood, Texas twice.

She's a Phd candidate in Sociology at Duke studying morality in her spare time and she's been featured as one of Esquire Magazine's Americans of the Year for 2012.

Jessica is also an active member of the Military Writers Guild. Photo: Courtesy of Buzz Covington Photography

Find her online at http://www.jessicascott.net

BOOKSHOTS
Dawn's Early Light

Printed in the United States of America

First Printing 2016

ISBN: 9978-1-942102-20-5

Author photo courtesy of Buzz Covington Photography

Cover Design by Jessica Scott

For more information please see www.jessicascott.net

ISBN: 978-1-942102-20-5